B53 065 688 7

KT-431-285

MOON CUTTERS

Recent Titles by Janet Woods from Severn House

AMARANTH MOON
BROKEN JOURNEY
CINNAMON SKY
THE COAL GATHERER
EDGE OF REGRET
HEARTS OF GOLD
LADY LIGHTFINGERS
I'LL GET BY
MOON CUTTERS
MORE THAN A PROMISE
PAPER DOLL
SALTING THE WOUND
SECRETS AND LIES
THE STONECUTTER'S DAUGHTER
STRAW IN THE WIND
TALL POPPIES
WITHOUT REPROACH

MOON CUTTERS

Janet Woods

This first world edition published 2013
in Great Britain and 2014 in the USA by
SEVERN HOUSE PUBLISHERS LTD of
19 Cedar Road, Sutton, Surrey, England, SM2 5DA.

British Library Cataloguing in Publication Data

Woods, Janet, 1939- author.
  Moon Cutters.
  1. Sisters–Fiction. 2. Orphans–Fiction.
  I. Title
  823.9'2-dc23

ISBN-13: 978-0-7278-8335-3 (cased)

All Severn House titles are printed on acid-free paper.

Severn House Publishers support the Forest Stewardship Council™ [FSC™],
the leading international forest certification organisation. All our titles that
are printed on FSC certified paper carry the FSC logo.

Typeset by Palimpsest Book Production Ltd.,
Falkirk, Stirlingshire, Scotland.
Printed and bound in Great Britain by
TJ International, Padstow, Cornwall.

One

'Gerrout of here, you thieving beggar!'

Keeping a tight hold of the loaf of bread she carried, Miranda dodged under the scrubbed wooden table and out through the kitchen door, knowing that the stout cook could do little more than waddle.

But she'd underestimated the prowess of the cook's throwing arm and aim. The wooden rolling pin bounced off Miranda's head with some force and for a moment her knees gave way under her. Lake, trees and the fancy house spun around her and she felt sick.

Miranda remembered that Lucy was waiting for her in the woods, and her sister was fevered. She gritted her teeth against the throbbing inside her skull. She had to escape and find them shelter for the night.

Drawing in some air, she managed to run. She tried to keep in a straight line as she followed her own footprints through the snow, but it was hard work and her legs began to buckle. As she made for the line of trees, the landscape slowly revolved. Earlier, the low mist had turned the crusty white landscape into watery slush. Now the mist had lifted and a chill wind blew. It stung her with ice needles borne on the wind. Breath scoured through her throat, and her body jittered with shivers. Miranda had never felt so cold.

Behind her, the cook kept on screeching. It reminded her of a gaudy parrot in an exotic land – a story her mother had once told her.

The immediate past seemed so far away now: the cozy house they'd once lived in, the father who'd died falling from a horse, and their mother – turned out by the new estate manager and losing her life while giving birth to a stillborn infant. Passing strangers had done the rest, robbing them of everything of value.

They were tired and hungry, and Miranda doubted if she could go any further . . . especially now Lucy seemed to be sickening for something.

As she neared the trees, she heard the shrill whinny of a horse and the excited bark of dogs. She closed her eyes.

'Please God, don't let them catch us,' she prayed, but although she could run fast, Miranda knew she'd never be able to outrun a horse or a dog.

She managed to gain the shelter of the woods and staggered on to where she'd left her sister, seated on a fallen log.

Lucy stood when she saw her. Her face creased up, as it did when she was going to cry, her eyes widened and her teeth chattered. 'You have blood on your face.'

Picking up the hem of her skirt, Miranda wiped the blood away. 'It's a scratch, that's all,' she said, and the fright drained from Lucy's eyes.

'Did they give you something for us to eat and drink?'

There was a rattling growl behind them and she turned to find a lurcher standing there. It was a handsome dog with a rough hairy coat and a lean body designed for speed. Another came to the left of her and growled softly in its throat. She saw the third one a little to her right, obviously endowed with the same parental mix. With the tree at her back, the dogs had her trapped.

Dread filled her. She wouldn't be able to outrun them.

Lucy gave a little whimper and clung to her skirt. 'Quickly, climb on to my shoulders and into the tree,' Miranda whispered, and her sister clambered over her with alacrity.

Miranda had no time to join Lucy on the branch; besides, it wouldn't take both their weights.

The dogs edged closer, yellow teeth bared and offering her rattling growls. Miranda daren't turn her back on them. Slowly bending from the knees, and not taking her eyes off the dogs, she groped around and picked up a stout stick. As she straightened, her head swam. She'd hardly righted herself when the first dog took a run at her. Judging it nicely, she rapped the stick sharply across its snout. It yelped loudly and backed away, pawing at its nose. The two beasts on her flanks attacked at the same time, as though they'd rehearsed it.

Borne to the ground by the weight of the dogs and trying to prevent the snapping teeth from tearing at her flesh, Miranda screamed and gathered the shawl round her head. The dog's teeth sank into her thigh, and at the same time her arm was gripped. She lashed out with the stick in her free hand. Above her in the pine tree, Lucy gave terrified moan.

The dogs pulled Miranda every which way, and above the snarls and screams she could hear the ripping noises as they worried at her clothing and tried to pull away the old shawl she wore, to get at her throat. One of them snatched the stick from her hand.

There came the thud of a horse's hooves, followed by a lively curse. 'Come here, the lot of you. Nero. Drop her! You too, Roma.'

Blessedly, the snapping, snarling teeth were withdrawn.

'Caesar. Leave that bloody stick alone and sit. *Sit*, I say!'

Footsteps scrunched through the soggy remains of the autumn leaves. The blanket was flicked aside with a braided-leather riding crop.

Everything swam as Miranda struggled into a sitting position. There seemed to be two of him. Two pairs of dark eyes gazed at her; two heads, with grey-flecked dark hair as tossed as a stormy sea, slowly came together as one.

One of the dogs dropped the stick in front of her and wagged its tail. When the man grabbed it up from the dog and threw it as far as it would go, the animals went bounding after it.

The man leaped from the saddle. 'You're bleeding, girl.'

'Your dogs attacked me.' She hugged the loaf of bread against her chest, slightly warm, moist and smelling of yeast, so that her mouth watered despite the predicament they were in.

'They wouldn't have touched you if you hadn't hurt their pup. They're trained to flush out the prey, not kill it.'

'That's a pup? It looks as big as a lion.'

'Yes, I suppose he does. He's not technically a pup, just *their* pup. Isn't that right, Caesar?' The dog wagged its tail at the mention of its name. 'Come, girl, I'll help you stand and we'll go back to the house.'

As soon as he laid a hand on her, Lucy's smaller figure hurtled down from the pine tree. She landed on the man's back, sending a surprised huff of air from his mouth. She began to pummel him. 'Leave my sister alone, else I'll tell the soldiers and they'll come and shoot you.'

He rolled his eyes, clearly exasperated. 'You didn't have to try to break my back, young lady. If you'd waited, I would have lifted you down. I daresay the soldiers would enjoy having an excuse to come here and make a salmagundi out of the place. Last week Nero ripped the arse out of the breeches of one of them, so I must make sure I stay out of their way.'

When the man began to rise, Lucy slid to the ground and scrambled over to where Miranda sat, her face screwed up with anxiety. Miranda couldn't bear to see her sister worried, so put an arm around her and held her close. Lucy's heat reached out to her and she had red fever patches on her face.

Miranda's head ached and blackness crowded in. She fought it, even though the thought of having someone else take responsibility for her and her sister was almost overwhelming.

'Allow me to see how badly injured you are. Are your ribs painful?' the man said, and when Lucy kicked out at him again, he told her, 'It will be dark in an hour or so. If you don't behave yourself, I'll leave you here. I won't hurt the pair of you, you know.'

'Enough, Lucy,' Miranda whispered, because she was all but spent and she sensed nothing sinister about this man, despite his air of toughness.

Indeed, his fingers were gentle against her scalp as he parted her hair. He probed the cut on her head before murmuring, 'That might need a stitch or two.'

Lucy burst into tears and snuggled close to her for comfort. She was shivering now, even though her face was hot. She began to cough. When she finished the spasm, she was exhausted and whispered, 'I'm thirsty. Shall I eat the snow? It's all dirty here and it makes my tummy feel like being sick.'

The man laid the back of his hand against Lucy's face and told Miranda what was obvious. 'Your sister is feverish.'

Miranda screwed up her eyes, trying to discover whether he was young or old. He was in his fifties perhaps. 'You won't hurt her, will you? She has a fever and needs help. It doesn't matter about me. A few dog bites will soon heal.'

'Unless they become infected – which they will if they're left untreated.' For a moment, she saw his face clearly. He wasn't exactly handsome. His features were firm, his expression stern, so you knew he would not take any nonsense from anybody. But his eyes, despite their dark secretive depths, were filled with concern. 'What should I do with you both? Custom dictates you should be handed over to the authorities?'

'They'll put us in a workhouse. Or, worse still, prison.'

'Prison? Have you committed a crime, then?'

She handed him the loaf of bread, now squashed, dirty and wet. 'We were hungry.'

'Hmmm . . . I suppose they would send you to prison, then. Both places are overrun with unloved and unwanted children, so two more won't make much difference. The board is governed by pompous, flatulent fellows with fat stomachs.'

Her splutter of laughter earned a chuckle from him and his eyes were filled with amusement. 'Perhaps I should tell you that I'm one of them, and a magistrate as well.'

Her heart sank, but she rallied enough to say, 'And perhaps I should tell you we were neither unloved nor unwanted but are perfectly respectable orphans. Why are the soldiers interested in you if you're a magistrate?'

'I've never met anyone who described themselves as perfectly respectable orphans before.' He slanted his head to one side and smiled. 'I don't believe I suggested you were otherwise. I suppose you could also be described as a perfectly respectable thief, with my loaf of bread tucked under your arm and still steaming from the oven. What have you got to say to that?'

She thought for a moment, then said, 'Well . . . there is thieving out of necessity and there is thieving because one can.'

'Good grief – such logic from such a small female! I shall have to find you a seat on the reform board. Oh, don't look so worried, girl. I will listen to your tale of woe when I get round to it, and we shall work things out to our mutual satisfaction. Once you have a roof over your head and a meal in your stomachs, you'll feel more lively.'

Miranda's resistance drained from her and her stomach growled like a wolf at the thought of a meal. She was so hungry she could gnaw the leg off a donkey. 'I'd be grateful if you'd just allow us to stay until my sister is better. Then we'll leave. The one thing she didn't want was to be parted from Lucy. She would be if they were turned in. We won't be any bother, I promise. I'll look after her and will work for you in return for our food.'

When he whistled, the hounds and his horse returned to him. Taking the loaf, he tore it into three chunks and threw them to the dogs, which gulped them down in a few tearing bites. He turned to her. 'There's no evidence you stole from me now. You have no choice but to trust me, you know. I'll take you in until I decide what can be done for you. Do you think you can hold your sister safely in front of you on the horse?'

She nodded. 'I feel dizzy at times and my head hurts. Your cook brained me with the rolling pin.'

'Nancy Platt usually wins the rolling-pin throwing championship at the county fair every year. We're quite proud of her. Consider yourself lucky it wasn't a carving knife she threw. Tell me if you feel dizzy, though it's not too far to the house and I think we shall manage. Come here and I'll give you a leg up.'

She put her foot in the stirrup he made with his hands and was tossed lightly on to the horse's back. He kept his hand on her thigh to stop her falling over the other side until her dizziness abated. 'All right?'

When she nodded, he lifted Lucy up to join her. Once they were securely settled, he began to lead the horse forward. The dogs ran on ahead, stopping to sniff the trail of blood spots she'd left on the ground or to mark the slush with a yellow scent for them to follow.

Sometimes the dogs looked back at the trio with the horse, giving small encouraging yips, their tails flaying at the snowflakes in the air like frayed ropes. Two of them were long-legged creatures in different shades of fawn. Caesar was handsome, his coat striped in brown and gold.

'Yes, yes, we're coming. Go and tell Jackson I'll need him.' He turned when the dogs raced each other towards the stables, barking loudly. 'Allow me to introduce myself. I'm Sir James Fenmore, and you will address me as Sir James. And you are?'

'Miranda Jarvis. This is my sister, Lucinda.'

He made a small bow as they approached the stable yard. 'Miss Jarvis, Miss Lucinda. I'm pleased to make your acquaintances. We will get you both settled and comfortable. I will expect an account of where you came from, when we're all ready. I will want to know where you intended to go on your winter travels, and how you happened to be trespassing on my estate and stealing from my kitchens. Be warned, young ladies, I will expect to hear the truth.'

Miranda was too tired to argue. Lucy was slumped against her and it took all of her strength to keep her secure. She figured that whatever she told him, he wouldn't know whether it was the truth or not. After all, nobody would report them as missing.

The night before, they'd managed to get a ride with some gypsies and had fallen asleep when they'd made camp. Cold had woken them to find the fire had gone out. The gypsies were gone and she didn't know in which direction. She didn't even know where she was or which county they were in. 'Yes, Sir James.'

Her head spun when he lifted her down.

'Good . . . as long as we understand each other.' He swore when she staggered, and put an arm round her for support. His other arm captured Lucy as she slid from the horse after her.

A stableman came out of the yard, followed by a boy in a flat cap who took the horse by the rein and led him away, the dogs dancing excitedly around them.

'Alert the house staff, lad,' Sir James called after him. 'Jack, help the older girl back into the house. I'll carry the younger one. She's running a fever and looks done in.'

'Yes, Sir James.'

Inside the hallway of the house, servants were rushing about as their master issued instructions, one after the other.

Miranda had an impression of swirling colour . . . embroidered tapestries, thick red and blue rugs. There was a life-sized statue of a woman with naked breasts and a wisp of cloth clinging to her hips. In the opposite corner stood a man carved from marble, his blank eyes gazing at her, his hair and beard a mass of curls.

From her half-reclining position on a sofa, Miranda could see under the statue's fig leaf. Did men truly look like that? How odd. Her cheeks warmed as she looked at it. Although she averted her eyes, they crept back to the protuberance, as though being drawn there. How brazen of her! Even more brazen was the fact that the statues flaunted themselves. The woman was a hussy! Miranda closed her lids firmly, thinking how utterly prissy of her, when they were actually works of art, a dedication to Adam and Eve in the Bible.

Her nose took over. The house smelled of polish . . . and a

spicy perfume, probably coming from a pastille burning in the bronze cassolette on the hall table. There was an odour of dog and a faint reek of tobacco smoke, all of the smells so familiar to her that she could be at home. She wanted to cry because they no longer had a home or a family to go home to. It occurred to her that the house didn't smell as though it belonged to a woman.'

She opened her eyes. 'Are you married, Sir James?'

'What an odd question to ask me on such a short acquaintance; do you intend to ask me to wed you when you grow up, then?'

She was sure her face had turned red and she placed her icy hands against her cheeks. She must not give away her age, which was eighteen, almost nineteen. Luckily, she and Lucy took after their mother, who had been small and neat in stature. 'Certainly not! You are much too old.'

'A pity; it's been a long time since I had an offer of marriage.'

A woman joined them, grey-haired and capable-looking. 'Shall I put your guests in the nursery wing, Sir James?'

'No, Pridie, it's too cold under the attic, and the younger girl has a fever. We'll use my sister's old room for Miss Jarvis. It will be convenient for the servants to come and go. It also connects to the maid's room, and Miss Lucinda can sleep in there until the fever subsides. Miss Jarvis will be near enough to her sister for them both to be reassured.

'But, sir—'

'Enough, Pridie. My sister has been dead a long time. There is no need to keep the room as a shrine, because she won't be coming back, despite you thinking you saw her ghost in that room. Perhaps you'll find some useful clothing there for the children to use.'

He led them up the stairs to a comfortable chamber.

'My guests will need a wash, and their clothing must be cleaned and repaired. You can get them something to wear from the cupboards. The hems can be shortened. Clean the wound on the older girl's head if you would. I may have to stitch it.'

Miranda's attention had been captured by a portrait over the fireplace. It was a lad, not quite into his manhood but confident in the beauty he'd inherited. His body was a long vibrant column, his slim hips thrust forward just a little – to emphasize his budding maleness, perhaps. Dark green eyes looked directly at her from slightly hooded lids, as though contemplating her, holding her gaze steady. But, then, he couldn't look away; only she could. It took a while. There was something a little derisive about his smile, but the softly curved mouth was quirked into a dimple at one side. His hair curled.

Sir James anticipated her question. 'No, it's not me when I was young. It's my sister's boy – my nephew, Fletcher Taunt. This was his mother's room when she lived. He and I had an argument two years ago, and the damned fool left to find his own way in the world. From what I gather, he's not making a bad job of it, either.' He fell into a moment of silent contemplation and then smiled. 'He wouldn't have changed much, I reckon.'

A little later, he pulled the edges of Miranda's wound together with strands of her hair, knotting them together over the top of the wound. He placed a pad and a bandage over the top. 'There . . . that's better.'

'I hope your nephew comes home.'

'Do you now? If he does, it will be after I'm dead and he inherits this place, unless one of us admits we were wrong.'

Which of them had been wrong about what? She was about to ask him what they'd argued about when he changed the subject abruptly. 'This might pull a bit, child, but it will be easier on you, and it will heal in a couple of weeks. Don't scratch it when it starts to itch, and keep it dry.'

'But my hair's sticky with blood.'

'And can stay that way. Once a scab has formed, the flesh under it will begin to heal.'

She was allowed some privacy while she washed herself and pulled on a large nightgown. Pridie treated the bites the dogs had left on her, bathing them in warm water, making tutting noises and pursing her mouth now and again. Miranda was glad he'd left that examination to Mrs Pridie, as she gently brushed the dark length of her hair that flowed out from under the bandage and then loosely braided it.

Sir James came in to question Pridie about Miranda's bites and examined a couple on her arm and hand before pronouncing himself satisfied that the wounds were superficial.

'There's one on her thigh that will bear keeping an eye on,' Pridie said. 'It's deeper than the others and might fester.'

'I'll make her a poultice, just in case. Are you dizzy, girl?'

Miranda's head thumped when she nodded, making her wince.

'You're concussed, which is why you're having dizzy spells. Your skull seems intact, but I want you to stay in bed for a few days.'

'How is my sister?'

'We shall go and find out. You come with me in case she takes fright. How long has she had this fever?'

'Two days.'

Lucy whimpered when she opened her eyes. 'My head feels wobbly.'

Miranda took her hand. 'It's all right, dearest. Sir James is just going to take a look at you.'

He examined Lucy's arms, legs and face quickly and efficiently. 'Does she have blisters on her chest, stomach and back?'

Fear thrust at Miranda. 'Yes . . . It's not smallpox, is it?'

'It looks to be more like chickenpox. Have you had it?'

'Yes, when I was an infant.'

'Miss Lucinda should feel more lively in a day or two when all the spots have appeared. You must tell her not to scratch the pustules, especially if they come out on her face; otherwise they'll scar. I'll find a soothing salve to help stop the itch.' He gave a bit of a laugh. 'I've got one I made for the dogs. It killed their fleas by suffocation and took the itch from their bites at the same time.'

'I didn't know fleas breathed.'

Giving her a quick glance, he chuckled. 'Didn't you?'

'You made that up,' she accused.

'Yes . . . but nature is fascinating. If you've ever examined a flea through a microscope, you would know that there's a strong probability that it takes air in through little openings in its side.'

That sounded more likely. 'So they get stuck in the salve and can't get air.'

His glance travelled over the shapeless swath of flannel she was wearing, and he grinned. 'You're a child – too young to know of such things, or have responsibility for yourself, let alone your sister.'

She didn't bother to enlighten him – to tell him she was nearly nineteen and her sister three years younger. She needed all the help she could get at the moment, and he obviously liked children. He wouldn't have allowed them inside if he was going to throw them out. He might fall back on convention if he knew she was of marriageable age.

Mrs Pridie said, 'Cook has warmed some chicken broth, but I don't think the younger girl will eat much. Nancy is upset about what she did to Miss Jarvis.'

'Perhaps you would tell her I'm not badly hurt, and it wasn't her fault; it was mine,' Miranda said immediately, which earned her a look of approval from Sir James as well as Pridie.

'I'll help my sister to eat her broth.'

Lucy shook her head and whined, 'I'm not hungry, just thirsty.'

'Could you manage some milk?'

When Lucy nodded, Sir James said, 'I'll send a maid up with some. In the meantime, you can try a little of the broth, Miss Lucy, since you need to get your strength up. I insist.'

Lucy managed a couple of spoonfuls before pushing it away. When the milk arrived, she only sipped at it at first and then found enough energy to gulp the rest down. Miranda sighed, wiping away her sister's creamy moustache when Lucy's eyes began to close. She tucked the covers over her, wishing she could set aside her cares and responsibilities so easily. 'Sleep, then, Lucy. Call me if you need me.'

Afterwards, Miranda wolfed down her own bowl of broth, though her head ached with every spoonful she swallowed. It was the most delicious soup she'd ever tasted.

'Into bed with you now, young lady,' Mrs Pridie said.

The bed was the softest she'd ever known, like lying in a cloud. The room was blissfully warm and the light from the flames sent shadows leaping and dancing across the room. She yawned. Now they were safe, she felt tired and falling apart, as if all the pent-up tension that had been keeping her together was draining away.

It was dark outside the windows. Mrs Pridie lit a nightlight and pulled the window hangings across. 'There's a bell on the table next to you. Ring it if you wake in the night and need anything. There will be a maid sleeping on the day bed and she can see to you tonight. Don't worry if you hear noises outside or see lights.'

'What sort of noises?'

'Could be men's voices, or thumping and scraping sounds, maybe. If you do hear those things, don't mention it to the master.'

'Why not?'

'It's not women's business, that's why, and he doesn't like people prying into his affairs. Course, it could be the apparition of the monk from the Abbey. He's seen from time to time walking abroad. The master gets angry if he's mentioned. Says it's twaddle.'

'And is it?'

She smiled to take the sting from her words. 'Who knows? Sleep well, Miss Jarvis.'

'Thank you, Mrs Pridie; you've been very kind.'

The woman gently patted her cheek and said in her soothing, almost musical voice, 'It costs nothing to be kind to a body. You're a nice young lady, with good manners. No harm will come to you and your sister here, though the master can be strict and expects to be obeyed. How old are you, dear – about fifteen?'

She shrugged as she avoided Mrs Pridie's eyes and mumbled something the woman couldn't possible hear clearly.

She said a small prayer for her mother, lying out there in the open air, oblivious to the cold. She must tell Sir James about her; he would make sure she had a decent burial.

'Mrs Pridie,' she said, when the woman reached the door. 'Where is this place?'

'Goodness, don't you know? We're in Dorset, my dear. And this is Lady Marguerite's House. If you lie as quiet as a mouse, you can hear the shush of the sea against the shore in Lady Marguerite's Cove.'

Miranda's eyelids began to droop. 'Why does Lady Marguerite have a cove named after her?'

'She drowned there. She was married to Lord Oliver Fenmore, who built this house for her. He was Sir James's great-great-grandfather. A proper love match, it was, and that over a hundred-and-fifty year ago. She loved the cove. But one day, when she was seated on a rock, a huge wave reared up from the sea and carried her away. Later, her body was washed ashore, tangled in the seaweed.'

'How sad.'

'It's said that Sir Oliver Fenmore was beside himself, and only the fact that he had a young son and daughter to rear stopped him from going insane. If you listen hard enough, when the moon is full and the night is calm, you can hear Lady Marguerite singing for her lost love to join her. Just remember that the dead can't hurt you.'

Miranda shivered and pulled the cover up round her ears as the door gently closed after the woman.

Two

Fletcher Taunt heaved a sigh of relief as the *Midnight Star* was tied securely to the shore. Although the ship was heavy with cargo, the tide was high. The flurries of snow-laden wind had thinned out enough for her master to safely berth the ship without having to anchor outside the sand bar that guarded the harbour.

His elegant ship nudged shoulders with vessels of lesser beauty: dusty colliers, a couple of ageing packets and several malodorous fishing smacks.

The *Midnight Star* was an aristocrat of ships. Her long lines and pointed prow balanced out her three tall masts, which thrust as straight as arrows into the sky. He'd won his uncle's half-share of the ship on the turn of a card. After the flaming row that action had produced, his uncle had accused him of cheating, something Fletcher would have challenged another man for. They'd traded insults and walked off in opposite directions – Fletcher to take possession of the ill-gotten gains that his bloody-mindedness dictated he now kept, and his uncle to his study, to brood over a bottle of good French brandy, no doubt.

They hadn't seen or spoken to each other since.

Fletcher had never really coveted the ship, and if his uncle had sought him out and apologized for his accusation, it would have been over and done with. As it stood, legally, his uncle still owned half the ship, while Fletcher owned the other half, purchased with the part of the legacy that had come from his father, and which his uncle controlled.

But James Fenmore hadn't pursued his claim. He'd stayed stubbornly silent and had informed his staff not to allow Fletcher entry to his home until he was ready to apologize – not even to collect his clothing.

He absently stroked his three-month growth of beard as the little steam tug chugged off in a fury of dirty smoke, leaving him and his ship to bed down for the night. It had been a long journey from Melbourne town, for on impulse Fletcher has asked the captain to divert, making landfall in Asia, where he'd filled every available space on the ship with anything oriental he could buy. The gold had already been unloaded in London the day before. It was a relief to get rid of it. Some people would do almost anything to get their hands on gold, even when it was destined for the Royal Mint. Taken from the ship by an official and guarded by several soldiers, it was quickly transferred from the ship to the new Mint at Little Tower Hill, where it had been weighed, recorded and receipted.

The wool bales were legitimate cargo, destined for Barrett and Son's auction warehouse in Poole, as were the oriental goods. They brought a good profit when sold at auction; so too the bolts of silk.

Passengers and crew were waiting to be given the all-clear from a doctor before stepping ashore. One of the crew was taking the luggage down the gangplank and stacking it on the quayside.

The doctor signed the log and the customs man gave it a cursory glance. Most of the customs officials were more interested in what was being smuggled across the channel, and left for them on the mud flats, than what Fletcher might have hidden in the hold.

There was a continuous battle of wits between customs and local shipping. What Fletcher carried ashore was nobody's business but his own. Those in positions of power who had involved themselves in the dishonest landing of goods had already taken their cuts and turned a blind eye.

'I can't see any nasty surprises lined up on shore, Fletcher,' George Mainwaring murmured on passing, and the captain took up a stance opposite the gangplank to help the ladies ashore. George Mainwaring was ten years older than Fletcher, and Fletcher had been taking instruction from him for the past two years. He travelled as the owner, not wishing to take over the management of the craft but learning as much seamanship and navigation as he could. Eventually, he would apply for a master's ticket, since they attracted the respect of the men who crewed the ships.

Another officer and two of the crew stood at the bottom of the plank, to offer a similar courtesy and help the passengers with their luggage. There were only a few passengers left, for some had disembarked in London.

Fletcher tried not to grin when Alice Puckingham brushed the back of her hand across his trouser front on the way past. She was a handsome woman, one skilled in many ways, and undervalued by her rather rotund husband. She looked well in a travelling dress and hooded cloak edged with fur, which was a little unfashionable. No doubt she would soon take advantage of her husband's wealth in that regard.

Alice had been sent to Australia after being convicted of stealing. She'd wed the wealthy woolgrower she'd been assigned to as a servant and was returning to England in the guise of a respectable woman of means. She fluttered her eyelashes at him. 'Thank you so much, Mr Taunt. It was nice to be in such . . . *expert* hands.'

Fletcher answered, 'It was my pleasure, Mrs Puckingham. The smooth running of the ship and the real safety and comfort of her passengers resides solely in her captain's specialized knowledge of the sea and his capable hands as he interprets the moods of wind, weather and tides.'

He reminded himself not to be so pompous when she gave a little grin and said, 'Oh, I've already thanked the captain for his management of weather and tides, his capable hands and his valuable services,' she cooed.

George Mainwaring allowed his left eyebrow to lift a fraction, but otherwise his face maintained an innocent expression.

'Which is more than I can call on myself to do, since I was sick for most of the way,' Mr Puckingham said sourly. 'I don't know how you fellows put up with all that bouncing around. As for myself, I'll be glad to get on dry land and have a bed that doesn't pitch and toss.'

Fletcher exchanged a glance with George. No wonder Alice Puckingham had been such a busy lady, he thought.

When the ship had been unloaded, the crew were given a chitty to take to the agent's office to collect their pay. He'd added a bonus. It would ensure that most of them would return. George Mainwaring set the ship's watch and proceeded to the captain's cabin, where George poured them a glass of brandy. Fletcher opened a wooden trunk with a false bottom and took out a box disguised as a book – one hollowed out and filled with small golden nuggets. He grunted as he set it down.

After a moment, the ship gave a barely discernible dip. The deck above them creaked, and there came a rap at the door.

'Who is it?' George called out.

'Seaman Baines . . . Sir Oswald is here, Captain.'

'Thank you, Baines; allow him to pass.'

A man entered, his face shaded by a tall hat. Removing it, he smiled at them both before his eyes fell on the box. 'How many ounces?'

George gave him an approximate. They all knew how much the box held; any adjustments would be made in the long term, should they be needed.

The man took a small wooden abacus from his pocket and did a rapid calculation. He named a price he was prepared to pay, then said, 'I take it the amounts will be deposited to the usual three accounts?'

Fletcher looked at George, who nodded at their visitor. The gold was transferred into two canvas sacks, and the book joined several others like it on a shelf.

When the man gave a low whistle, two men came in and the gold was carried outside. So gently that they barely heard a scuffle, it was lowered into a dingy on the harbour side of the ship.

The man smiled. 'I have on me the deeds to Monksfoot Abbey. The quicker the purchase is finalized, the sooner you can take up residence, Fletcher. I can redirect the draft and witness your signature now if you like.'

When Fletcher murmured his assent, the man pulled pen and inkstand towards him and wrote a figure on two bank drafts. He pushed the pieces of paper across the table. Fletcher took possession of the deeds and smiled. 'It feels surprisingly good to own some property of my own at last.'

'Congratulations on the purchase, Fletcher,' the man said. 'Even though Monksfoot Abbey is in need of some repair, you got it at a bargain price.'

'Silas could have got more from my uncle for it.'

'He could have, but he decided not to sell it to him. Somebody told him your uncle intended to pull the place down.'

Fletcher grinned. 'Sir James is given to odd notions at times. I believe Silas's heir is in America doing missionary work, much to his disgust. According to him, the man's got no intention of returning to Britain. Silas is disgruntled by the thought that his relative is a preacher, and the man intends to spend Silas's hard-earned cash on the poor when he dies. However, kin is kin.'

'Quite. However, not everything in this life always goes as planned.' Sir Oswald took out his watch and gazed at it. 'It's been a pleasure doing business with you, sirs. I must warn you. I've heard you're due a visit from our friends in about half an hour.'

George said with a sigh, 'Thanks . . . That's ruined my plans for the evening.'

And those of Fletcher, who looked at his watch and also heaved a sigh. 'I hope they get it over with quickly so there's still some light left. You go ashore, George. I'll stay. You got a good thumping last time, I seem to recall, so it must be my turn. I do understand my uncle's need to disrupt my life as often as possible, though. I wish I had the means to reciprocate.'

George shrugged. 'You won his share of the ship fair and square. I was there – and I wasn't the only one who witnessed it. But you know as well as I do that this harassment will continue until one of you gives in. No . . . I'll stay with you.'

Unexpectedly, Oswald asked, 'Will they find anything?'

'It's highly unlikely, but last time they ruined a couple of sails for no reason at all, and they cost a fortune to replace.'

'Then I'll stay, too. There is no man more respectable of reputation than I. You can pour us a brandy if you would, George. Fletcher, you can break out the cards.'

It was not long before feet thumped across the deck and down the short ladder. The cabin doors were flung open with some force, and Fletcher found himself looking down the barrel of a pistol. He took a mildly indignant stance in case the owner of the pistol had a nervous trigger finger, and gazed up into a pair of steely blue eyes. 'What the hell's going on here?'

'Customs. We're looking for contraband.'

Fletcher jerked his thumb at George Mainwaring. 'The master of this ship is there. I'm merely the owner.'

George didn't even turn a hair. 'The revenue men have already inspected the cargo in London. I have the certificate.' George threw a card down on the deck and reached for several sovereigns. He slipped them into his waistcoat pocket. 'I'm afraid you're out, Sir Oswald.'

'Damn and blast it, Captain; that's the second time tonight. The interruption put me off my stroke.' Sir Oswald looked up at the customs officer and scowled. 'Oh, it's you, is it, Mr Bailey? Haven't you got a home to go to?'

'I didn't know you were on board the *Midnight Star*, sir.'

'There's no reason why you should know, is there? I should think it was none of your damned business. Point that gun somewhere else, would you; else I'll haul you up in front of a magistrate for using threatening behaviour.'

Bailey did as he was told. 'I'm sorry, sir; we had a tip-off that the *Midnight Star* was carrying gold.'

Fletcher stood, stretching lazily to his full height, a hard-muscled six feet. 'Of course we were carrying gold. We're licensed to do so by the Royal Mint. For obvious reasons, we usually keep such a consignment quiet. Would you mind telling me where you got your information from?'

'I'm afraid I'm not at liberty to say. Where is the gold now?'

'I have no idea. Safely in the Royal Mint, I should imagine. Your informer forgot to tell you it was off-loaded in London early this morning.'

Bailey lost his air of authority, and Fletcher almost felt sorry for the man. After a moment, he suggested, 'Hurry up and do your search if you must. I intend to go ashore once I've won my money back from Mainwaring. Why don't you join us? It's your deal, isn't it, Oswald?'

'Let's up the stakes, shall we, gentlemen?' Sir Oswald expertly shuffled the cards and began to deal them.

Bailey said quickly, 'Count me out, Sir Oswald. I've got other business to take care of.'

Sir Oswald didn't look up. 'What about your search, Bailey? I've received complaints from ship owners that you've been a little too zealous on occasion and have caused unnecessary damage. One or two are thinking of presenting a case before the magistrate's court to seek redress. I've told them to count themselves lucky that we have an honest and fair man in charge of the port, and one who doesn't court favours.' Oswald gazed up at him, his eyes sharp. 'You *don't* court favours, do you, man?'

Bailey fiddled with his cuffs for a moment. 'Mistakes and accidents can occur from time to time, but one does one's best. My men have a good record at catching the thieving bastards who bring illicit goods into the country without paying the due taxes.' His mouth pinched with frustration. Being honest could be a liability since everyone knew that several of those working under Bailey were on the take. Then the man's glance flicked to Fletcher and his eyes narrowed as he grated out, 'Now I must go. Another time perhaps, Mr Taunt. Obviously I was given the wrong information this time. I must warn you, though: my pistol cannot tell the difference between a smuggler and a gentleman.'

Sir Oswald gazed up at him. 'Nor mine between an officer of the crown and a beggar. Are you threatening us?'

Fletcher chuckled after Bailey turned on his heel and left. 'There's nothing more tedious than a man who justifies his faults by imagining he has more integrity in him than the other fellow, when really he just has less humanity. I sense my uncle's hand behind this. I wonder what he'd do if they found something and threw me in jail.'

George clapped him on the shoulder. 'Sir James knows damn well you'll never be caught, and he still wants his half of the ship back. If you were arrested for smuggling gold, he'd make sure he was the magistrate hearing the case, and he'd seize the *Midnight Star*.'

Oswald chuckled. 'Your uncle will have a fit when he discovers you've bought Monksfoot Abbey, lock, stock and barrel.'

Grinning, Fletcher patted the deeds, now held safely in the deep, inside pocket of his waistcoat. Monksfoot wasn't a large residence, but it was of comfortable size. He calculated that in another eighteen months or so, if his luck held, he'd have enough money to repair the place. I'm taking the dingy into Axe Cove. I'm going to tie her up next to the *Wild Rose* and say hello to Silas.'

'Silas was hoping you'd visit. Don't put it off, because he has something he needs to say to you, and little time in which to say it.'

'Likewise. I enjoy his company, and have done since I was a boy. I used to enjoy hearing about his travels then; now he enjoys hearing of mine, though mine are not as embellished as his. What about you, George? Come with me if you like.'

'I'm going to seek out a pot of ale and a willing woman for a fond farewell, and in that order.'

'Anyone I know?'

George grinned. 'Strike while the iron's hot, I always say.'

'Just be careful the iron doesn't rise up and strike you first,' he said.

A thin mist vaporized from the cold grey surface of the sea, and Fletcher pulled his greatcoat around him as he made his way round the coast. The wind was fitful, his progress slow, and he wondered if he'd made a mistake in using the *Midnight Star*'s dingy. The light was fading rapidly as he rounded an outcrop of rock.

As luck would have it, the tide turned and began to surge back towards the shore. The current carried him straight into Axe Cove. The small harbour was aptly named. Viewed from the top of the cliff, the cove was shaped like the head of the tool it had been named after. The narrow end was a deeper passage worn in the sea bed, and the blade end fanned out into a curving sandy beach.

Where the cliff dipped towards the water, there was a jetty, and a track that meandered up towards Monksfoot Abbey and past the drying shed. A strong smell of seaweed lingered in the air. Axe Cove trapped the weed, especially after a storm. Gathered up by the villagers, it was soaked to rid it of salt, then dried in a long shed before being crushed and sold to farmers for fertilizer.

Monksfoot Abbey came into sight. It was a solid, oblong building with a coach-house and stables off to one side. It had an air of secrecy about it. As he strode along the track, a light appeared in the porch and a pair of dogs headed towards him, barking rustily. They were well past their prime and had never been blessed with proper names. They were known as Dog and Dog.

He stopped, allowing them to inhale his scent and recognize him as friend or foe. As they nosed at his ankles, their tails began to wag. Only then did he take the liberty of fondling their ears. When he got closer, a man with a pistol trained on him stepped from the gloomy depths of the porch. 'Identify yourself.'

'Fletcher Taunt . . . I've bought the place.' Fletcher patted his pocket, reassuring himself. 'I have the deeds to Monksfoot here, with my name on it, and not a penny owing.'

'Aye, so I'd heard.'

'So soon? I've just finalized the transaction. How are you, Tom?'

'Fair to middling, I reckon. The cold gets to your bones this time of year. I thought it might be you, Mr Taunt. We saw the

Midnight Star sail past earlier. Silas said he hoped you'd come to see him tonight.'

'Can you manage a meal and a bed?'

'Reckon so, seeing you own the place now.'

'How is Silas? I hear he's been poorly. I thought to share a jar and a tale with him.'

Tom Pepper grinned widely. 'He's as sour as a witch's tit and hates being confined to bed. There's life in the old dog yet, though, especially now he knows he won't have to leave his home to a stranger. Got instructions for you about his funeral, too.'

'Which are?'

'He wants to be tied to the mast of the *Wild Rose* and be towed out into the channel and set fire to. He's reckoned the times and tides, and tells me his ashes will float back into the cove if you do it right. That way he'll be able to keep an eye on you.'

Fletcher chuckled. 'I'll have to try to talk the old fool out of that one. I don't want him floating around the place telling me what to do every five minutes. Besides, the *Wild Rose* is too sweet a lugger to waste on a funeral.'

'He thought you'd say that, but it won't hurt to humour the bugger. He wants to take Dog and Dog with him for company.'

'We can use the old dingy instead. It's been beached for over a year, so a small amount of encouragement and it should go up like a torch.'

Five minutes later, Fletcher greeted Silas with as much cheerfulness as he could muster. 'The best you'll get from me is to wrap you in your shroud, take you out into the channel in the dingy and bury you at sunset. I might take the preacher to say a sermon over you, as well.'

'Do that and I'll come back to life and kick the pair of you overboard,' Silas growled.

Fletcher was shocked by the change in Silas. He couldn't be more than sixty, but he'd lost weight and his cheeks had sunk over his bones. Fletcher could almost hear his lungs flapping for air against his rib cage, and his breathing was painful to listen to. He looked like a skeletal child in the large four-poster bed. It was plain to see the Grim Reaper had placed his mark on him.

'I get tired of lying here.' He grimaced as he shifted from one hip to the other. 'I can't eat, I can't pee, and I can't . . . well, never mind. Just thinking about women hurts. All I can do is fart. It feels as though rats are chewing away at my guts. And I hate having nobody to talk to.' Silas gazed at him through eyes filled with pain and fatigue, his manner all at once piteous. 'Will you stay a few days, Fletcher?'

Fletcher felt sorry for the old man, who seemed desperate for company. 'I can stay longer. George can manage to sail the *Midnight Star* without me, especially on the American run. After all, he's the one in possession of the seamanship qualifications. If you like, he could inform your nephew of your illness – bring him back, perhaps.'

'Nay, lad . . . the man won't be coming here to visit.'

'Is there anything I can do to make you feel more comfortable, Silas?'

'Apart from shooting me through the head like you would a worn-out nag? Take me out on the *Wild Rose* tomorrow. I want to smell the salt and feel the wind on my face just one more time. I asked Tom to take me over to Cherbourg on the next run, but the miserable old bugger refused.'

'We could go into Poole, and Tom can come with us to help sail her, but only if the snow lets up. George Mainwaring will need the ship's dinghy back before he sails. I'll ask the doctor if you're fit—'

'Sod the doctor. He can't cure me; he just fills me up with laudanum to keep me quiet. The medical fraternity like their patients to die in a dignified manner and without kicking up a fuss.' Silas plucked at Fletcher's sleeve like a magpie. 'What did Oswald say to you?'

'Nothing I didn't already know. He took my payment for Monksfoot and gave me the deeds. Bailey came sniffing around, looking for trouble, but with Sir Oswald there he couldn't do much. I think Bailey is in the pay of my uncle.'

'Could be, but I doubt it. Simon Bailey is as straight as they come. He's always been a loyal servant to the law. Take my advice, Fletcher. Heal the rift with your uncle before it's too late and get him out of the smuggling business. It's getting out of hand. Bailey is one of the new type of law enforcers. He's an outsider who doesn't have an emotional connection to the Dorset coast or our local customs. And the authorities are getting tougher. They'd shoot you in the back first and ask the questions afterwards. Give your uncle his half of the ship back. He bought the *Midnight Star* to give you and your mother a legitimate income.'

'I will . . . when he apologizes for calling me a cheat.'

'It doesn't matter which of you is in the wrong. You're all he's got. He brought you up and you owe him some respect.'

'He gets all the respect he deserves. I've put aside the money he would have earned from the *Midnight Star*. It's in the bank under his name, so if anything happens to me, he won't be able to accuse me of stealing from him. As for giving up the game, I intend to, Silas, just as soon as I've earned enough to repair this place and give me something to fall back on. It should take me another eighteen months or so to get on my feet.'

'You're just as stubborn as he is, but he's a wiley old fox.'

'Aye, Silas, there's no doubt that I am. He taught me well.'

'There's more to running an estate than house and land. You need a woman to warm your bed and children to feed your soul. They're like pups. They rely on you, take all you can give them and love you in return.' His eyes took on a dreamy look. 'When all's said and done, it's people who matter . . . not fame and fortune. Family turns an ordinary man into a good man who knows how to love and forgive.'

'But a man needs to be able to earn the means to provide for them.' Remembering that Silas had lost his wife and two children to typhoid, he said, 'But aye, you're right, at that.'

'Then you'll reconcile with your uncle?'

'I'll think on it, Silas.' He grinned at him. 'I come here to pay you a visit and in five minutes you've already arranged a pleasure cruise for yourself, a wife and a litter of youngsters for me, and a reconciliation with my uncle. I wouldn't be surprised if you had a woman hiding in the cellar waiting to be carried off. Now, stop nagging me and get some rest.'

'Time enough for that when I'm dead.' Silas yawned. 'Come to think of it, I am a bit weary. Go and explore your new home, lad; everything in it is yours, including the dust and dog turds. At least I can die knowing Monksfoot is in good hands. And Fletcher . . .' Silas said when he reached the door. 'I forgot to mention earlier that my nephew in America has died. One of those redskins he was trying to convert had the good sense to fire an arrow through him. Apparently, it went in one ear and out through the other.'

A huff of laughter escaped from Fletcher. 'Please accept my condolences, if you feel you have need of them.'

'I don't. I just want you to know that I've made you my heir.'

Fletcher turned to stare at the man, wondering if he'd heard that right. 'Say that again, in words I can understand.'

'You heard, all right. I had to leave it to someone. Apart from Tom, who's already been taken care of, and the lawyer man, you're the only one who knows that I've made you my heir.'

'What I want to know is why, Silas?'

'There's a possibility that we're related.'

'How much of one?'

'Enough for me to think you're entitled to have my fortune. There will be no further discussion on this. Shut the door when you go out, would you, lad?' And Silas turned on his side and began to snore.

Three

Deep in the heart of the house, a clock struck the twelfth hour in a regular baritone. It penetrated Miranda's slumber and brought her awake.

The fire had burned low and the room was filled with a pale, eerie light. Getting out of bed, she scrunched the bottom part of the nightgown into her hand so she wouldn't trip over it, and moved to the window.

The wound on her head was a constant drumbeat under the bandaging, and the muscle on her thigh ached where the dogs' teeth had penetrated below the skin.

There had been a fresh fall of snow while she slept. The sky was low and heavy, threatening more. The air in the room was cool, and the nightlight on its saucer fluttered like a frenzied moth trapped in a pool of molten wax.

Anna was asleep on the daybed, but Miranda didn't wake her. The woman had to work all day and needed her rest. She settled a couple of medium-sized logs on the fire and replaced the spark guard.

Her sister's breathing was laboured and harsh, the sound reaching her from the room next door. Now and again, a rattling cough disturbed its rhythm. Miranda lit a candle from the nightlight to guide her to where Lucy slept. She placed the back of her hand against her sister's heated skin.

'Mama . . . I'm thirsty,' Lucy whispered.

Mama! Tears sprang to Miranda's eyes as she filled a glass with water from a flower-patterned white china jug. The image that came to her mind, of her poor mother lying under the snow in the cold with just the dead infant for company, saddened her.

Lucy tried to gulp the water down and then began to cough.

Propping her sister's head against her shoulder, Miranda said, 'Sip it slowly, my love.'

'I'm hot. I can't breathe and everything itches.'

'You'll feel a little better in a day or two. Sir James left me something to help stop the itch. He said that, however hard it irritates, you mustn't scratch the spots; otherwise they'll leave scars.'

She gazed at the pot of salve Sir James had left on the table. What had he said? It had killed the dogs' fleas and taken the itch from their bites. He'd laughed when she'd asked him if fleas breathed.

Removing the lid, she inhaled its fragrance. It didn't smell in the least bit sinister, but seemed to consist of aloe juice with lavender mixed in. She spread the concoction on Lucy's skin. 'There, does that feel better?'

Lucy nodded. 'It feels nice and cool. Miranda . . . I thought I saw our mother standing at the end of my bed.'

The hairs prickled up Miranda's arms and into her neck. 'It would have been the maid checking on you, I expect. She's asleep on the day bed now.'

'Do you think that man will let us stay here?'

'I don't know. He seems nice, but he can't take in everyone who is homeless. Perhaps he'll give us a job. Or he might decide we must go into an institution for the poor. Our mother was taking us all to the workhouse. She had no choice.'

Lucy's nose wrinkled. 'I don't want to go into a workhouse.'

'I know. But it might be the only thing we can do to survive. We can't wander around the countryside in winter without shelter or food. We probably wouldn't have to stay there for long. I might fall in love and get married, and then we would have a home.'

'Perhaps you could marry Sir James.'

'Don't be silly, Lucy. He's old enough to be my grandfather.'

'No, he's not. He's only fifty-four. I asked the maid.'

She shrugged. 'If you don't think that's too old, you can marry him. Now, settle down to sleep. Sir James might want to talk to me tomorrow, so I want to make a good impression and remain alert.'

'What will you tell him?'

'I'll answer any question he asks with the truth. He's already indicated that he's not the type of man who would tolerate a liar. He's also a magistrate, so would not allow one to stay undetected for long, either. Then where would we be?' She kissed her sister's cheek. 'Go to sleep now. Goodnight.'

The logs had begun to burn and sparks flew up the chimney as they snapped and cracked. Firelight caused the shadows to leap like puppets dancing on the wall.

When she was settled in bed again, Miranda's glance was drawn to the portrait of the young man. His face was in shadow, but his greenish eyes glittered in the firelight. She smiled at him and whispered, 'Perhaps I'll marry you.'

A log cracked and then flared up. Something shifted in a corner. There was a moaning sound and she caught a glimpse of a pale gown.

Heart bumping, she gazed at it. 'Who is it? Who's there?'

The maid sat up. 'Is everything all right, miss? Do you need anything?'

'I've just got back from making my sister comfortable and thought I heard someone groan.'

'It's the draught blowing under the door. Usually it happens when one of the outside doors is opened. I expect the master has let the dogs out before he retires for the night.'

As if on cue, there came a bark from outside, and the gruff voice of Sir James calling them back. Miranda relaxed back on to her pillow with a sigh of relief.

'You get used to the ways of this house after a while, miss. You go back to sleep now, and your body will soon mend.'

Miranda did, but not for long. Just as she was about to drift into sleep, she heard a snuffling, panting sound along the bottom of the door. Suddenly wide awake, her heart began to pound again.

A soft whistle from the depths of the house was followed by a whining yawn and the scrabble of feet on floorboards.

One of the dogs, thank goodness. Heart returning to its usual rhythm, she sighed when the maid began to snore, and pulled the covers over her ears to block out the noise.

'I hope you enjoyed a good night's sleep,' Sir James said the next morning.

Did he? Did he indeed, when he'd recently woken her up from it? Her head felt as though it was full of feathers. She managed to contain a sharp retort; even managed to release a polite smile to accompany her lie. 'Yes, thank you, Sir James.'

'I want to examine that head of yours again. Does it still ache?' He leaned forward and parted her hair, his fingers gentle against her scalp.

'Just a little.'

'You were lucky, Miss Jarvis. Focus on my finger, would you?'

His face was a few inches beyond the end of her nose, and her gaze wandered away from the slowly moving finger. His dark, guarded eyes were fascinating, flecked with little streaks of brown and grey on the surface and with nothing but darkness in their depths.

'You're supposed to be looking at my finger,' he said, and he sat back. 'You know, young lady, if you look into a man's eyes like that when you grow up, you'll be in serious trouble. Another day in bed for you, I think. It will keep you out of mischief. I'll have your sister brought through to keep you company.'

'Lucy was thirsty during the night.'

'So she told me. She still has a fever, but I think its heat has reduced somewhat. I'll send up a dose of willow-bark, which will help reduce it further. I can make you a dose to help ease your headache, too. By tomorrow, all of your sister's spots will have emerged and she will feel much better. Having a warm bed to sleep in has helped. My housekeeper is going to make you both some ginger cordial. It's a cure-all.'

'Like your aloe and lavender salve? It soothed Lucy's itches very quickly. Are you a doctor?'

'You could say that I doctor people sometimes. I'm interested in the healing qualities of plants, and I record my findings when I get the time.'

The door opened and the three dogs pushed their way in, tails wagging. Placing his head on the bed, Caesar lifted first one brow and then the other, his glance going back and forth.

'So, you've managed to reach the door knob and open doors now,' Sir James said to the dog. 'I hope you've all come to apologize to the young lady for the fright you gave her yesterday.'

Caesar whined, and when Miranda cautiously stroked his head, he licked her hand. Sir James smiled. 'There. Now it's your turn, Roma. Do your pretty parlour trick.' The bitch sat up on her haunches and waved her front legs in the air. 'Good girl.' Sir James patted her. 'Nero, you can shake hands like the gentleman you are.' Nero seemed to grin when he held a paw up to be shaken.

She laughed. 'They're nice dogs.'

He sent them packing. 'They're trained to guard the house and roam free in the place at night. Make no mistake: they would tear the throat out of an intruder if I ordered it. Caesar settled himself down outside your door last night. Perhaps he intended to eat you for supper. I hope he didn't wake you.'

'I was already awake. I thought it was a ghost at the door.' Her glance wandered to the corner of the room and she grinned. There was a gown draped over the back of a chair and a needlework box on the table. The hem was tacked up ready to be stitched into position. 'Is it still snowing?'

'Off and on, but the wind is coming off the sea and the snow isn't heavy enough to form into drifts. It will clear by mid-morning.'

'There's something I must tell you, Sir James. Our mother died in the woods, near the road, giving birth to a stillborn baby four days ago. She is still there, I think.'

'I see. Did nobody stop to help her?'

'A man and woman stopped, supposedly to help us, then helped themselves to everything of value our mother had on her. They took us to the village church and left us there, but we were turned away. The gypsies gave us a bowl of rabbit stew to eat, and somewhere to sleep. But they left in the morning. The smell of food led us to your kitchen. That is why I stole the bread.'

His eyes darkened. 'I'll make enquiries about your mother. Do you have a father?'

'He was estate manager to the Earl of Parbrook. Our father died after a fall from a horse and we had to leave our accommodation to make room for the incoming manager.' Tears filled her eyes. 'I can't bear the thought of our mother left there in the woods. She and the baby need to be buried.'

His forehead crinkled in a frown and, awkwardly, he patted her shoulder. 'Which road were you on?'

'I don't think it had a name. We started out on the main track from the Parbrook Estate, and then left it to take a lesser track. Our mother said there was a barn she knew of where we could shelter, which was a day's walk by foot away from the Earl's home. But we couldn't find it, only a shepherd's hut. We stayed there for a night. My mother said the barn must be across the fields, and the track took us into the woods. Then the infant started to arrive . . .' Tears scalded her eyes at the recollection of what her mother had gone through.

'Can you remember what those people looked like?'

'They were ordinary, except the woman had ginger hair, a rusty colour.'

His mouth twisted in a smile. 'She shouldn't be too hard to find if they're still in the district. Strangers with red hair will be noticed in these parts.'

'Oh, I remember, too, that the woman took a blanket made of knitted wool squares in different colours. Lucy and I had made it for the baby.'

'All the better.'

'You won't be too hard on them if you find them, will you? They were hungry and cold like us, and looking for work. At least they didn't leave us there.'

'You have a soft heart, Miss Jarvis. Do you have anything that might have your mother's scent on? My dogs are very good at tracking.'

She indicated her mother's shawl. 'It will have all our scents on; I hope it doesn't confuse them.'

'It won't. They already know your scent and where you are. They'll be looking for the strange scent.' He stood when a knock came at the door and picked the shawl up. 'That will be the housekeeper to see what you want for breakfast.' He smiled at Pridie when she entered. 'Bring her sister through. The pair of them can sit at that little table by the fire. Miss Lucy might be able to manage some gruel and a glass of milk. We will try them on coddled eggs and a little ham, and some toasted muffins and gooseberry preserve. And send up a jug of hot water so they can wash, if you please.'

After the woman left, he smoothed his fingers over the shawl. 'I'm sorry your folk died. That must have been hard. What was your mother's name in case I need it for the parish register?'

'Anna Louise Jarvis. Her family name was Jefferies. Thank you; you're very kind, Sir James.'

Now he looked embarrassed and said gruffly, 'I wouldn't turn a starving dog from my door without a meal in its belly, let alone one suffering from a fever. I haven't decided what I'm going to do with the pair of you yet.'

'I can work. I'm very accurate with figures and my father taught me to keep the Parbrook Estate ledgers in good order.'

'Did he now? I'll bear that in mind if I'm ever in need of a clerk. At the moment, our conversation on your futures must be set aside to a later date, as it seems I have other, more urgent business to attend to. We must find your mother's body and see her decently buried.' He left, and shortly afterwards there came a faint sound of hammering from the direction of the stables.

When they'd finished their morning toilette, the maid cleared everything away and breakfast arrived. While they ate, Miranda heard men call to one another and the occasional bark or howl from the dogs. The hammering stopped.

Afterwards, they knelt on the window seat and watched several men on horses move out, leaving dirty trails through the slush. Sir James was easily recognized by his size.

A man driving a small cart followed the men on horseback. The cart had a crude box on the back, probably in which to place the bodies of their mother and the infant. That's what the hammering had been for. Someone had made a burial box.

'Is that box for Mama?' Lucy began to cry.

Miranda put an arm around her and cuddled her close. 'She would want us to be brave.'

Two men left the main group and went in the opposite direction.

'They've gone to look for the body of our mother and those people who stole from us,' she said, smoothing Lucy's hair when her sister leaned her head against her shoulder.

'What will they do if they find them?'

'I don't know. Send them to prison, I suppose.'

They watched until the men went into the woods. Their breath steamed up the window and Miranda wrote their names in it with her finger. She gazed at her sister's face and smiled. 'I'll put something on your spots to stop them itching. Do you still feel feverish?'

'Yes, but it's not as bad as yesterday. I still feel tired, though.'

Her sister was far from her usual robust state. 'Except for breakfast today, you haven't eaten for several days. You must go back to bed and rest as much as possible.'

'Can't I lie on the day bed? It's lonely all by myself. You could read to me.'

'I haven't got a book. Besides, Sir James wants me to rest, too. The bed's big enough for two.'

'Do you like Sir James?'

Miranda had reservations. There was something about him that she didn't quite trust, but she couldn't say what. It was just an instinct.

'I don't know. He said he's a magistrate, so I think he'll be strict when we get to know him. I'll tell you after I've talked to him.' She thought about it while the housekeeper came in to build the fire up. When the woman had gone, Miranda told her sister, 'I've offered to keep Sir James's books, like I did for our father. If we can be useful, he might allow us to stay.'

'What can I do? I'm not very good at anything.'

'You can play the piano and sing better than I can. I saw a piano downstairs when we arrived. Perhaps he would enjoy listening to it.' Taking up a brush from the dresser, she gently tidied the soft brown length of Lucy's hair. When her sister's eyelids began to droop, she laid her back amongst the pillows, then joined her in the bed.

Her gaze was drawn to the portrait of Fletcher Taunt, and she smiled and said, 'You resemble your uncle greatly. Are you as tall, I wonder?'

The cold had kept the woman suspended in rigor mortis. She looked as though she was carved from marble, for the blood had pooled on the underside.

James moved a wet strand of hair from her face with his forefinger. Like the rest of her hair, it was sodden from slush.

She'd been a beauty in life, like her two daughters. The infant was in her arms; its skin was dark, as though it had strangled on the cord before it could take a breath.

They reminded James of his own wife and daughter, taken in the same manner all those years ago, except they hadn't had to experience the indignity of dying in the open air. He hadn't mourned that loss too keenly, since the marriage had been an arranged one. His wife had been a little on the dull side and had offered him no companionship of note, and she had been an unwilling partner in bed. James had been left with a son then. Barely five years old, William had died from typhoid six months later, and James had thought his heart would break. How many times could it be broken, though? He wondered. Now it was Fletcher's turn to break it. He must make matters right between them. The argument had been his fault. He'd said some hard things to Fletcher, and he missed the boy.

Still, the young must defer to the old, and Fletcher would come to realize it.

He was tidying the woman's skirts when he felt something hard along the hem. Taking out a knife, he slit along the fold and removed a heavy gold ring of the type a man would wear. There was a second ring to fit a woman's hand, with a small, inferior diamond in it, and a couple of golden guineas. He searched the rest of Anna Jarvis's clothing thoroughly and, finding nothing else, turned to Jack Pridie, the general foreman of the estate and husband of his housekeeper.

'It's a small amount for a legacy, Jack.'

'Aye, it's little more than a keepsake. What do you intend to do with those youngsters, Sir James?'

'I don't know yet. Perhaps there will be room in the charity school.'

'They're already overcrowded, I believe.'

'They could probably fit them in for an extra fee. They couldn't afford to pay from this legacy.' He spun one of the coins in the air and laughed. 'Have you shifted that stuff yet?'

'It should be gone tonight. We could do with some extra storage.'

'If Silas Asher sells me Monksfoot Abbey, we could use that.'

'Aye, but somebody told him you intended to pull the Abbey down and mine the clay and gravel out from under it.'

'I'll have to convince him otherwise. Who started that rumour anyway?'

'I don't suppose we'll ever know for sure, sir.'

James grunted as he grumbled, 'I have a bloody good idea.'

They gently lifted the still figure into the makeshift coffin and wrapped it in the linen sheet he'd lined it with. Placing the woman's head on a small cushion, he covered her face.

Jack said, 'She was a bonny-looking woman . . . neat, but nicely built.'

'That she was, Jack. I fancy the older girl takes after her. Come. Let's go.'

They would hammer the lid on after the older girl had identified her.

The others had returned from town. There had been no sign of the couple from the road, but the authorities were keeping a look out for them.

There was other news. One of the maids, who had just come back from town, was brought before him by Pridie.

'What is it, Pridie?'

'It's your nephew, sir.'

'What of him?'

'Maisie here overheard something in the market, and I thought it was important enough to bring her to you so you could hear it from her own mouth.'

'What is it, girl?'

'I overheard the Monksfoot coachman tell someone that Mr Fletcher Taunt had purchased Monksfoot Abbey, lock, stock and barrel.'

James felt as though he'd been punched in the midriff, and spluttered, 'He's what?'

'He's purchased—'

'Yes, yes . . . I heard you the first time. Thank you, girl. Pridie, give the girl sixpence as a reward for keeping her ears open.'

Going into the drawing room, he slammed the door behind him. So that was what Fletcher was doing behind his back – using the extra money he'd made from James's half of the ship to buy the very building that he'd always coveted.

Smoke billowed into the room from the chimney in the down draught he'd created and he began to cough. He poured himself a brandy and sipped it slowly while the dogs whined outside the door and scratched at the panels.

It was Mrs Pridie who found the courage to approach him. 'What shall we do about the woman's body, sir?'

James's anger had forced the task at hand from his mind. 'The elder of the two girls must identify her, and I'll tell the doctor to issue a death certificate. Ask Jack to arrange for a plot to be dug in the local churchyard and to tell the preacher I'll expect him to say some words over the body tomorrow morning.'

'Reverend's Swift's wife turned the girls away from the parish . . . said they didn't belong to ours.' Pridie's sniff displayed her affront. 'Anyone would think she ran parish affairs.'

'She does, since her husband is a sot. I don't blame him with that nagging shrew as a wife. Tell the good reverend to lay off the holy wine. And if he doesn't put in an appearance, sober or not, I'll personally fetch him. I'll haul him out of his pulpit by the scruff of his scrawny neck, tie him behind my horse and drag his skinny arse along the highway to the cemetery.'

'Yes, sir.'

'And Pridie?'

'Sir?'

'Tell Jack to say none of those things, just that we need his services to lay a body to rest in the old cemetery. We must leave him with some pride.'

Pridie smiled.

'Also, ask your husband to get in touch with the quarry for an estimate. I want the walls and gatehouse reinstated between my property and the Monksfoot Estate, where the road passes through my land.'

'But the folks at Monksfoot Abbey won't be able to . . . What about the public right of way?'

'There was no public right of way until my grandfather provided one. I'm about to withdraw the favour. They and their visitors can use the long way round.'

Her smile faded as the purpose of the wall sunk in. 'Anything else, sir?'

'See if the older girl is awake. Wrap her in a warm rug and I'll carry her to the stable to do the indentification. Let's get this business over and done with. She might need a bit of comfort afterwards, so make sure she has it.'

'Yes, sir.'

'Once she's properly identified the woman and infant, we'll leave the body in the carriage house tonight, ready for burial in the morning.'

Pridie nodded and turned away.

'And, Pridie, rid yourself of that disapproving expression. If you need to place any blame, it can rest on the shoulders of my rascally nephew, Fletcher Taunt.'

Four

It was the second funeral in as many months. In that time, March had come in with a boisterous roar of wind and was beginning to calm its temper.

The first funeral hadn't attracted much attention, Fletcher thought. It had been the body of a vagrant woman. The ceremony had been attended by his uncle, a couple of house servants and a worker from the Monksfoot Estate who had been passing by and stopped to pay his respects, Fletcher had been led to believe.

The deceased's two children had also attended.

A modest stone was erected, with the date of death recorded. It stated that Anna Louise Jarvis died in childbirth and was buried with her stillborn infant.

'"Beloved mother of Miranda and Lucinda" had been etched on the stone when I went back to have a look at it. They were pretty little maids,' the worker had told Tom Pepper. 'Almost grown.'

Tom had made further enquiries at the local inn before he'd approached Fletcher with the information. 'It's said Sir James has offered the children temporary accommodation while they recover from the privations their exposure to the cold had brought about.'

His uncle was known for his occasional philanthropic acts, and Fletcher nearly lost interest until he remembered Sir James's shady business interests and the fact that the children were two young girls who had nobody to protect them.

Sir James owned the deeds to several waterfront investment properties along the coast to Southampton, and a couple in London. He rented them out for an enormous amount, closing his eyes to what went on in them, his reputation buffered by several lawyers, agents and rent collectors in his pay. Some were the haunt of smugglers and press gangs; others were houses of ill repute.

Not that Fletcher was himself totally pure in body and mind, but it was possible the 'pretty little maids' would end up in one of those houses or, worse, sent overseas and sold to the highest bidder.

Fletcher's interest was piqued. His uncle's guests would get short shrift once they no longer amused him, and he intended to keep an eye on the situation. He knew his uncle well, and out of sight usually meant out of mind with him.

Silas Asher's funeral was vastly more spectacular than Anna Jarvis's had been.

The evening weather was uncertain as to mood, for though the clouds and sea were stippled with the last reflections of a glorious setting sun, mad blusters of wind invaded the evening calm, sending coat skirts flapping and hats flying.

Silas had been a popular and colourful character in the district, despite being feared. He'd been the last in a long line of wreckers and smugglers, a man who'd carried on his family tradition without scruple. Half of the local law enforcers had their hands in his pockets.

Silas had blood on his hands. That's the way he'd been brought up, and his defiance of the law collected only admiration, with little thought given to his victims and their families.

He'd been more notorious than Sir James Fenmore, who guarded his own privacy scrupulously and hid his deceit behind an honest front.

Silas had known too much about everyone, and there had been a couple of attempts to end his life. Fletcher had always got on with him, and his uncle had never objected to the relationship he'd formed with the man, as long as Silas didn't lead him into danger.

Were they related by blood, as Silas had hinted? Fletcher wondered. It was entirely possible. He'd never met Adrian Taunt, who'd been a soldier of fortune without family or means – one who'd conveniently died abroad, leaving Fletcher's mother a widow.

There were no paintings or sketches of Adrian Taunt for Fletcher to compare himself with. His mother would never discuss the man, except to say, 'It was a marriage of convenience. He's dead and gone, and good riddance.' Fletcher's looks were annoyingly like those of his uncle, except for the difference in eye colour.

Word of mouth had spread the news quickly. The cliff top was lined with onlookers gazing down into Axe Cove. Two of the house staff served brandy. Another preceded Fletcher and Tom Pepper, lighting flares as they carried the body of Silas down the path and settled it in the old dingy that was to be his pyre.

Everything smelled strongly of lamp spirit and the brandy Fletcher and Tom had poured into Silas to help incinerate him from the inside. Silas was as pickled as a dead man could get.

Fletcher turned to Tom. 'I think we're going to be half-seas-over on the fumes if we don't hurry and get it over with. Did Silas intend for us to go up in flames with him?'

Tom chuckled.

The lugger, the *Wild Rose*, was fully manned, but she displayed only half of her sails on her three masts and headed for the harbour entrance in a manner so confident as to suggest she could find it by herself if need be.

In the dingy carrying Silas's body, Fletcher hoisted the sail, and Tom freed the little craft from the shore for its final voyage and jumped in after him. The dingy was sluggish when compared with the *Wild Rose*, like a duck with one paddle.

Silas's shroud was weighted down with heavy ballast bricks, secured to his body with chains. The weight would carry Silas's remains down into the deep and away from the currents that might drag him back to shore.

Beyond the mouth of the Axe, the revenue men's cutter came into view, almost blocking the entrance on the other side when it dropped its sea anchor. She was similar in style, and fast, but not as fast as the lugger in full sail. They didn't risk coming through the entrance on this occasion.

Fletcher swore. 'Don't tell me they're going to search the boats and the body for contraband. It will start an instant war.'

'Bailey isn't that daft; he's just being provocative.'

The crew of the *Wild Rose* ignored the cutter and sped for the gap with the air of one who had every intention of sailing right through the revenue men's ship. The cutter's crew scrambled to pull on the anchor rope, leaving just enough leeway for the *Wild Rose* to sail alongside her with barely a gap between them. The crews hurled insults at each other, even while Fletcher admired both skippers for holding their nerve.

When the *Wild Rose* reached the designated spot, they dropped the sea anchor. By the time Fletcher got there in the valiantly struggling dingy, the water was up to his ankles and the funeral craft was leaking like a sieve.

He saw Bailey on the deck of the cutter, telescope held to his eye.

Fletcher put a finger to his cap in acknowledgement. He could have liked the man if he'd been a trifle less honest.

'Signal to the *Wild Rose* to send their dingy over, else we'll be going down with Silas,' he said.

The sky was beginning to darken. While Tom signalled, the staff on the cliff top began to light flares. Fletcher saw his uncle, outlined against the sky, and affection for him arrived in an unwanted surge. He wished they'd got on better. Perhaps Sir James would come to the house later, and he could mend the rift between them, though he didn't see why he should make the effort when it was his uncle who was in the wrong.

Fletcher used a flare to light a fuse and stepped from the funeral boat into the *Wild Rose*'s dingy with Tom. The oarsmen rapidly rowed it away.

They'd barely made it on to the deck of the *Wild Rose* when flames ran up the mast of the dingy containing the body, and the sail exploded into a raging fire. A cheer went up from those on shore, followed by silence as they watched the boat burn.

He glanced to where he'd last seen his uncle. He was watching him through a telescope. There was another man with him; from his outline he appeared well built. 'Who's that with my uncle, Tom?'

'Murdoch Barnstable. Your uncle employed him three months ago as second coachman, and he sometimes rides with him as a sort of bodyguard. I've heard that he's good with his fists.'

Fletcher acknowledged his uncle's presence with a lift of his hand, and the telescope was slipped into the man's pocket. It would do as a start.

Eventually, someone began to sing in a deep voice. '*Rock of ages, cleft for me, let me hide myself in thee.*'

The rest of the mourners waded in with great gusto. '*Let the water and the blood, from thy wounded side that flowed.*'

Fletcher joined in the singing. '*Be of sin the double cure, save from wrath and make me pure.*'

Tom snorted loudly. 'Silas will come back and haunt you if he hears that.' He began to bawl out a sea shanty from the top of his voice. '*Come all ye young fellows that follow the sea, and pray pay attention and listen to me to me . . .*'

'*Blow, blow, blow the man down,*' everyone roared.

Even the crew of the revenue cutter joined in, throwing another hymn into the ring as her crew hauled in her anchor and she flirted her tail as she turned in the wind. Soon the words flowed back and forth between sea and shore, with no rhyme or reason.

Somebody cursed. Words were changed. Another threw a punch.

The leaking dingy, fuelled by the body of Silas, was a roaring ball of crackling flame. It was a fierce fire.

'He's going up like a hog on a spit,' Tom said, fifteen minutes later.

'Time to go back before the brandy disappears, gentlemen, so let's leave him to it. Besides, we're missing a good brawl going on ashore.'

The *Wild Rose* lifted anchor and made for her mooring, her crew eager to enjoy the fun.

Fletcher was halfway up the path when he heard a hiss. He turned in time to see the funeral pyre carrying the charcoaled remains of Silas Asher disappear beneath the water. For a few seconds, he saw a flame burning under the surface, and then it was extinguished.

The revenue cutter was hauling sail. Soon it would head for its berth at Poole. There would be no business done in this part of the coast tonight; everyone would be at Silas's wake.

There came a sudden shout from the cutter, and those on shore ducked when the crew raised their rifles and a rattling fusillade of gunfire filled the air.

Instinct made both men drop to the ground.

'Bloody varmints,' Tom said, sounding embarrassed as he rose, brushing the chalky dust from his jerkin.

Fletcher sprang to his feet and laughed. 'You've got to admit the man has a grim sense of humour. Silas would have liked that touch.'

'He would that.'

When they reached the cliff top, Fletcher's glance wandered over the crowd to where he'd last seen his uncle. Damn, he'd just missed him, he thought, watching the rear end of his uncle's horse disappear into the gloaming.

James had to admit that Fletcher had put on a good show with Silas's funeral. He'd been tempted to stay longer, but approaching his nephew was out of the question now.

Fletcher knew how much he'd wanted Monksfoot Abbey, and James intended to teach Fletcher a lesson, in more ways than one.

He stabled his horse and poured himself a brandy, his temper still too uncertain to trust. He had guests coming for dinner – Bailey and his widowed sister, Sarah, plus his legal representative and his wife.

Then there were the two Jarvis children, who were now recovered completely from their misadventure. He'd decided to give the pair an airing, see how they acted in a social situation.

'Are the children suitably attired for a social dinner, Mrs Pridie?'

'As to that, we've managed to alter a gown or two for them, but the older one prefers her own clothes. She's determined not to be beholden to you.'

'That's her pride speaking. I won't have her wearing those rags to dinner. Tell her she must change into the suitable clothes that have been provided for her, else I'll assist her to.' He gave an indulgent smile. 'Young Lucy has asked me if she can play the piano and sing for our entertainment.'

'I hope you're not getting too attached to those youngsters, sir.'

'Why not, pray? They liven the place up and amuse me no end. Lucy is as lively as a flea, and the too-dignified Miss Jarvis beat me at chess the last time we played – and had the bad manners to crow about it. Miranda is quick-witted and clever. She seems to have gathered a lot of knowledge in her short life.'

'May I ask what is to happen to them in the future?'

James *had* allowed himself to become attached to the sisters. He hadn't had female company in the house for a long time and found them a distraction from the seriousness of his business life. He'd considered the various options open to them and hadn't liked any of them.

'It's possible that I'll make them my wards, furnish them with a dowry and find them suitable husbands when they turn sixteen – which can't be that far off. It will give me a purpose in life. I often notice something gracious and womanly about the elder girl; she's mature beyond her years. Sometimes she seems more woman than child.'

'But, sir—'

'Enough, Pridie. I'm a man and I know exactly what I'm about where women are concerned.'

Pridie grinned. 'Do you, indeed, Sir James . . . I often wonder if you see beyond the end of your nose.'

Filled with fatherly feelings towards the youngsters he'd rescued, he said, 'Go about your business now.'

'No!' Miranda said, knowing full well that if she wore the blue brocade gown Mrs Pridie offered, she would no longer be able to disguise herself as a child and they would be sent packing.

Lucy had no such scruples. Her spots had now faded to little more than a trace, and she danced across the room with a wide smile on her face in an ankle-length swirl of pink chiffon over satin. She wore a big bow in her hair with flowing ribbons dotted with little silk rosebuds.

Mrs Pridie sighed. 'The master is not in the best of moods, luvvy. Take my advice. It would not be wise to put your head in that particular lion's mouth tonight.'

'Then I won't go down at all. Tell Sir James I'm unwell.'

'He won't believe it when you displayed no evidence of it earlier.'

'He'll have to, because he wouldn't drag me down the stairs by my ears.'

Pridie's lips pursed. 'I wouldn't be too sure of that, young lady. On your own head be it, then.'

Miranda didn't want to spoil Lucy's enjoyment. 'Take Lucy down with you, Pridie. She can tell me all about it when she comes up to bed. Be on your best behaviour, Lucy. Don't forget your manners.'

Advice she should have given herself, she realized, when a few minutes later the door opened and slammed back against the wall.

Dropping the book she'd just started, Miranda jumped up from the chair and stammered as she backed towards the bed, 'What . . . do you think you're doing?'

He came to stand in front of her, a solidly handsome figure gazing down at her through eyes that glowed like fiery coals. 'In this house, I give the orders and you obey them.'

'I'm not hungry.'

'That's a lie, since you missed lunch. I expect you to put on the clothing I provided you with, and come down to dinner like any other civilized young woman.'

A quiver of nervousness crept into her voice. 'I prefer my own clothes.'

'Do you . . . do you indeed?' Reaching out, he grasped her ragged dress in both fists and split it asunder.

His eyes widened in surprise as his glance ran over her exposed body, which she tried to cover with her hands.

He drew them aside, and she closed her eyes and drew in an agonized breath, almost paralyzed by shock, when his hands gently cupped her breasts, before sliding lightly down over her belly to flatten against the dark thatch of hair at the apex of her thighs.

'Don't do that,' she pleaded, her voice low with the shame of being handled, and she found the courage to push his hand away.

His breath expelled with some force, 'My God, you're a grown woman . . . and an exquisitely formed one at that. How the hell did I miss it? You've been lying to me all along, missy. How old are you?'

'I'll be nineteen next month.' Face flushing, she jerked the torn edges of her clothing together and turned her back on him. 'I never suggested I was anything different from what I am. Go away; you've shamed me.'

The heat from his body lessened, and the tension between them cooled. He stepped back, created some space between them, but something had changed in him because his eyes held the knowledge of her nakedness.

'Why didn't you enlighten me on the numerous occasions I referred to you as a child? Why didn't you tell me, Miranda?'

She shrugged. 'I thought you might turn us out, and Lucy desperately needed help. I intended to tell you when we had our meeting.'

'Which meeting was that?'

'The one where you said you wanted to know everything about us.'

'Ah . . . that meeting. I've been a bit busy of late, and it had slipped my mind. In view of what's happened, we shall schedule that meeting for eleven o'clock tomorrow morning in my study.'

His footsteps echoed across the floor and he opened the door. 'Now your charade has been *exposed*, there is no more need for subterfuge, is there? Nobody will learn from me of what happened here this evening. I'll send Pridie up to help you dress. If you want to be silly and wear the remnants of your own clothing for the occasion, go ahead, but I'll be disappointed if you do. I will expect you in half an hour at the latest. Is that clear, Miss Jarvis?'

'Perfectly, Sir James,' she said, wishing she'd listened to Mrs Pridie in the first place.

The door was almost shut when he opened it again. Gruffly, he said, 'You took me completely by surprise and have nothing to feel shamed about, girl. That particular honour goes to me on this occasion.'

Five

The gown was slightly old-fashioned, its skirt flaring out over a stiff petticoat and decorated with a pretty lace trim, but it suited her. Anna arranged Miranda's hair into a topknot, decorating it with a posy of silk flowers. Heated tongs were used to create ringlets at either side of her face.

'There, don't you look lovely?' Mrs Pridie said, turning her towards the long oval mirror. 'Sir James was right taken aback . . . that he was. And serve him right for seeing only what he wanted to. I tried to tell him before, but no, he wouldn't listen.'

A stranger looked back at Miranda, and she was made immediately aware that her parents would never have been able to afford
a gown like this for her.

The bodice hugged her waist, stomach and ribs, and had enough
stretch in it to allow her to breathe, but not to slouch. She remembered laughing with her mother over an advertisement for one in
the *Ladies Journal* – seven shillings for a waist no more than eighteen
inches in circumference and sixpence per inch extra for larger
ladies.

That had been before her father's accident, when her mother's
expanding waistline was becoming noticeable. They'd been looking
forward to having a new baby in the house. How swiftly everything
had changed.

The young man's portrait on the wall was reflected in the mirror,
too, standing just behind her shoulder as if they were a couple.
They looked so realistic together that she nearly returned his wry
smile.

She ran downstairs when the clock struck half past the hour, in
case Sir James took it into his head to fetch her himself. Taking a
deep breath, she opened the drawing-room door.

It seemed to Miranda that every eye was upon her when she
entered the room.

She shook her head, trying to dispel the younger image of
Fletcher Taunt that still lingered on in her mind. It was hard to
do when Sir James approached her with his similar, older face. His
eyes expressed both approval of her appearance and an apology.
'You look delightful, my dear.' Placing his hand under her elbow,
he led her towards the guests. 'May I introduce Simon Bailey and
his sister, Sarah Tibbets. Simon represents the customs revenue
service in the district.' He turned to the older couple. 'And this is
my legal representative, Andrew Patterson, and his wife, Mary. Miss
Miranda Jarvis. You've already met her younger sister, Lucinda.'

'A delightful young lady,' Andrew Patterson said, sending Lucy
a smile. 'I believe Miss Lucinda is going to entertain us after dinner.
I'm looking forward to it.'

Seated on the sofa, Lucy looked shy and self-conscious in her
finery, and in the company of so many adults. Both of them wore
black armbands to signify their bereavement, for they had no
mourning garments. 'Two pretty butterflies should not be covered

in ugly black, and wearing only an armband will not cause any disrespect to your mother,' Sir James had said.

Both couples scrutinized Miranda without seeming to. Their glances flitted from her dress to her hair, and to places in between, like curious birds. In the case of the men, they lingered on her breasts, their eyes vaguely predatory. The women's gazes were more critical and somewhat speculative, as though they were wondering what sort of relationship she had with Sir James.

Sarah Tibbets's smile faded when she looked at Sir James. 'I thought you said they were both children, James.'

He gave her an easy smile. 'At my age it becomes harder and harder to differentiate. Girls seem to change into women overnight.'

'The younger, the better – aye, Sir James?' Andrew Patterson said with chuckle.

Miranda blushed, remembering her host's hands on her exposed flesh.

'Not a subject fit for the drawing room, Andrew,' Sir James said firmly, and he held out his arm for her to take. 'Shall we go in to dinner? We've already kept the cook waiting for twenty minutes.'

To which Miranda replied, seeing an opening for her to hit back at him, 'It was entirely my fault, Sir James. I couldn't decide between the suitability of two gowns. Then I discovered a huge tear in one and was forced to change into the other. I apologize most profoundly for keeping everyone waiting.'

His eyes narrowed in on her. 'Apology accepted.' He beckoned to Lucy, who took his other arm. 'You look pretty tonight, Miss Lucy. You'll sit on my left hand and Miss Jarvis on my right. Promise me you won't grow up as unexpectedly as your sister did?'

Lucy offered him a smile filled with hero worship. 'I promise.'

Mrs Patterson chuckled. 'You're such a wag, James. You've only known these lovely girls for a couple of weeks. How much growing up can be done in that short time?'

'You'd be surprised.'

Sarah asked, in a rather imperious tone for a guest, 'And where shall I be seated, pray?'

'Wherever you wish, Sarah. It's a large table and the dinner is informal, which is why I've allowed you the liberty of using my first name on this occasion.'

When they were seated, Sir James rang a little bell before turning to Simon Bailey. 'What did you think of the funeral and sea burial for Silas?'

'It was interesting, but I thought there was a little too much romance attached to the demise of such a rogue. Silas was born dishonest and should have been hanged years ago. The world would be a better place without the Silas Ashers of this world littering it, like so much rubbish.'

'The old families hereabouts tend to follow tradition. Silas's family came from a long line of Vikings; smuggling was part of his blood.'

'So was murder, but that doesn't make it right.'

'Come, come now, Simon. Silas was a good man in his way. He kept many of the local men in work when they could have starved in the gutter, and he was honest in his dealings with his equals, even when he was being dishonest in the eyes of the law. Sometimes one has to measure a man's worth to the community and turn a blind eye to his foibles.'

'You may have the clout to turn a blind eye on occasion. I must work within the law, Sir James. I cannot weaken my stance towards those who seek to grow rich by avoiding the taxes legally due to the crown.'

'Oh, the crown benefits from taking her share of vagrants from the prisons. Most of those pressed into Navy service are smugglers. Every smuggler given decent employment to atone for his sins is replaced by a dozen more.'

Andrew Patterson joined in. 'Meanwhile, the prisons are filled to capacity, and wives and children are left with no means of support, which encourages more crime in their struggle to survive. To remove crime altogether would be to encourage anarchy.'

'Nonsense. As long as there is a network of honest men in government, there will be checks and balances. I have no compassion for such felons. It's up to a man to support his family, but not by criminal acts. If his wife and children suffer, that's his business, not mine. What say you, Miss Jarvis?'

Miranda thought Simon Bailey was rather forceful in his manner, however honest he professed to be. Nevertheless, she felt sorry for the man for having been exposed to such contrary opinions from those supposed to uphold the law.

She couldn't help but offer an opinion, albeit rather timidly.

'The wives and children of felons are also victims. If it hadn't been for Sir James, my sister and I would have perished in the snow two weeks ago, along with our mother. Not that my father was a felon, of course. He died when he fell from a horse.'

Bailey offered her a smile and his voice softened with what seemed to be genuine sympathy. 'My commiserations, Miss Jarvis . . . a different circumstance altogether. Females are notably soft-hearted about such matters. I have seen them weep at the gallows over the demise of the most disgusting and notorious of villains. With respect, women have very little understanding in such matters, since they are governed by their emotions.'

Into the sudden silence, Mary Patterson declared, 'Sir James is a saint. I have always thought so.'

Her husband exchanged a glance with their host, whose upward thrust of a single eyebrow made him look more devilish than saintly.

'I must get my halo out and polish it,' James said lightly and changed the subject, saying to the lawyer, 'Has the rector chosen the design for the new chapel window?'

'He is indecisive, but his wife leans towards the most expensive, I've heard.'

James huffed with laughter. 'And why not, when the money for it is coming out of my pocket. Perhaps I should donate the money for a new cutter for the customs service instead. A dedicated window is poor reward for such selfless acts, and I heard you had an encounter with a Frenchie, Mr Bailey, and had to turn tail and run.'

Simon didn't look too pleased to be reminded. 'He was armed to the teeth and intent on ramming us.'

The cook and the serving maid came in, carrying a steaming tureen. 'Ah, here comes the first course. That smells delicious, Nancy.'

Nancy beamed a smile at him. 'It's your favourite, Sir James. Chicken and mushroom.'

Roasted lamb and vegetables followed the soup, and the pudding was a tart made with a filling of preserved gooseberries, covered in creamy custard.

Lucy ate little, but Sir James coaxed her with a few spoonfuls.

As if he were her father, Miranda thought uneasily, because Lucy was impressionable, and it seemed as though Sir James was acting a part.

After dinner, the three men disappeared into the billiards room for port and cigars, and the ladies sipped coffee and liquor in the drawing room.

Sarah Tibbets began the conversation. 'I was unaware of the circumstances of you residing here, Miss Jarvis.'

'Are you implying Sir James *should* have made you aware of them?' Mary Patterson said. 'I've known him since we were children, and he usually keeps his private business to himself.'

Sarah didn't back down. 'If his guest sees fit to blurt out the reason of her being here in the middle of dinner, then I don't see how he can complain if his business becomes common knowledge.'

'To which guest are you referring? You can be certain that neither Andrew nor I will blurt out anything that's said at our host's dining table; am I wrong in assuming that you and your brother will offer him the same courtesy?'

'Of course not.' Sarah Tibbets stared at Lucy, who had shuffled her feet. 'Do stop fidgeting, child.'

Miranda was grateful to Mary for drawing the woman's attention away from herself, but she wasn't going to allow Sarah Tibbets to pick on Lucy. 'My sister has been ill, and she's beginning to tire.'

Just then, the door opened and the men came in. Sarah cried out, as if Lucy was five years old, 'The child should be sent to bed, James. She's tired and she's being a nuisance.'

Lucy coloured and tears moistened her eyes.

Sir James handed her his handkerchief. 'I doubt very much if Miss Lucy could ever be a nuisance. Besides, she has yet to do her turn. Mop those eyes, Miss Lucy. I'm sure Mrs Tibbets didn't mean to make you cry, did you, Mrs Tibbets?'

Sarah almost snorted and said brusquely, 'Of course not. Girls are overly sensitive these days. They shouldn't be pandered to.'

His eyes glinted when he turned to Lucy. 'Do you hear that, Miss Lucy? Thank goodness I have a mind of my own that tells me I'm too old and ugly to be dictated to by guests in my own home. What say you?'

Lucy giggled. 'You're not ugly, Sir James. As you said earlier, you're nearly as handsome as your horse and he's a dandy.'

'There we are, then. Seeing as how one cannot have an argument with oneself, it stands to reason that I must be right, and so must you be. You shall play the song we rehearsed, and I'll sing it with you. Then you must say goodnight and your sister can take you off to bed.'

Taking her place at the piano, Lucy played a lead-in to Benteen's song, and sang the first line. She had a clear, pleasant singing voice. *'How can I leave thee, how can I bear to part?'*

'That thou hast all my heart, dearest believe,' Sir James answered in a gravelly tenor that had abandoned the drawing room some years since.

A few moments later and Lucy took her bows to polite applause. Sir James lifted her hand to his mouth and kissed it. 'Well done, my dear. Off you go now. Miss Jarvis. Please don't forget to return to us when you've tucked her in.'

There was a chill in the air after the drawing room, and Miranda noticed that the door was open and cold air was streaming in. She remembered that Caesar had learned to open doors, and she smiled. She'd better leave it open in case the dogs needed to get back in. She'd mention it to Sir James.

Lucy's eyelids were drooping by the time they got upstairs, and she was almost asleep when she whispered, her voice slurring, 'It was fun tonight, wasn't it? You looked so lovely in that gown that it made that ugly woman jealous.'

'I enjoyed it, and you mustn't say that about Sir James's guests.' She pulled the nightdress over her sister's head. 'Into bed now.'

'Will you stay until I'm asleep? I get scared by myself sometimes, in case I see the ghost again.'

'It was your fever that caused that, but of course I will. I'll sit on the window seat.' Out in the darkness, she saw a blue light winking on and off. Then, not long after, she saw a steady light shining on the cliff top. Perhaps it was a pair of lovers, or a fisherman signalling to his wife as he headed back to harbour.

Lucy's breathing had become soft and even. Miranda lit the nightlight and went on to the landing. She heard the dogs fretting in a room on the other side of the landing. Caesar must have let them in.

Quietly, she entered the room. The dogs pushed damp snouts into her hands and gave little huffs of welcome.

'What are you doing in here? You should be downstairs. Off you go to the kitchen now and get your dinners.'

The dogs pushed past her and headed off. She stayed.

The room had a musty smell to it. The curtains were drawn back and she drew in a delighted breath at the sight of a shining round moon framed in the window.

Moving across to the window, she gazed dreamily out at a garden bathed in moonlight. Gradually, she became aware of something else. The sea perhaps, shushing on the shore. But no, this was another's presence. There was a soft feathering of breath that competed with her own, and a whisper of a heartbeat, like the regular beat of a far-off drum. She remembered the place was supposed to be haunted. Did ghosts breathe? Did they have heartbeats?

Of course they didn't. They were dead and didn't need either. 'Who's there?' she murmured, cursing the fear that made her voice quaver.

Prickles raced through her body and her throat closed when the door clicked shut. Fear paralyzed her and she could neither speak nor move.

There was a movement of air as something moved past her. Grasped by a strong arm, the other hand covered her mouth, smothering her involuntary whimper of fright. A man's voice materialized, like a curl of smoke against her ear. 'Don't scream, I won't hurt you.'

Though frightened half to death, the voice was reassuring and Miranda believed him. Even while she nodded, she thought, *No dead spirit, this.* The hand was warm and alive, and it smelled of brandy, as though he'd recently held a glass of the spirit in it. When she sank her teeth into the pad under his thumb, he jerked it away, cursing, and turned her to face him. He struck a vesta and applied the light to a candle.

She got a good sight of him then, the angled planes of his face accented in the moonlight, his hair a torrent of dark unruly curls. Not Sir James . . . no, not him, yet like him. This face had greenish eyes that glinted in the moonlight, and the hint of a wry smile, exactly like the image of him on her wall. But far from being an image, the living warmth of his body embraced her, invited her closer.

She could taste traces of brandy on her tongue, left there when she'd bitten his hand. She couldn't move, couldn't speak. He was the living, breathing image of Fletcher Taunt.

They stared at each other, and she thought her curiosity must be as apparent in her eyes as his was to her.

Slowly, a smile inched across his face and he drawled, 'Dear God, it's a young woman in my bedroom. Didn't anyone tell you I don't sleep here any more, so I can only imagine your delights? Tell me your name.'

She felt a blush creep into her cheeks. 'Miranda . . . Let go of me, please, Mr Taunt. What are you doing here?'

'I was looking for myself, but found you instead.'

He ran his hands down her arms and took her hands in his, gently pulling her to him across the few inches of space between them, his intention clear. There was no force from him. Slowly, he leaned forward, his gaze on her mouth, allowing her time to avoid him before it gently settled on hers.

She could have moved away, slapped him or screamed for help. She could have said no. She did none of those things. Legs rooted to the spot, she slowly disintegrated, allowing him the delicious liberty of stealing a lingering kiss from her lips, now sensitized beyond reason. Fire darted through her veins and every vulnerable part of her absorbed the living essence of him and quivered with anticipation.

A puff of air extinguished the candle. 'I want to know all about you and must see you again,' he whispered. 'Try to come to the stile next Thursday at ten.'

After a while, her mouth cooled. Miranda realized he was gone, quietly and without so much as a creak of a floorboard or a stair. Still she stood there, only God knew how long, enjoying the bouquet of the brandy on her tongue and experiencing his warmth embracing her inside.

Eventually, she opened her eyes and moved out to the landing window. The moon gradually rose and the night was saturated in its light. Shadows elongated in the garden.

She wondered if he might have walked out of his painting and she'd imagined him, after all, except she suddenly saw him in the shadows below the window. He was heading towards the woods at an easy lope, the three dogs silent shadows at his heels.

He stopped in the shadow of a horse chestnut – one that had recently delighted her by unfurling feathers of spring greenery from their brown sticky casings. He turned and blew her a kiss.

There was a whistle from beneath her. The dogs turned, sniffed at the air and then headed towards the noise at speed. She must go down before Sir James came looking for her and caught her in this room.

'So that was Fletcher Taunt,' she whispered, smiling as she quietly closed the door and floated downstairs on knees that seemed as liquid as water after the confrontation.

'Ah . . . there you are. I was just coming up to find you,' Sir James said from the hall below, making her jump. 'Have you seen the dogs?'

Sir James occupied a space patterned by ribbons of incandescent moonlight reflecting from a mirror. The air was filled with tension. As if he'd suspected his nephew had been here!

She hoped her breathlessness wasn't apparent in her voice as she raced to tell him, 'The dogs rushed out past me when I went upstairs. I'm sorry if I took too long. Lucy asked me to wait until she fell asleep, and from our window I could see a blue light winking. I thought it was a lantern on the shore.'

'Was the light steady or sparking?'

'Steady, I think. What was it?'

'A reflection of the stars on water, I should imagine.'

She nodded. 'My attention was then captured by the light coming through the window of the landing. The moon is so large and pretty tonight, and as bright as day. The dogs were over near the woods by then.'

'The front door was standing open. Did you open it?'

'No. I thought one of the dogs had managed to open it, until they pushed past me upstairs. I was about to tell you about it. Do you think it was an intruder?'

'If there had been an intruder, the dogs would have let me know. Either it was someone they knew or, more likely, they opened it, went out and came back. Caesar hasn't learned how to close it behind him yet. I'll have to get down on my hands and knees and demonstrate.'

The dogs scrabbled at the door and it slowly opened. They tried to push through it at the same time, a dozen legs sliding and scrabbling on the stone doorstep.

Miranda laughed. 'He must have heard you.'

He harshly addressed the dogs, 'You're not supposed to use this entrance or provide entertainment for my guests. Into the kitchen and stay there, you pests.'

They headed across the hall in a race of heated bodies and panting tongues, their tails between their legs.

As Sir James watched them go, a lump gathered in Miranda's throat. It was obvious he was as fond and indulgent with his dogs as he would be with children, if he'd had any. Lucy had grown fond of him, which worried her a little. He was lonely, and Miranda wanted to hug that from him. She wouldn't, of course. Although something about Sir James instinctively drew pity from her, another instinct feared him.

When they went back into the drawing room, Sarah Tibbets gazed from one to the other suspiciously. 'You were a long time.'

'Miss Jarvis was captivated by the moon on her way down the stairs, and I was distracted by her joy in the sight of it. It's full. There is something quite enchanting about a young woman standing looking at the moon, as though she's bidding farewell to her lover.'

He offered her a guileless smile when she gave him a sharp look.

Andrew Patterson was more practical. 'Not a night for smugglers, then; they'll be cursing the moon tonight.'

'Aye, there's that, and those who attended the sea burial will be overcome by the brandy they've swallowed this night,' Simon Bailey said complacently. He smiled without mirth, his teeth a perfect spread. He was not unattractive and looked fit. 'It means that my men can stand down and pay some attention to their families . . . except for the watchmen on duty, of course.'

Sir James's eyes glinted. 'The dogs have just come back from their rounds. You can relax, Simon. They'd let me know if any strangers were about, or if anything was amiss.'

Sarah Tibbets sniffed. 'We're not really strangers here, yet they wouldn't let us out of the carriage.'

'Dogs are like humans. They don't take to everybody. Mainly, they're animals that are faithful to the pack, and the pecking order of that pack. My youngest dog, Caesar, has taken mightily to Miss Jarvis here. He dotes on her.'

'Well, I think dogs are smelly, unreliable creatures and they should be kept out of the house. I prefer cats.'

'I admit, cats can be amusing, especially when they're cornered. They're plucky little creatures.' He chuckled. 'All I can say is I'm glad I'm not your dog . . . nor ever likely to be. I believe it is your turn to entertain us, Sarah. Edgar Allan Poe's "The Raven", isn't it?'

'Such a long poem,' Mary trilled. 'How on earth will you remember it all?'

'Sarah has been rehearsing it all week, and she has an excellent memory,' her brother told them.

Sarah offered a confident smile, 'I admit to being blessed in that way. But I do have the poem in a small volume of his works with me if I need to refer to it.' She cleared her throat and took up a stance. *'Once upon a midnight dreary, while I pondered weak and weary . . .'*

Eighteen weak and weary verses later they were all glassy-eyed from boredom. Sarah was certainly word-perfect, but the drama of the poem was lost in her style of narrative that plodded along like a herd of nodding donkeys.

Andrew Patterson suppressed a yawn and gave a theatrical shiver. 'I hope a raven never comes tap-tapping at my door.'

Sir James turned to Mary Patterson. 'Perhaps you'd be kind enough take a turn at the piano to round off the evening, Mary. Then I shall get you to recite a poem. In the meantime, I'll send a maid to fetch your cloaks, and you'll have the moonlight to guide your way home.'

Six

Fletcher was only slightly inebriated. He was a moderate drinker and always recognized the point when he needed to stop before his wits became too addled for him to function properly.

The moon was too bright for smugglers to go about their business. It was as though Silas's death had put a curse on it. But it was just right for lovers who wanted to be moonstruck. And he was obviously in the mood to be.

'Where did that delectable little female come from?' he asked himself, turning his face up to the glowing orb. 'Who is she?'

Her mouth had been as soft and melting as a bowl of butter,

her body firm and small. Her deliciously upthrusting breasts had almost invited his tongue to tickle the virginal nubs pushing against her bodice.

What was she doing at his uncle's home? Had she come with his dinner guests or was she a house guest? She'd been there long enough for the dogs to be happy with her presence.

The thought that she might be his uncle's guest caused him more than a little disquiet. His reasoning went off at a tangent, so he didn't have to follow where that particular thought was leading him. It was possible the girl was a new maid. He shook his head. Not in the gown she wore or the way she spoke. It was more likely that his uncle had brought her home for his weekend entertainment. There . . . he'd thought the unthinkable.

Miranda of the violet eyes hadn't looked, smelled or tasted like a trollop.

She'd been delectable, innocent . . . bloody scrumptious. In fact, she seemed to have woken latent cannibalistic tendencies in him!

He adjusted his trouser seam, which had begun to strangle his balls, and, straddling the stile, thought he'd far rather have a woman between his legs. He gazed back at Lady Marguerite's House. He hadn't found what he'd been looking for – the correspondence between lawyers that had surrounded his birth . . . the papers Silas had told him about, but wouldn't discuss with him. The only place left to search now was the attics . . . and his uncle's study. He frowned. No, not that. He did have some scruples.

It wasn't the first time he'd been back to his uncle's house over the past two years, but it was the first time he'd been detected. He could have stayed hidden in the shadows, but somehow she'd sensed his presence. Her breathing had quieted and she'd gone on alert, her senses twitching like the whiskers on a mouse.

His room was as he'd left it, his clothes still hanging in the wardrobe or folded neatly into the drawers, as though he was expected back. No dust had been allowed to gather on the surfaces of the furniture.

Would the girl tell Sir James he'd been there? He wondered, and then remembered the talk about his uncle taking two orphaned children under his roof after he'd buried their mother. The girl he'd met hadn't been a child, though there was certainly an air of innocence about her.

He'd left his horse just at the end of his own property, the boundary of which was on the other side of the copse. The gelding snickered softly when Fletcher approached and called out his name.

The wake for Silas was still going on in the seaweed drying-shed when Fletcher got back to Monksfoot. Some of the mourners were singing out-of-tune but vulgar sea shanties as he took his horse to the stable to bed him down for the night.

He heard the cook giggling and shushing in the darkness of the hayloft and a man grunting. He grinned. He hadn't ridden a woman for a while. Although there were a couple of attractive woman amongst the house staff who'd made sheep's eyes at him, it wouldn't be wise to take his pleasures so close to home if he wanted to keep the respect of his workers. As it was, one or two of them resented him taking over from Silas. Not even the faithful Tom had managed to take his measure yet.

'Miranda,' he said, tasting her name on his tongue. His grin widened as he wondered if he'd swallowed a tad too much brandy and had imagined her.

There was no sign of Tom or some of the more able-bodied men about, but the *Wild Rose* had gone from her berth. It surprised him that Tom would take her out on such a bright moonlit night. But then he remembered that Simon Bailey had been dining with his uncle. The revenue would not expect a run when the master of the house had just been buried, and most of the workers had been as drunk as fiddler's bitches.

Making his horse comfortable for the night, he went indoors.

The house staff were absent too, but the kettle was steaming on the hob and the lid rattling. He made himself some tea and slapped thick slices of ham and cheese between two slices of bread, eating his supper at the scrubbed pine table.

When he went up to bed, Dog and Dog were outside their former master's door. Glancing up at him, they whined.

He hunched down on his heels and fondled their ears. They stood, going through a stretching ritual and sniffing him, making growly noises as they detected the alien scent of his uncle's dogs on him. They seemed to waffle between doggy menace on behalf of the late Silas and pleasure at his attention to them.

These battle-scarred old hounds without names didn't move far from the house now. They'd belonged to Silas since they were pups. They'd pine for him, but Fletcher hadn't been able to carry out the instruction from Silas to shoot them and send them off into hell with him.

'Sorry, but your master isn't coming back, dogs. You can sleep in there if it gives you some comfort, just until you get used to his absence.'

One of them barked when someone bade the cook goodnight in a deep voice.

'Shush, Murdoch; someone might hear you.'

Fletcher knew he'd recognize the man by his voice alone, if they met.

The dogs disappeared through the door when he opened it, tails wagging in expectation of seeing their master there. If they were disappointed, they didn't look it, taking up their usual position on the rugs by the bed.

Fletcher propped the door open with a chair under the doorknob so they could get out if they felt the need.

—

The next morning, most of the servants were suffering from an excess of alcohol consumption. The cook must have overslept. Fletcher went to the kitchen, to find her bleary-eyed and short of temper.

He accepted her churlish apology and overtly gazed at her when she turned her back on him to examine the contents of a pan. Most of Silas's servants were too familiar for Fletcher's liking. This one was about thirty, and as slim as a reed. She had light brown hair pulled back into a knot. Her lack of hip spread was overshadowed by an abundance of bosom. All in all, she was passing fair, and a competent cook. The kitchen was grubby, though. Food scraps had been swept into a corner and left to go mouldy.

'Is the *Wild Rose* back at her mooring, Bertha?' he asked.

A pair of tawny eyes were turned his way. 'As far as I know, she hasn't been anywhere, sir.'

'Her berth was empty when I got home last night.'

'The brandy must've made you see things that weren't there. Or perhaps it made you not see what *was* there. Then again, the *Wild Rose* might have gone out to catch a tasty fish or two for your breakfast.'

If it had, there was no sign of them. 'And perhaps you were

too busy entertaining a man friend in the hayloft to notice.' He didn't let her know he was aware of the person involved, but it would bear watching.

'You should learn to keep what you see to yourself, master, lest someone chop off your nose.'

Lifting the lid from a pot, she grinned, stirred it with an iron spoon and aimed a dollop of oatmeal into a dish. She spun it across the table to where he stood. 'There, that will put hairs on your chest. Oatmeal was Master Silas's favourite breakfast.'

And she would learn, right now, that she had a new master, one who would demand politeness from his house staff. Gently, he pushed the bowl aside. 'Gruel is for invalids and children. I'm neither. Taking into account the upset to the household of Silas's demise, I will overlook what has just taken place between us. But if your intention is to remain in my employ, from now on you will not address me with such familiarity. Is that understood?'

Her mouth tightened; her gaze slid away, then came back. 'Yes, sir.'

'Good. Make sure you remember it. I'll have fried ham, eggs and bread. Serve it in the dining room, please. And get this kitchen cleaned up.'

'I haven't got time to do everything, with no help to speak of . . . sir.'

'I'll get you some help if you need it. When Tom returns, tell him I want to see him. And here's a word of advice for you, Bertha: I'm not the fool you think I am, so take care.'

She hesitated for a moment, and then, under his steady gaze, she murmured, 'Yes, sir . . . sorry, sir.'

He spoke to Tom in what passed as a study, though it was more like a junk room with piles of paper everywhere and the surfaces of the furniture dull and scarred. He hadn't been able to make head or tail of the account books, except to notice that they had been neglected for several years before the accounting ceased altogether. Receipts were piled high, and he might have to employ a clerk to deal with it and sort the books out.

'What's your function round here, Tom?'

Tom scratched his head and then grinned. 'Most everything

now, I reckon. I started off doing the outside work when I was little more than a boy. Then I went on the boat and learned how to sail her. Now I keep things running, as well, 'cepting for the kitchen. There hasn't been a manager for the farming side for some time. That's gone by the by, I reckon.'

'Have we got a housekeeper to oversee the domestic side?'

'We did have once . . . a long time ago, I reckon. She was a distant cousin to Silas, I recall. Blood kin or no, Silas fancied her. After a while, she went off to work in London, as your mother's maid. There was talk that she had some idea in her head of becoming lady of the manor.'

'And?'

'Not long after, they come back from London and you were born. One day Rosie Jones upped and left without telling anyone. I was just a kid then, about ten. There was a bit of talk because the last baron had died about the same time, but there were a lot of changes going on with Sir James taking over, so it soon faded. Silas named the *Wild Rose* after her.'

Fletcher couldn't help but grin at Silas having such a romantic thought over a woman. 'Do you remember my father – Adrian Taunt?'

'Adrian Taunt?' Tom scratched his head. 'Can't rightly say I ever clapped eyes on him. Went abroad and died there, I heard.'

'He left my mother and me without support.'

'Reckon that's the way it was, then.'

Fletcher's mind jerked him back to the present. 'As far as I can see, we have several maids, but, judging by the state of this house, they don't seem to do much work.'

'It never bothered old Silas.'

'A lot of things that didn't bother Silas bother me. Would any of the present maids be suitable to take charge of the household?'

'Flora Targett. She's not flighty like the others, and does her best to keep up with the work. The others laugh at her when she complains.'

'Then let's give her some authority. Tell her I want to speak to her. I'm giving you fair warning, Tom. Things are going to change from now on. My main income will come from the *Midnight Star*, and I intend to make the land productive again as soon as I can find a good manager who I can trust. Are you that man, Tom? Let me know when you've thought it over.'

'Could be that I am.'

'Where did you take the lugger last night?'

Tom took his pipe from his pocket and deliberated for a moment, taking a couple of empty sucks before he tucked it away again. 'We used the rowing boats to do a grapnel creep for fifteen hundred casks we'd lost a week ago, and we dropped fifty pounds of tobacco and several hundred pounds of tea disguised as seaweed fertilizer into Marguerite Cove.'

Fletcher whistled. 'Right on my uncle's doorstep . . . last night . . . and under the nose of Simon Bailey?'

'Silas was always hand in glove with your uncle, and your uncle has more nerve than most. He didn't do it for the money but for the excitement. For Silas, it was a way of life, but he knew he was ill and he wanted to get out of the business.'

'Then why didn't he?'

'Your uncle had something on him, I reckon. Silas would have sold Sir James the estate except your uncle kept driving the price down. Besides, it's a way of life for most of the men. Silas and your uncle had a two-way split after the workers got theirs. Your uncle always did have a nose for business.'

'How many people know about this?'

'Everyone except Simon Bailey, I imagine. Sir James will find some way of involving him before too long if he can.'

His uncle would take advantage where he could; that was the nature of the man. Charismatic he might be, but neither friendship nor kinship was allowed to interfere with his business arrangements. Everything came at a price. 'What was it that my uncle had on him, do you know?'

The man's eyes lit on him, considered him. Then he sighed. 'I reckon old Silas didn't trust me with that one, Mr Taunt.'

Tom knew something, but Fletcher wasn't about to push him. Instead, he changed tack. 'Do you know who those two young women staying with Sir James are?'

'I heard that the dogs ferreted them out after the older one stole a loaf of bread from the kitchen. The mother was dead over the other side of the woods with a stillborn in her arms. The younger girl was ill, and both were starving.'

Fletcher frowned at that. 'What does he intend to do with them?'

'As to that, we'll know when he does it. Happen you might want to attend church on Sunday. Perhaps he'll give them an airing. Sir James rarely broadcasts his intentions beforehand.'

Fletcher knew that all too well. He nodded. 'I want this estate put to good use. I do understand that the estate workers need a little extra on the side for their retirement, but so much activity and bloodshed along the coast has attracted an increase in the number of officers to deal with it. Even the French are getting involved. And have been for some time. The *Midnight Star* had to run the gauntlet of French boats on the way in – and they're heavily armed. Those who work for the crown are getting more coordinated and more ruthless. The coastguard service is run by fully trained officers of the Royal Navy who are fearless, and, with the soldiers on land, they are slowly but surely set to wipe out most of the smuggling along the coast.'

'Aye, Silas was of the same mind, but it remains to be seen if they can.'

'The land here has good pasture for sheep, and wool is in great demand as well as the meat. I'll be establishing a flock, and I hope to buy a second clipper in the future. In short, I want my business dealings to be clean.' He remembered the gold and grinned. 'Well, almost clean.'

Tom grinned in return. 'Silas was of the same mind.'

'I'm aware that smuggling is a game to my uncle, but just because I've inherited Silas's fortune, it doesn't mean I'm going to take up his way of life and the risks that go with it.'

'Aye, Mr Taunt. Silas—'

'If you tell me he was of the same mind again, I'll pick you up by the seat of your britches and throw you into the cove,' he said fiercely, and then realized Tom had been leading him on and he'd been preaching to the converted.

Tom chuckled.

After he'd finished interviewing Flora Targett, Fletcher sorted the house staff problem out and the cook had an assistant to help in the kitchen. He was a little perturbed about the cook's relationship with his uncle's second coachman. He would keep an eye on that relationship. But at least things should run a little more smoothly in the house now.

He needed to go into Poole and talk to Oswald Avery, to find out how much his legacy was worth. Then he must put out feelers for another ship, via the agent in Southampton. He should be able to pick up another ship fairly cheaply as the big shipping companies changed to steam, and she would pay for herself in a year or two.

After Fletcher got things clear in his mind, he would go and see his uncle. It had always been his uncle's intention to unite the two estates. While Silas had made it possible for him to be independent of his uncle, there was no reason why they shouldn't work together and remain on good terms, as long as he made the effort to restore and maintain their former relationship.

Apologizing for something he hadn't done went against the grain, though.

And he had a good future to look forward to now. He grinned, looking forward to his tryst with Miranda. Would she turn up or would she not?

Seven

Aware that Sir James disliked being kept waiting, Miranda joined him in his study on the last stroke of eleven.

He was seated behind a polished desk, writing in a ledger. Without looking up, he waved her to a chair by the fire. 'I won't be much longer. You can pour us some coffee if you would.'

The dogs were asleep in an untidy heap. Nero lifted his head and thumped his tail against the floor. Roma yawned, and Caesar opened one eye and shut it again before rolling inelegantly on to his back with his back legs splayed open.

It must be nice to be a dog and unaware of how comical you looked at times. But, then, perhaps Caesar thought she appeared just as silly folded on to a chair.

Miranda looked around her while she waited. The room was half-panelled, with shiny gold embossed paper decorating the top half. Leather chairs and a floor-to-ceiling bookcase gave it a manly feel, as did the portraits of horses and dogs. Above the stone fireplace was a picture of a ship in full sail. She had a long hull and three masts, and the water arched realistically where her prow sliced into the sea and foamed along her side.

'Beautiful, isn't she?' Sir James said, and he placed the pen on the inkstand and came round the desk to take the seat opposite her. 'She's named *Midnight Star*.'

'What a lovely name for a ship; she's a clipper, isn't she?'

'She is. She was built and designed by Donald McKay, who is a noted designer in North America. Her captain is George Mainwairing, the son of a former business acquaintance.'

'Is she your ship, Sir James?'

He hesitated, and then said firmly. 'I'm a part-owner with a fifty-per-cent share in her. My nephew owns the other half. He runs the business side of things.' Taking a sip from his coffee, he said, 'Tell me about you and your sister, Miss Jarvis. Who educated you?'

'We went to church school, and our parents encouraged us to read and answered any questions we had. My father taught me numbers.'

There wasn't much to tell that he didn't already know, but when she finished, he said, 'Do you have any relatives who would offer you and your sister a home?'

'None that I know of.' Her heart sank. So he was not going to allow her to work for him, as she'd hoped. 'Is this because of what happened yesterday?'

'Is what about what happened yesterday?'

'You're going to turn us out, aren't you, because you think I lied to you?'

'The thought crossed my mind, but after talking to my lawyer last night I have tentatively made other plans.'

She sat forward. 'What are they?'

'I will inform you when they are finalized and I think you need to know.'

The rebuke brought colour to her cheeks. 'I will need to have some consideration in any plans concerning myself and my sister.'

'Then I will tell you that, up until the revelation of your position in life, I was considering making you both my wards.'

She should have felt heartened by such a generous gesture from a man she'd tried to steal from, but uneasiness came to the fore. 'Why would you go to such lengths when Lucy and I are strangers?'

'If you are looking for an ulterior motive, there isn't one. To be honest, your plight touched me.'

'And now?'

'You seem to be a capable young woman, and you are right about having consideration. Perhaps you could now *consider* your plight and tell me what I should do with you?'

'As I said before, I'm good with figures and have learned how to keep ledgers. You could employ me. And Lucy and I could sleep in the maid's quarters. She could make herself useful in the kitchen, perhaps. We wouldn't be a nuisance.'

'I keep my own books; that way I'm sure everything is above board. I don't look upon you or your sister as nuisances, but rather I enjoy your company. Neither do I need another employee. I was thinking of getting married again.'

'To Sarah Tibbets?'

He raised an eyebrow. 'I've considered the possibility. It would be useful to be related to her brother. But do I look like a man who would marry Sarah Tibbets? My preference in brides would be a young woman – one pleasing to the eye and biddable. Do you know anyone like that?'

He said nothing more, but nothing more really needed to be said. Even so, she struggled to absorb the shock of it and she stared at him, wary of what her mind was telling her. No . . . he couldn't . . . she wouldn't.

He could!

'Think about it, Miss Jarvis: you would have a comfortable home here for life, and so would your sister until she married. You would also have a social position, an income of your own and jewellery. Neither of you would want for anything, and I'd treat you well.'

'But we hardly know each other.'

'Look on it as a business arrangement – most marriages are, you know. I would be your means of support and would provide you with a generous allowance. In return, you would afford me certain privileges.'

'You would expect . . .?' She blushed and gazed down at her hands.

He lifted her face with a firm finger under her chin. 'Not only would I expect, but I would insist, since the purpose of marriage is to breed and create a family. There is much pleasure to be found in the bed-chamber, as you are yet to discover. The act that leads to creation need not be unpleasant; in fact, there is much to be gained from desire and anticipation, and the act of loving for its own sake. Men have needs beyond copulation for heirs alone. I'm many years older in years and experience than you are, Miss Jarvis, but I still function, and I do require an heir as a matter of urgency. I think it possible I'll live long enough to raise a child or two into adulthood.'

Panic struck Miranda, making her feel twitchy. Her throat constricted. There was something cold-blooded about what he was saying. She felt trapped, and forced out, 'I hadn't expected this.'

'I know, and I won't push you for an answer just yet, since I don't want you to feel pressured. Just promise me you'll think about it.'

She couldn't see past the surface of his eyes, as though they had captured a dark soul in their depths. They reflected the firelight – two flames dancing in unison . . . as though he'd come straight from hell. She jerked her head away, took a step back. 'What will you do if I refuse your offer?'

'To be honest, a refusal is not something I've given serious consideration to, but I'll think on it. There are other options in which your debt to me could be addressed, no doubt. I will expect an answer by the end of June at the latest.' He brought out two coins and two rings from his waistcoat pocket and dropped them into her skirt. 'I found these sewn into the hem of your mother's skirt. Obviously they were precious to her, and I thought you'd like to have them.'

He could have given them to her earlier. She picked them up and folded her hand around them. 'They're my parents' wedding rings.'

'Not much of a legacy, I fancy. Perhaps they'll serve as a reminder of what poverty is like. On the day our marriage is consummated, I'll give you a thousand such coins . . . and a thousand more when you produce an infant. I imagine your mother and father would approve of such a match for you. It would be a considerable step up in your status.'

But rather than consider Sir James's desires and needs, or any need of her own for an improvement in fortune and her status, Miranda was thinking more along the lines of how far she and Lucy could travel on the two coins she already had.

At least he'd given her several weeks to plan their escape if she needed to.

He moved back behind his desk, the barrier making her feel more comfortable. 'Before you go, my dear, under the circumstances I'd prefer that this be kept to yourself rather than have it provide exercise for idle tongues.'

As if she would want it to become common knowledge! When she reached the door, she turned.

An eyebrow arched. 'Is there something further you wish to discuss, Miranda?'

So, he was sure enough of her to start using her Christian name. 'I thought you already had an heir – your nephew.'

'Did you . . . did you indeed? Unfortunately, he has chosen to turn his back on me.' His smile was polite but regretful. 'Shut the door on your way out, my dear.'

About to do so, she stayed the motion when he said, 'Lucy tells me it's your birthday in a week or so.'

'Yes.'

'Good. I'll be going into Poole on Thursday if the weather is fine, and I thought that you and your sister might like to have an outing in the carriage. There are several shops in the High Street, and I daresay we could find you an outfit or two as a gift . . . Lucy as well, of course. I don't like seeing the pair of you wearing my late sister's clothing.'

When she opened her mouth to speak, he said, 'You'll disappoint me if you refuse without due consideration. Having two young ladies in the house is a source of pleasure to me.'

Her heart fell. She'd been going to meet Fletcher Taunt on Thursday.

'That's very kind of you, Sir James.'

Thursday came quickly. To Miranda's relief, Sir James rode astride his horse while she and Lucy had the carriage to themselves. Lucy was exuberant with excitement. 'Two new outfits – imagine that, Miranda! Sir James said I should pick a gown the colour of bluebells, to go with my eyes. Oh . . . do look at the daffodils; they're so pretty! I love it here, don't you?'

Daffodils reminded Miranda it was April and she only had until June to think of a plan to escape. 'Yes, I do, but we can't live on

Sir James's goodwill for ever; we must soon go and look for work so we can earn some money to support ourselves.'

'He doesn't mind supporting us.'

'We are not his kin, Lucy.'

Lucy opened her mouth and then shut it again. Her eyes slid away. 'What if we were his kin?'

'That would be different.' Miranda made an attempt to steer her sister away from the subject of Sir James. 'Do you remember the stone jug that sat on the kitchen windowsill, the one our mother always kept filled with flowers?'

Lucy smiled. 'I wonder what happened to it.'

'Everything belonged to the Parbrook Estate. Mother loved daffodils. She said it wasn't really spring until they were in flower. We must pick some to put on her grave.'

'You can, Miranda. Life is so exciting now; I don't want to fill it with sad memories of the past.'

'Honouring our mother's life can't be sad. You must never forget she gave us life and loved us dearly.'

'Then why did she go off and leave us?'

The small note of petulance in Lucy's voice dismayed Miranda. 'It wasn't her fault that she died. Don't you miss her?'

'Sometimes, especially just before I go to sleep, but I try not to. Death is so horrid and solemn. You're not allowed to laugh or smile in case people think you have no respect for the dead, and crying makes your eyes looked red and watery. I'm never going to wear black. Sir James said I'm too young and pretty to wear such a colour.'

Their host was turning her sister's head. 'You mustn't get too attached to Sir James.'

'I don't see why not. I like him a lot. He said he'd always wanted a daughter like me. Besides, you're not my mother, so you can't tell me what to do.'

'Lucy, what's come over you?' Miranda said with some annoyance, and warned, 'You're not Sir James's daughter, and we might not be welcome here for much longer. And if you disrespect our mother again, I'll . . . well . . . I'll slap you!'

Lucy hugged her. 'Stop being so cross with me. I'm sorry; I didn't mean to be disrespectful. It's just that I like it here. We have warm beds, good food, and pretty clothes to wear, which is more than we ever had with our own parents. That might sound selfish, but nothing is going to bring them back. I can even use the piano. Sir James is going to teach me to ride a horse.'

Sir James the wonderful! Miranda was tired of it. Anyone would think he was God. 'Our parents did their best on the money our father earned honestly.'

'I know . . . but that doesn't mean I've got to live that way, does it? I'm not going to leave here, not ever. You'll see.' Lucy shrugged and, folding her arms over her chest, gazed fixedly out of the window.

Miranda could have slapped her sister for being seduced by Sir James's surroundings and generosity. But, then, Lucy was of an age where such things would impress her. They also impressed Miranda, but now she knew she'd have a price to pay for it.

'Sorry,' Lucy mumbled after a while, and because Miranda didn't want to spoil her sister's day, she kissed her sister on the cheek and made up.

The next day, Miranda left Lucy and the maid exclaiming over the contents of the boxes and parcels that had been delivered by a man in a smart delivery wagon. She went to the kitchen, where the cook provided her with a chipped vase.

'It don't matter if you leave this one there, Miss Jarvis. Sir James told me to throw it away, and nobody will want to steal it anyway, the ugly thing. You can fill it with water from the little stream running alongside the road. There's lots of water flowing from the April rains, so be careful you don't fall in.' Nancy avoided her eyes and said rather tentatively, 'Is your head all better now, miss?'

'Yes, it is, Nancy. It wasn't your fault.'

'All the same, I'm sorry. I didn't mean to hurt you. Sir James told me that if I'd broken your head and killed you, I'd be hanged from the gallows, and it would serve me right. He said I'm to remember that hanging ain't worth the cost of a loaf of bread.'

Miranda kissed her. 'I'll remember that the next time I feel like stealing a loaf of bread.'

Sir James waylaid her in the hall when she went to fetch her blue velvet jacket and bonnet from the hallstand. 'Where are you going with that old vase?'

'I'm going to the cemetery. I intend to place some daffodils on my mother's grave. The cook gave me the vase; she said you wouldn't mind because you told her to throw it away. My mother loved daffodils.'

'It's a lengthy walk.'

'Yes, but the countryside is pretty and I need the exercise . . . and the solitude,' she hastened to add, in case he took it into his mind to escort her.

He helped her into the jacket, tying the bow of her bonnet against her left ear. The lock of hair left exposed was twisted in a loose tendril around his finger and laid against her face. 'You have lovely skin, Miranda. So soft.'

She took a step back. 'Thank you.'

Three clicks of his fingers brought a dog to his side. 'Take Caesar to look after you and make sure you stay on the road. Don't forget the urn.'

It was an ugly object: grey-marbled and etched with bunches of grapes. Curved Lizards formed the handles.

When she pulled a face at it, he laughed. 'It used to be a pair. It was a wedding present.'

'What happened to the other one?'

'My nephew broke it in a fit of temper.'

'Did you punish him?'

He shrugged. 'Probably. It was a long time ago.' When he opened the door, he eyed the sky. 'The rain is unpredictable; you might need to carry an umbrella.'

'The urn is enough to carry. Besides, I can shelter under a tree if there's a shower.'

She was aware of his gaze on her back all the way down the drive, but she resisted the urge to turn.

She crossed paths with several wagons filled with stone coming from the opposite direction, the plodding carthorses labouring under their load. She supposed the stones were to repair the gaps in the walls.

Caesar took his duties seriously, growling under his breath at every wagon and every man who tipped his hat to her. She didn't know what she'd do if he attacked someone.

She fondled his ear as she stopped to pick some daffodils. 'You don't have to be quite so conscientious, Caesar. Not everybody is out to do me harm.'

She turned into a track that led to the cemetery. It was a peaceful spot overlooking the sea. The tombstones had been weathered by many storms and leaned all ways, like friends having a conversation.

Rainwater bubbled along in a brook on the side of the track, and there was a stone bridge across it to mark the entrance of the burial ground. The stream had been formed over many years of rainstorms and it disappeared into the hill further down, eventually soaking out into Lady Marguerite's Cove.

Miranda filled the urn with water and carried it carefully to the corner where her mother was buried. Her tablet was the only new one there. Sir James had told her that the dead were buried in the church grounds now, but there were a couple of plots in the cemetery on his land, and he was sure her mother would prefer it there.

Caesar jumped up on to a nearby grave, his length covering the oblong of stone afforded to the occupant in death. He spread out on the surface to absorb any heat the moss-covered stone had retained from the day. She could just make out the words. *Big George Grime, pickled in brine for his smuggling crime when he drowned in seventeen hundred and nine.*

Her smiled faded when she remembered her mother's burial. The rector had stumbled over his words, though they were not lacking in sincerity. To make up for it, Sir James had said words over the grave and read a passage from the Bible. He'd mentioned the stillborn child, saying that the little girl would have been given a place in heaven as an angel. Up till then, Miranda hadn't known that the unfortunate infant was a girl.

She arranged the flowers, smiling when she noticed the hundreds of daffodils spearing through the earth and the early bloomers already bobbing their bonnets in the breeze. She had never given a thought that the daffodils were everywhere at this time of year.

There was a lovely view over the sea to the Isle of Portland from here. Her gaze went to the faint line between sea and sky. A strand of clouds lay like a string of misty black pearls to herald another oncoming shower.

Miranda thought of her mother. So near, yet so far and unable to comfort or be comforted. 'I wish you were here to advise me, Mama. I don't know what to do. I always thought I would follow my heart, fall in love and wed, like you and Pa did. Now I find myself in the position of needing to surrender my freedom so Lucy and I can have a future.'

A twig snapped, and several birds flew from the opening of a neglected family tomb a couple of plots away. It looked like a small church. A rusty metal gate hung crookedly ajar, revealing a flight of steps that descended into the dark yawn of an interior. A lantern hung from a hook over the portal stone, its candle sunk into a pool of melted wax and dripping with greasy icicles.

Caesar came down from his vantage spot to press against her leg, quivering and alert as he raised his snout to cast for alien scents in the air. His tail began to whip back and forth.

Miranda couldn't see anything untoward, though her sight was being drawn towards the tomb. It was irrational, but she'd feel better if the gate was shut.

She shrugged off her uneasiness. If the gate was closed and there was a ghost that wanted to haunt her, it would simply float through the bars. 'It's nothing, Caesar . . . unless it's the spirit of the dead.'

'I'm no ghost.'

Almost rooted to the spot, Miranda pressed a hand against her mouth and stifled a little scream.'

Caesar went to greet the intruder.

Miranda spun around. 'Fletcher Taunt,' she yelped.

The breath rushed from her body in one long gasp and she struggled to breathe, so she felt dizzy. He was no longer the elegant young man of the picture hanging in her bedroom, or the shadowy intruder who'd introduced a measure of romance into the night of the full moon. In daylight, his height and muscular body was reassuring rather than threatening. Twice as handsome in maturity and dressed all in black, he nevertheless had a slightly sinister air, like his uncle. Instinctively, her glance searched through the dark ruffled curls on his head in search of a trace of horns.

There were none.

How had he got here? It seemed as though he'd risen up from the grave. She was still struggling to get a breath after the fright he'd given her.

'Miranda of the violet eyes, we meet again,' he said, his smile robbing her of her remaining breath.

She was taking a step towards him when she tripped over a

tussock. Her knees gave from under her and she landed on some-thing soft.

Eight

Miranda recovered from her stumble only to feel lightheaded.

Fletcher was seated with his back to a headstone, and she was cradled in his arms, her head against his shoulder, his jawbone barely an inch away from her mouth. If she moved just a little . . .

Dash away the thought! They hadn't even been introduced and all she could remember from their accidental first meeting was his kiss. He removed her bonnet and the wind blew through her hair so she felt like a wild creature he'd captured. She'd become part of him, and both were part of the wild landscape.

He looked down at her, laughing. 'Young ladies don't usually throw themselves into my lap.'

She doubted that was true as she struggled against his strength. 'I must get back.'

'Of course you must . . . but not yet, just when I've found you again.'

'I wasn't lost.'

'Not yet, but you will be if you stay in my uncle's house for much longer.'

She shivered, knowing she would be more lost staying here wrapped warmly in his arms. Feeling compelled to defend his uncle, she said, 'Sir James has been good to us.'

'Of course he has, but he does nothing without reason, and he is full of trickery. Hush, woman; stay quiet until you recover your wits.'

She suddenly remembered her host's reason for being good to them – marriage and children to repay the debt they owed him. It was a large price to pay, but her sister's life was worth it.

As for recovering her wits, dread filled her again and she felt as though she were falling into a deep, bottomless pit. His fingers stroking gently through her hair was a long way from producing the relaxing effect he seemed to be aiming for. She'd thought she knew her own feelings, at least well enough to be able to differentiate between what was real and what was not. At the moment, she was filled with an ocean of tumultuous urges towards this man and she didn't know how to get them under control.

'I can't stay like this . . . here with you. It isn't right or . . . or even decent and you are making me blush.'

'I'm not making you blush – not yet.' This accompanied by a grin. 'Either the colour is returning to your cheeks after your stumble or you've discovered your thoughts aren't as pure as you imagined or as society dictates, my lovely.' He gave a delightfully wicked chuckle. 'As for it not being right, it feels right to me, and being indecent can be fun. We must try it some day.'

'We certainly must not.'

'It's inevitable.' He had long, dark lashes and they suddenly swept up to reveal his eyes, gazing directly into hers, dark green like the pine trees growing in the copse. 'I think you're beginning to like me, Miranda.'

She did like him – she liked him too much. And he was right: her thoughts were not pure. No doubt she would think about him when she was almost asleep and the moon was shining through the window and making her restless. He'd lit a fire under her by just being alive.

She dredged up some calm she didn't feel. 'I'm quite recovered now, so you must let me go, Mr Taunt.'

'If I must uphold convention, then I shouldn't leave you disappointed.' He kissed her, and it was a longer, more intimate kiss than before, one that brought honey rising in her mouth, slicked her body with perspiration and made her aware of the most sensitive and secret desires of her body. How could she crave so much for his touch, the scorch of his mouth and his tongue turning her own into a melting flame that was a sinful conflagration of desire?

Then he opened his arms, leaving her feeling utterly abandoned, and entirely and delightfully wicked. 'Fly away little bird.'

She scrambled away from the danger of him and began to rearrange the daffodils. Seating himself on a tomb, he watched her, one leg bent at the knee to support his head, the other dangling in its scuffed black riding boot.

'I recognize that urn.'

'Your uncle said you broke its twin in a temper.'

'Yes . . . I threw it down the stairs.'

'What were you in a temper about, Mr Taunt?'

'Call me by my first name. It's Fletcher to my friends.'

'Fletcher, then.'

He smiled. 'It sounds like silk rolling from your tongue.'

'You're changing the subject.'

'Yes, but it's really not that important. You should ask my uncle, perhaps.'

'He said he couldn't remember.'

Fletcher shrugged. 'It was stupid really. I was fifteen, and it was over a woman. I was too old to be beaten, yet he instructed two of the stable hands to tie me to a tree trunk and called on the staff to witness it, and he took a birch to me – it was humiliating for both of us. He went too far, and my skin was split and bleeding. It took months to heal, and I still have some scars. Throwing the pot down the stairs was an act of defiance.'

The unconscious hurt in his voice touched her soul. A dagger of pity pierced her heart and she almost experienced the shame of that moment. 'Did you love the woman?'

'Lord, no, it was a case of nature leading a young man by his . . . *nose*.'

'What happened to her?'

'I don't know. She was a servant and she just wasn't there the next day. I imagine he sent her packing. Perhaps he killed her.'

She gasped. 'He wouldn't do such an awful thing.'

He shrugged. 'Perhaps not . . . though he's a man of many moods and can be irrational at times. Nevertheless, my relationship with my uncle changed after that. We were never easy with each other again. It was as though he regarded me as his rival. I set out to prove that I intended to be that. Males are like that you know. They butt heads to prove they're right.'

'What if they're not right?'

'There's that, of course.'

'It was a stupid reason to cause such a rift between you.'

'There's more to it than that. Two years ago, we had an argument. It started out as a game. A piece of property was wagered on the turn of a card, which I won. My uncle couldn't bear to lose to me in public, so, with bad grace, he accused me of cheating. He threw me out of the house and, by rights, should be the one to apologize.'

'Can't you swallow your pride and make it up with him yourself?'

'I keep meaning to try, but if I did, it would look as though my uncle had told the truth, and I had cheated. That stops me. The same would apply to him if he approached me. It would be like telling everybody that he'd lied.'

'Someone should bang your heads together,' she said, using the phrase her father had used on the odd occasion she'd quarrelled with Lucy.

Laughter huffed from him. 'That's not the first time I've been told that, but the first time from a woman. It might be too late for us to reconcile. There's been water under the bridge since. I've inherited the property my uncle had set his sights on, and I'm making my own way in the world.'

'Do you miss his companionship?'

'I do, even though he was a difficult man to live with. He lost his own wife and son.'

'It must have been hard for him to lose them.'

'He took my mother, Elizabeth Taunt, under his roof, where I was born. She died of consumption when I was still a child.'

'Did you miss her?'

'I imagine I did at the time, but I can't really remember her. She paid me very little attention and was almost a stranger to me. With my uncle, there's always a price to pay. My mother chose to pay it, so that I would have an education and a good home.'

'Then you owe him your gratitude, if nothing else.'

'So he kept telling me.'

'Where was your father?'

'Adrian Taunt? You tell me.' Her companion got to his feet, standing tall against the sky. 'I've never known him, and I've never been able to find any record of him to say he existed. My mother told me he was a soldier of fortune who died overseas. She wouldn't discuss him, but said he was a wastrel. That's why I was in the house the other night – looking for papers to confirm who my father was.'

'What sort of papers?'

'Letters . . . anything really.'

'Don't you believe what you've been told?'

'No. All my life people have been evasive about him, or avoided the subject altogether.'

Sympathy flared in her and she placed a hand on his arm. 'From your appearance, there is no doubt that you are related to Lord Fenmore. Does the rest matter?'

'It wouldn't, if only it hadn't been turned into a closed subject. That piqued my curiosity.'

'I think your uncle suspected you'd been in the house the other day. I find it difficult to be deceitful when I was brought up to be honest.'

His hand closed warmly over hers for a few precious moments. 'Honesty is layered in these parts.'

'What do you mean?'

'If a poor man commits a crime, he's considered guilty until proven innocent. If he happens to be wealthy, it's the other way round. Money is power, however it's earned, and there are very few totally honest people around – just those who would like to be honest if they could afford to be.'

'Are you telling me that your uncle is dishonest, when he's a respected magistrate?'

'Nobody can afford to be wholly honest, and I suspect you're already closing your eyes to some things. My uncle's good at getting the truth out of people. Don't lie to him on my account, Miranda. He's a powerful man and he won't thank you for it if he finds out.'

Her back was turned to the sea and the wind was pushing against her with powerful salty thrusts. The air seemed to be more exciting in Fletcher's presence – more robust and sharp, and spiced with the tang of seaweed. Her loosened hair flew in all directions, crackling with tumultuous energy, so that her scalp prickled.

She closed her eyes. 'I've never been so close to the sea before.'

He smiled and said, 'There's something I'd like you to experience. Will you trust me? Will you close your eyes now and keep them shut until I tell you to open them?'

He turned her round when she closed them, and began to walk her forward towards the edge of the cliff. The tide was in because she heard the waves smashing against the base of the cliff, and it sounded louder now her eyes were closed. Her heart began to thump and her legs began to resist. 'I'm not very good with heights.'

They came to a halt and he slid an arm around her, to hold her against his side when she'd rather have been turned into his body. Caesar pressed against her other side, whining, pulling at her skirt as if warning her not to go any closer to the edge. He didn't like heights, either.

'When can I open my eyes?'

A kiss landed on the corner of her mouth, then another against her ear. He whispered, 'Now, my lovely.'

She opened them to the sight of a clipper ship in full sail beyond the entrance to the cove, yet framed by it. Miranda's breath left her body in one long rush as she said, 'How lovely it is. Is it the *Midnight Star*?'

'Aye, she's on her way to America this voyage. I'd be sailing on her if Silas hadn't died. Being responsible for an estate tends to tie you down . . . but it's about time. How did you know her name?'

'Your uncle has a painting of her in his study.'

'Ah yes, I'd forgotten. He owns half of the ship.'

She tried to get her hair under control. He laughed. 'Leave it flying free; it reminds me of a Selkie maiden.'

'What's a Selkie?'

'A creature from Scottish folklore that comes from the sea and sheds its skin so it can take on human form.'

'Why should she want to do that?'

'She fell in love with a human, and he fell in love with her. The last Selkie seen here was Lady Marguerite, who was plucked from that ledge below us and carried away when the sea claimed her as one of its own. See, that's where she was seated, on that top slab above the water line where the sea doesn't usually reach . . . not even in a storm.'

Miranda looked down to where a knotted rope was pegged to the cliff face at intervals to secure wooden stretchers designed to support the feet. It led down to a series of flat rocks lying one on top of the other. With the tide already high, the oncoming waves washed over the bottom five slabs, then cascaded down into the churning sea, dragging long strands of brown seaweed with it. The sixth slab was considerably higher than the others, and there was a clearly defined high-tide mark well below it.

She shuddered. 'Lady Marguerite must have been brave to go down that ladder. I don't think I'd like to be a Selkie.'

'The original ladder became unsafe. My uncle put that one there. It's maintained, and quite secure if you're careful. It can be pulled up if needed.'

They withdrew from the edge and watched the ship move out of their sight. The band of grey clouds had now moved above their heads. It began to rain, a soft, playful patter of drops that painted the wavering bands of sunshine around them with a silvery sheen.

'Come on, it's time to go before my uncle comes looking for you.'

She was reluctant to part with him. 'Must we?'

He smiled. 'I don't want to part with you, either, but I was on my way into Poole when I saw you turn in here.' He picked up her bonnet and placed it on her head, and, much like his uncle had, he tied the ribbon in a bow. Fletcher kissed her to go with it – a caress that was long and lingering to savour in her dreams.

They walked across the bridge, and he stopped to kiss her again.

'Are you going to kiss me every five minutes? If so, it will take me a long time to get back to the house,' she said, laughing, because, if nothing else, Fletcher Taunt made her feel happy.

Amusement filled his eyes and they narrowed, in a way that reminded her of his uncle. 'Would you like me to?'

'It would be forward of me to say I would.'

'Yes, it would be. Are you going to be forward?'

'Not as forward as you'd like me to be, I imagine. You are not as irresistible as your confident demeanour suggests you think you are.'

'Ouch!' He chuckled and took her hand in his. They broke into a sprint when the shower got heavier, and they were out of breath when it stopped, laughing together. As they gazed at each other, his smile faded and he lifted her hand to his mouth. 'I'd forgotten why you were here today. I'm sorry about the demise of your parents, and apologize for intruding on you.'

'It's kind of you to say so, and to apologize. I enjoyed the time I spent with you today, and admit it took my mind off the reason I was there. I just needed to be near my mother while I thought about the situation I find myself and Lucy in.'

Fletcher had tethered his horse up near the road. It gave a little neigh and did a dance on the spot when it set eyes on him.

'May I see you again?' he said.

She was troubled, wondering how this would affect his uncle's plans. 'I'm sure we'll meet again. Perhaps in church, where we can be introduced properly.'

He made a face. 'My uncle is at the Dorchester assizes all next week. We could meet here again on Tuesday. I will have finished my business in town by then.'

She should tell him that his uncle had offered her marriage. But just because he had, it didn't mean he had any claim on her yet. She was still trying to think of what to do. If she and Lucy left, where would they go?

'Why so pensive?' he said.

'I don't think Sir James would like me going behind his back, and I don't want to deceive him.'

'Then tell him you've met me, if you must. Just remember that you're allowed some privacy, even if you are his house guest. It's not your fault we were in the same place at the same time. I'll be here on Tuesday, anyway. In the meantime, I'll consider an approach to my uncle in an effort to heal the breach between us.'

He mounted his horse and turned the handsome creature's nose towards Poole. He turned in the saddle and waved, and suddenly it seemed a long time until Tuesday, when Miranda would see him again.

Fletcher was thinking much the same thing as he took one last look at Miranda Jarvis before he rounded the bend and she was out of sight. He'd never met any woman who'd affected him quite so profoundly. Usually, he judged a woman by her physical attributes and her willingness to contribute to his pleasure. This young lady was something different. There was something guileless and sweet about those deep blue eyes, and his emotional reaction to her was tender rather than base. He wanted her – *God, how he wanted her* – but he also wanted to protect her.

'Miranda,' he whispered, tasting her name on his tongue, and he smiled when his horse's ears swivelled back towards him. Then he laughed out loud, shouting exuberantly, 'Miranda!'

A thrush sounded an alarm and birds abandoned their young and flew like a panicked cloud out of the hedge, so to confuse a would-be predator. His horse sidestepped in alarm. He got the gelding under control. 'Sorry, Rastus, but I think I'm falling in love. *I am in love!* With Miranda.'

He'd shouted her name so the whole world knew, and the hedges and fields became suddenly brighter. He noticed the satiny white ladies' smocks, golden primroses, and violets entwined like lovers in the hedges. Beyond the hedge, lambs sprang into the air and bleated in alarm for their mothers. A couple of painted lady butterflies meandered by on brown and yellow wings.

He turned his horse round and went back at a gallop. She hadn't got very far, and she turned to gaze at him, a half-smile on her face and her cornflower eyes filled with curiosity as well as laughter.

'I forgot to tell you something,' he said, leaping from the horse on to the ground. He blurted it out like a youth in the first throes of passion. 'I've fallen in love with you.'

He hadn't known that a woman's eyes could open quite so wide and capture the sky in their depths. Worriedly, he asked her, 'What do you think?'

From the woods came the clear fluting call of a bird. It was the first call from that particular bird he'd heard this year, and it couldn't have been more apt for the occasion with its mocking *cuckoo . . . cuckoo . . . cuckoo!*

For a moment she stared at him, startled, and then her lips twitched and she began to giggle.

He felt like the fool he was. 'It's not funny.'

'Don't you like being in love?'

'I don't know; it's something new to me. I haven't come to terms with it yet.'

'You fell in love rather quickly and it seems to have stunned you. I won't hold you to it, as you obviously have an impulsive nature. Think about it a little longer, if you would.'

He slanted his head and grinned at her. 'I have no need to.'

'Do so, anyway, Fletcher.' The giggle she gave turned into laughter – not a titter behind her hand, or a stutter, but a full-blooded belly laugh that had her arms cradled over her middle and her hands clutching her elbows.

When Caesar lifted his snout and howled into the wind, she laughed even more.

Eventually, she stopped, though her eyes still brimmed with enough amusement to make him believe it wouldn't take much for her to start laughing all over again.

'I think I feel honoured by your admission, Fletcher Taunt, and will treasure this moment for the rest of my life,' she managed to say between leftover giggles.

He'd wager she would, and if this affair went any further than her lighthearted rejoinder, this minx would never let him forget it, either.

'Hah! There's only one way to silence you.'

Drawing her into his arms, he kissed her with all the love and tenderness he could muster.

The defeated little sigh she gave afterwards and her lips seeking his to return the kiss wrenched his heart from his chest and put his manly parts on alert.

He could either drag her under a tree, kiss her senseless and have his way with her, or play the gentleman. He had a fierce need on him and an uncomfortable ride ahead if he did the latter.

'Do you know what you've done to me, woman?' he grumbled.

Her eyes gave the merest of flickers down to where his erection flaunted itself. At least her instincts were right.

Her eyes widened as they flicked up again, and she blushed a fiery red.

'Hussy,' he said.

She giggled and covered the blush with her hands, but he saw the gleam of her eyes through her fingers when she said drily, and with more mischief than guile in her voice, 'I'll also treasure this moment.'

Nine

Fletcher's heart dropped as he gazed at the battered, medium-sized clipper tied to the end of a jetty in a Southampton boat yard. The air reeked of mud for the tide was almost out.

'That's the *Agnes O'Dare*, Oswald? You've brought me all this way to look over a wreck? She has hardly any rigging left and the paint is flaking. Look at her draught; someone forgot to replace the ballast when the cargo was unloaded.'

He also noticed that her masts were raked back slightly for balance and her bowsprit had a mermaid with flowing hair.

Miranda with her hair flowing in the wind . . . The image

entered a space in his mind, along with her teasing departure. He smiled.

Sir Oswald broke into his reverie. 'If you say so, Fletcher. I have it on good authority that she's generally sound. She needs refitting and cleaning up.'

'If she's sound, why has she been left to rot at the end of a jetty?'

'The yard owner went bankrupt over a year ago and the ship was seized. Unfortunately, they didn't secure her, and some of the sails and many of the fittings were stolen. The insurance company wants rid of it – at any price – after she failed to attract a single offer at auction.'

They gazed at each other and Fletcher grinned. 'Any price?'

'That's what the man said.'

'Then, by all means, let's look her over.' The ship gave a little bob and a loud creak when they went on board, as if she was complaining over her lot. She smelled of neglect and the deck needed to be caulked here and there. They went below. The hull was dry inside and he couldn't see any rot or wormholes. Her three masts were secured solidly to their mortises. Both planks and masts rewarded him with solid thuds when he knocked them. His heart began to beat a little faster. 'She seems free of worm, and her hull is still coppered.'

'Her log is with the agent, as is the sale. You can inspect it if you're interested.'

'I am.' He was more than interested. He already had a strong urge to own this shabby little princess and reveal her beauty to the world.

'The dinghies are missing.'

'Somebody had the foresight to place them in the boatshed.'

Fletcher grunted, trying not to sound too eager, though restoring the ship would be a worthwhile project. He found a concealed compartment under the bunk in the captain's cabin. It was empty, but big enough to hold a couple of pounds of tea, some gold or cash. It was the captain's prerogative to skim a little off the top for his retirement. He probably shipped his own cargo, too, especially to Melbourne, where domestic goods and ladies' trinkets could be auctioned off for gold.

Oswald smiled, as if satisfied with Fletcher's response. He took out a notebook and pad. 'Let's do a rough calculation of what she'll cost to refit. We might as well go there with an estimate of cost, and well aware of what we'll be up against. All the lanterns are missing to start with.' He wrote down a sum on his pad.

'At least the wheel has been left intact.' Fletcher ran his palm over the wood.

It was oak, and although it had lost its shine, it was well patinated from past use and only in need of some varnish. 'She needs new paintwork, and some of her bright work is missing. She'll have to be dry-docked to paint her hull.'

The list grew – and so did the cost.

Finally, they gazed at each other, and Fletcher gave his companion a wry smile. 'I'm beginning to think it would be cheaper to buy a new ship.'

'By the time it was built, this one would have earned her cost many times over.'

'Can I afford it? Have we factored in the crew's wages?'

'Yes and yes.'

Fletcher nodded. 'I'll offer the agent fifty pounds, but I won't shell out more than five hundred for her.'

Oswald chuckled. 'This I must see. Five pounds says you won't get it for fifty.'

They spoke to the agent, and Fletcher presented him with a list of the ship's defects and the cost to him. 'It will be several months before she's fit for work, and she'll drain me of money in the meantime. I'm prepared to make an offer of . . . fifty pounds, say?'

The agent didn't bother to try to get more out of him.

A little later, Oswald handed over a fiver, grumbling, 'I'd forgotten how lucky you are.'

'It's not luck on this occasion; it's the ability to read a situation. The agent was prepared for failure after the auction brought no result. The list of what needed doing and the estimated cost of the repairs reinforced what was already in his mind – that the ship was defective. He was so eager to get it off his books that he didn't stop to consider. Remind me never to use that agent to represent me for anything.'

Oswald left Fletcher to sort out the finer points and headed off to pay a visit a female relative.

'I didn't know you had a relative living here.'

Oswald had chuckled.

Fletcher spent a night at the boarding house and the next couple of days making arrangements.

He tracked down the former captain, a man called Joshua Harris, who was aged about forty.

'We'd been at sea for several weeks and the authorities seized her as soon as we tied up. They confiscated her cargo of wool, and there wasn't enough money left to pay the crew.'

'Was that all she carried?'

'Apart from some mail, yes. Her cargo was seized and sold off to recoup costs.'

Fletcher paid him his back wages and rehired him. 'When she's refitted, she'll be sailing on the Hong Kong, New York and London route, and you'll take turn and turn-about with our other ship on the Australian run.'

'Aye,' Harris said comfortably. 'I might be able to rehire some of her former crew. My first mate is still looking for a berth, and some of the crew. Those with families are having a hard time of it.'

'Tell them I'll pay them a year's back-pay if they sign on. I'll ask my agent to pay the womenfolk after they sail. The other half they'll get in their wages when they get back. It might stop them deserting. And I should be able to find a couple more strong young men from my estate with a yearning to enjoy the adventure of going to sea first-hand.'

'Experienced?'

'They've worked on a lugger from time to time and lived to tell the tale.'

Harris grinned. 'I get your drift.'

'Make no mistake. I'm an honest man and expect honest dealings in return, though I will overlook the occasional captain's commission. She's your ship, Captain Harris, so I'll leave you in charge. She has to leave her mooring by the end of the month. The yards are still intact, so get the rigging done first, and find enough sail, crew and ballast to help move her round to Buckley's Hard for repairs and a refit. You've heard of it?'

Laughter snorted from the man. 'Who hasn't? Nelson's Navy wouldn't have got very far without it.'

'I'll drop in there on the way home and tell them to expect

you, and I'll inform my shipping agent, Whitchurch and Sons. They will act in my stead with regard to payment of accounts, though I'll turn up now and again, I daresay.'

'I've had dealings with them before.'

'By the way, if any of the original fittings happen to turn up on the ship in the meantime, there will be no questions asked and a small reward . . . say, five per cent of their value to replace.'

Captain Harris remained impassive, though there was more than a gleam of interest in his eyes. 'That would save you a lot of money, I daresay.'

'You daresay right. Perhaps ten per cent would get me a better result.'

'Aye, I'll remember that and keep an eye out for them.'

'I'm going to rename her, and she'll be registered to the Fletcher Taunt Shipping Company as *Lady Miranda*.'

'As is the *Midnight Star*, she's George Mainwaring's ship, isn't she?'

Fletcher was surprised by the captain's knowledge. 'You know a lot about shipping.'

'It's my business to know, Mr Taunt. Shipping is my profession. Besides, I used to sail the same routes.'

'Is there anything you feel you should know about me?'

'I attended naval college with George Mainwaring. He has told me that you're fair-minded, and what you see is what you get. I also know of your differences with your partner, Lord Fenmore, and sincerely hope they will be resolved. There's nothing more unsettling for a crew than a partnership with the directors at loggerheads. A man cannot serve two masters.'

'So I've heard. My uncle owns a half-share in the *Midnight Star*. Far from being at loggerheads, he leaves the business side to me and the shipping company provides a great deal of my income. The *Lady Miranda* now belongs to the same shipping company, but I'd be obliged if you kept that to yourself for now, until she's ready to sail. When she's ready, bring her to Poole, flying her colours, which I'll get to you. There she can be provisioned. I'll try to have a cargo of domestic goods ready. I'll visit the shipyard in six months' time to see how much progress has been made. Expect her to undergo rigorous customs inspection in the Poole port. The customs service seems to be overly attentive there.'

Captain Harris grinned. 'If you don't mind me saying, sir, you've purchased a well-mannered ship, despite her current appearance. She's a sprightly lass and a pleasure to handle.'

Which immediately made Fletcher wonder how the flesh-and-blood Miranda would feel to handle. She was quick-witted and certainly not afraid of him . . . or his uncle, come to that.

But he doubted if his uncle had displayed his true personality – not yet.

Buckley's Hard was about four miles from the Solent on the Beaulieu River.

Fletcher made arrangements for the *Lady Miranda* to be restored as near as possible to her original state. The shipyard employed the kind of people who possessed a long history of expertise to bring her up to scratch. It was going to be expensive, but the work would be thorough.

Satisfied that the ship would be with people who loved sailing ships as much as he did, Fletcher then headed for the road through the New Forest, knowing he'd done his best for her.

The New Forest was several hundred years old. It had been created for William the Conqueror so he could hunt deer. His life had been claimed by an arrow in his chest, though whether by accident or design was never quite determined.

Fletcher cantered along at a comfortable pace for his horse, thinking alternately of Miranda the ship and Miranda the woman. He enjoyed the ride. The air was fresh and pleasant, with some light showers. The landscape was a delight, the day alight with daffodils and the clearings dotted with the small herds of wild ponies that lived and bred in the forest.

Just as the soft, purple light of evening began to tint the air around him, he saw the inn up ahead. Moreover, he was hungry, and the tantalizing smell of a roasting pig came to his nostrils, so he cast his nose in the air like a hungry dog and his mouth began to water.

Turning Rastus over to the ostler, who would see to his comfort, Fletcher spotted Oswald's horse. He was pleased to find Oswald inside the inn. It meant he'd have company for the rest of the journey, which was always safer than being alone.

Oswald was just as happy to see him. 'My horse threw a shoe, and by the time I'd walked him to the nearest smithy and he'd been shod, it was too late to carry on. I was hoping you'd get here before dark.'

'As you see.' He accepted a tankard of ale from the landlord, who sent his wife scuttling to ready a room for him, then asked, 'How did you find your female relative?'

Oswald grinned, 'Most accommodating. I stayed a day longer than I intended. 'You should get a female relative for yourself.'

Fletcher gave him a pained smile. 'I've just fallen in love, Oswald.'

'May I ask, with whom?'

'You may.'

'Is that all you've got to say?'

'Pretty much.'

When darkness fell, the inn filled up with locals. The buzz of talk and the fug of tobacco fumes increased, and the laughter grew more raucous. Oswald and Fletcher kept to themselves, talking business, mostly about the new acquisition, and aware of the glances coming their way, for strangers were always looked upon with suspicion.

Dinner arrived: a plate of pork with crackling, roast vegetables and rich brown gravy. It was followed by a large slice of pie filled with preserved apples and rhubarb, and swamped with creamy yellow custard. They ate in companionable silence.

When they finished, Oswald belched and patted his stomach. He said to the landlord, who'd come to collect the dirty dishes, 'Your lady is a fine cook.'

'That she is, sir. Can I fetch you something to round your meal off properly? We have recently purchased a fine drop of French brandy, and you look like two gentlemen of discernment.'

'Undoubtedly,' Oswald said.

Fletcher didn't even blink an eye. 'Thank you, landlord, a measure or two of your best would be appreciated.'

They sipped it slowly, savouring the fruity taste on their tongues. Oswald raised his glass in a toast. 'To the *Lady Miranda.*'

'Have you ever thought of buying a stake in a ship, Oswald?'

Oswald laughed. 'That type of investment is too risky for the likes of me. I'm more like a seagull. I earn my wealth, and my enjoyment, from the simple act of arranging other people's affairs and scavenging from them an extortionate rate of commission.'

'I have to say, you're the most honest scavenger I know, but it sounds quite a dull way to enrich yourself.'

'But it's safe. Wait until you get my account for this little endeavour . . . then tell me how dull I find it when you start hollering about usury.' He yawned. 'It's been a long day. I think I'll go up to bed.'

Fletcher rose, too. 'I want to make a good start, since there's someone I must meet.'

'Anyone I know?'

Fletcher could hardly contain his smile. 'I shouldn't think so. She's a rather delightful young woman.'

The horses were rested and springy with energy. Fletcher's horse did a couple of bucks when he mounted. Fletcher reined him in. 'Settle down, Rastus; we have a long way to go yet.'

The air was clean and damp, with a faint wisp of smoke from the inn's chimney to tickle the nostrils. The horses snickered at each other.

There was a mist rising from the forest floor when they set off into a grey and yellow dawn just before sunrise. Everything was pearled with dew. The new bracken hearts curled tightly into themselves, waiting for the touch of the sun to entice them to unfurl.

It was midday when they reach Poole. As usual, the port was a bustle of people. Oswald went his own way, and Fletcher decided to have a meal in an inn before continuing his journey.

He was across the heath and ambling along, enjoying the peace and quiet of the bright day, and drowning in his own thoughts, when the horse began to dance under him.

'What the hell!' he muttered.

Across the road, an elaborate construction with sturdy pillars obviously designed to support gates was in the process of being erected. He approached a burly man who seemed to be in charge of the construction. He'd never set eyes on him before. 'What the hell's going on here?'

'I've been instructed to restore the gatehouse to the original plan.'

Fletcher was unaware of the fact that there had ever been a plan, let alone a gatehouse there, and although he didn't need to ask who'd instructed the man to rebuild it, his disbelief made him stutter, 'Who advised you to do this?'

'Lord Fenmore. And who might you be, sir?'

'Fletcher Taunt; I own Monksfoot Estate, which adjoins this one, and I'm Lord Fenmore's nephew. This has always been a public right of way.'

The man was perfectly polite. 'Not always and not any more, Mr Taunt. It's always been private land. Lord Fenmore has decided to close it to the public. I'm afraid you'll have to go the long way round. So will anyone else who intends to visit you at Monksfoot Estate from now on.'

'I live there and this is my uncle's estate. Let me through.'

'I'm sorry, Mr Taunt. It can't be done, since the other side of the estate has already been walled off in similar fashion. Besides, I have my instructions.' The man brought up a blunderbuss and laid it on a slab of stone within reach of his hand, making it quite clear what those instructions were.

Fletcher measured the wall with his eyes, wondering if Rastus could clear it. He probably could if pushed, but Fletcher couldn't risk it. The horse was tired, his muscles sore, and it wouldn't be fair to him. He needed a good rub down and a feed. But it was no use blaming one of his uncle's minions for his own predicament. He should have known his uncle would retaliate.

'Tell my uncle I'd like to see him on Sunday, after church. It's about time we sorted out our differences.'

'Yes, Mr Taunt.'

Fletcher turned away and headed back to Wareham, his happy mood scattered to all parts of the compass. He felt alienated from the only family he'd ever been able to call his own, as though a gust of icy wind had blown through his body and taken his Fenmore blood along with it.

Retracing his steps, he returned to Wareham and took the inland road. This act of pettiness on his uncle's part was something entirely unexpected. He couldn't believe the man would deny him access to Monksfoot.

It then occurred to him that he'd now be late for his meeting with the delightful Miranda, and his heart sank even further. Would she wait?

Ten

While Miranda delighted in the blue gown trimmed with Brussels lace that she wore, she also felt uneasy about taking anything from Sir James.

She couldn't say what bothered her. She and Lucy had a comfortable existence in the home of a man who was generous, and obviously honourable in his intentions, for he'd proposed marriage.

Yes, he was more than twice her age, but was that such a bad thing, apart from the fact that he'd expect to bed her and get her with child — and he looked healthy and muscular, as though he might be rather vigorous in that pursuit. It was not that she was afraid of the union between man and woman, but rather that she'd wanted to give that particular favour to a man she loved.

The alternative was to leave. But where would they go, and how far would they get before they ran out of money? They'd already experienced what poverty was like, and the danger that came with it. The truth was, their lives had become a comfortable trap, more so for Lucy, who lived for the moment and was being given everything her heart desired. Miranda sensed danger in that, and knew that the longer she avoided making her mind up, the harder it would be for both of them to abandon a life they were rapidly growing used to.

Sir James was at the Dorchester assizes this week, presiding as magistrate.

Lucy was practising the piano. The notes floated through the house as Miranda pulled a shawl around her shoulders and tied her bonnet. She didn't ask Lucy to join her for a walk, because she'd tell Sir James that Fletcher had been there.

Luckily, her creatively inclined sister preferred indoor pursuits. Lucy was writing a novel that featured a ghost, for she'd found a tattered, water-stained journal hidden behind a sliding panel in the window seat, which had sparked her imagination. The author of it hadn't put her name to it. Lucy read short passages of her work out to Miranda. It was rather melodramatic, and Miranda marvelled at her sister's fertile imagination.

She picked up a sketching block and pencil, in case anyone suspected her of motives other than walking. It struck her that she'd become suspicious of everyone else's motives lately. There was no reason why she shouldn't meet a young man to walk and talk with him.

And kiss him, a little voice inside her mocked.

'There's that, but actually he kissed me . . . I just didn't stop him,' she said quietly and grinned.

Caesar followed her down the stairs, his tail whipping dust motes into the air. She laughed. 'Yes, you can come, too.'

The dog seemed to have attached himself to her, and followed her everywhere, much to Sir James's amusement, for he'd said, 'Caesar must have liked the taste of you when you first met.'

And, indeed, she had a scar on her thigh to remind her of that meeting.

Seeking out Mrs Pridie, Miranda told her she was going out to sketch wildflowers, and would take Caesar with her.

'Will you be long, Miss Jarvis?'

She wondered if there was anything behind the seemingly innocent query, and then dismissed it as guilt over her secret assignation with Fletcher. 'I don't suppose I'll be more than an hour or two.'

'Well, best you stay within the bounds of the estate. We can't have you getting lost.'

'I assure you, Mrs Pridie, I have quite a good sense of direction.'

'Sir James doesn't want you wandering around the countryside by yourself. There are too many felons abroad.'

'He hasn't said so to me directly. I promise you I'll stay in the grounds. Besides, I'll have Caesar with me.'

Mrs Pridie placed a work-worn hand on her arm when she turned to go. 'Take care. Some people are not what they appear to be.'

Annoyance filled her. 'Are *you* what you appear to be, Mrs Pridie?'

'I'm what I have to be to survive. I promise you this: if you ever need to confide in anyone, and you might need to one day, you can trust me.'

Her voice was so sincere that Miranda softened towards her. 'Thank you, Mrs Pridie; I'll remember that.'

The afternoon was calm and quiet, the air warm and moist for spring. Disturbed by her passing, clouds of midges rose from the hedges and performed a frenzied dance in the air.

Despite the calm, everything moved. She jumped when she disturbed a grass snake soaking up the sun, mistaking it for a viper at first. It slid greasily off into the undergrowth. The sudden intrusion of the reptile into the territory of the hedge sparrows caused a noisy burst of agitation. They began to dive at it, chasing it off.

Everything settled back into calm. High in the sky, a hawk circled. Along the banks of the stream, wild arum and soft purple sliced through the undergrowth to join the golden lady's smock.

Caesar ran on ahead, marking his territory and investigating the other scents. He backtracked now and again to check on her.

The cemetery stood in its own state of dilapidated quietude. There was no sign of Fletcher.

She swallowed her disappointment. Had he been flirting with her? Perhaps he'd had no intention of keeping their appointment. She blew a kiss towards the corner where her mother lay. The small patch of ground she occupied was no longer raw brown earth, but a bed of different coloured wildflowers that nature had woven into a small quilt for her. A tendril of ivy from the adjoining plot had stretched friendly fingers across to cling to her stone, as if welcoming the new neighbour.

She busied herself sketching flowers and the ancient headstones in the warm, hushed air.

After a while, her glance fell on the largest tomb. The rusty entrance gate still hung open on its hinges and the lamp was still there. Yet there was something different about it. Her gaze went back to the lamp. That was it – it had a new candle!

Why on earth would a tomb need a candle over the entrance? Bumps prickled up her arms and into her neck. There was something about that mausoleum and it seemed to call to her. She didn't even know who was interred there. As she approached it, the world seemed to hush, as if holding its breath. She felt uneasy and her blood began to pound against her eardrums.

'Don't be silly; the dead can't hurt you,' she whispered, the sound of her own voice giving her a small amount of comfort.

The Fenmore name was etched into the lintel.

Three steps down and she was in a cold, clammy half-light. It was a large space that accommodated about fifteen stone coffins of various sizes, set in alcoves. Placing her drawing tablet and pencil on a coffin, she moved to read the names of the occupants. She could only just make out the writing on the closest stone coffins, which were nearer to the door.

Further inside were three more recent-looking ones. *Bella Fenmore. Elizabeth Fenmore* . . . then there was *William Fenmore, beloved son of James and Bella.* An empty coffin waited for Sir James, the lid leaning against the wall. She shivered at the macabre thought that this was a family gathering. Was the drowned Lady Marguerite, after whom the cove was named, buried here?

Her mind switched from one woman to another. Elizabeth Fenmore must be Fletcher's mother. So why wasn't she buried as Elizabeth Taunt?

There was a noise, like a faint whisper of voices and a sudden draught of air. The gates scraped a series of rusty discordant notes on their hinges as they swung together and latched, like a mouth closing around its prey.

Panic welled in her as her imagination took hold. What if she couldn't get out and she was trapped, kept prisoner by grisly, grinning corpses?

Miranda sucked in small gasps of air, trying not to give in to a scream, expelling it in breathy squeaks when a shadow moved in the entrance and blocked the sunlight. Caesar gave a rattling growl, pawed at the gates and barked urgently at her, as if he'd picked up her panic.

There was a drift of sensation, a faint pressure, as if somebody had touched her shoulder in passing. There was something comforting about it.

The gate was latched on the outside. After all, which of the occupants had the ability to open in, even if they wanted to let themselves out? She managed to squeeze a finger through an elaborate scroll in the wrought iron and push the latch up, resisting the urge to look over her shoulder. The gate opened.

When she scrambled into the fresh air, Caesar's ruff was pricked up around his neck and ridged along his back. When she smoothed it down, he wagged his tail, looked past her and gave a bit of a huff.

'All right, I'm here, Caesar,' she said and, pulling the gates together, she latched them and turned.

Fletcher Taunt stood a short way away, grinning from ear to ear.

She yelped, and tripped over a tussock, her knees nearly buckling with the fright he'd given her. The giggle she gave bordered on hysteria. Was he real or an apparition?

'Why is it that the sight of me makes you trip over your feet? Come here.' Looking delightfully dusty and dishevelled, he put out an arm to steady her and gathered her close. 'Christ almighty! You frightened me half to death coming out of the family plot. It's not All Hallows' Eve, is it?'

Instinct made her place her face against the steady beat of his heart. An apparition couldn't be this warm. Then she remembered she hardly knew him and drew back.

'Don't move away, Miranda; it feels as though you belong there.' Cupping his palm against her face, he gently pulled her back. 'You and I both know how we feel about each other,' and to remind her in the most practical of manners, he tipped up her chin and kissed her.

She was scared of the tumult of feeling rioting through her. How could she feel like this about a man she hardly knew? How did she know it was love? She just did. He laughed when she sighed in defeat and murmured, 'Yes . . . I suppose I do know.'

'I'm glad we've sorted that out. May I ask why you're visiting my deceased relatives?'

'Curiosity, I suppose. There's a new candle in the lantern and I wondered why.'

'Ah . . . I see. You have sharp eyes. Did you come up with an answer?'

'Not yet . . . and then I began to wonder if Lady Marguerite was laid to rest here. The light was so dim I couldn't read the names. I thought I heard voices, and there was a sudden draught. The gates squeaked and then closed by themselves. See, somebody moved the stones propping them open.'

His eyebrow arched and he chuckled. 'You heard a ghost or

two having a conversation? It was a gust of wind, that's all, and it pushed the gates aside and they moved the stones. You made a good job of scaring the hell out of yourself as well as me.'

Gazing at the trees, she reminded him, 'There's no wind – the trees are barely moving. You didn't close the gate to give me a scare, did you? It was eerie . . . It felt as though someone touched my shoulder.'

'No, I've only just arrived and came along the cliff. The sea breeze has just started to come in. If you follow the ripples, you'll see the water change as the breeze sweeps them before it. It was just a stray gust, I expect.'

Miranda felt much braver now Fletcher was with her, and she shrugged, ashamed of being so weak and willing to bow to his male reasoning. 'You're probably right. I allowed imagination to get the better of me.'

'I'd expect nothing less from a young woman.' Taking her hand in his, he drew her away. 'Let's get out of here. A cemetery isn't a very romantic place for a private tête à tête. There's a nice sheltered little spot back along the cliff near the copse. We can sit there unobserved and talk.'

There was a large boulder, and they sat with it against their backs and gazed out to sea, Caesar lounging at their feet.

'I'm sorry I'm late,' he said. 'I've only just arrived back and haven't been home yet; that's why I'm so dusty.'

'You weren't very late.'

He gave a bit of a frown. 'I would have been on time if my uncle hadn't disallowed me access to my estate via his. He's had a wall and gate built across the road, and there's an armed guard. Using the long way adds another five miles each way to the journey.'

'Isn't it a public highway? I did see some traffic on it – wagons with stone on them – and I thought he was having the wall repaired. Why would he do such a thing as close the road?'

'He wanted to buy Monksfoot Abbey cheaply, and intended to pull the house down. My offer was accepted instead, although, as it turned out, Silas Asher ended up leaving me everything when he died. But let's not talk of my relationship with my uncle. Let's just enjoy each other's company.'

When he put his arm around her, she leaned comfortably into his shoulder.

'I bought another clipper a couple of days ago. She's little more than a hull and has been stripped of most of her fittings. She'll be at a shipyard for repairs by the end of the month.'

His voice had warmed when he'd spoken of the ship, and she prompted him, 'Will that be expensive?'

'Yes . . . but it will be worth it and I got her very cheaply. She's a young ship, but honest when stripped down to her skin. There is a grace and dignity about her that needs to be exploited.' He gazed down at her, the expression in his eyes still warm and now laced with tenderness, so she knew his words were describing her. 'I've named my new ship after you – *Lady Miranda.*'

She touched his face. It was a small caress, the only one she dared to offer him at this time. 'I've never had a ship named after me before.'

He took her hand and placed a kiss in the palm. 'I'll take you to see your namesake when she's trim and tidy and ready to receive visitors.'

Her smile faded and she idly traced a circle on the back of his hand. 'I'm your uncle's guest, Fletcher. He's been good to me and my sister, and I don't like deceiving him.'

'Yes, I know, and my association with him seems to be growing worse, rather than improving. I'm going to do something to heal the breach between us, and have sent a message to say I intend to see him on Sunday after church. After all, we are business partners. Does he ever talk of me?'

'He's mentioned you on occasion.'

He engaged her eyes and looked amused. 'But not with any great enthusiasm, aye?'

'But not with rancour either.'

'Thank you for that small kindness.'

'It's the truth.'

'Before I went to Southampton, I told you I was in love with you, Miranda. Do you remember?'

'How could I forget, when only a few days have passed?' she said, with a grin. 'It was a totally impulsive act. But you were very dashing, and you nearly swept me off my feet. I told you to think it over. I hope you have, and have come to your senses.'

There was something boyish about his grin. 'You laughed at me, and that was cruel, because it dented my feelings considerably.

I just want you to know I have thought it over, as you advised. Nothing has changed. I still love you . . . only I love you madly now. There's nothing like resistance to sharpen a man's appetite.'

'It's too soon for . . . love. We've only met three times.'

'I feel as though I've loved you all my life. Don't be so sensible, Miranda. Run away with me.'

'I can't . . . I have responsibilities. I have my sister to consider as well as myself. Also, I don't want to be involved in a scandal.'

'You're in the wrong place to avoid one, I fear. Your sister could run away with us. After all, it's not very far to the next estate.'

'I would prefer it if the argument with your uncle was resolved. I don't want to spend my life on bad terms with the people around me. Shall I talk to him on your behalf and urge him to reconcile your differences. I needn't mention that we've met.'

'I'm not a man to hide behind a woman's skirt, and would prefer to speak for myself.'

'As you wish, Fletcher. You certainly have more than your fair share of arrogance.'

'I can't deny it.' He ran his finger down her nose. 'Are you very annoyed with me?'

'No. I have something else on my mind.'

'Ouch . . . I must be losing my appeal.'

To answer in the negative would be playing into his hands, so she ignored it. 'Sir James is holding a supper party for me a week next Saturday. It's my nineteenth birthday. Perhaps he'll invite you.'

'If he did, it would have an alternative purpose. My uncle is not what he seems, Miranda. He has two faces, and he has many informers. Just bear that in mind.'

'Informers?'

'He's a magistrate, and he makes it his business to know what's going on in the district.'

'Is that so bad?'

He rose and, holding out his hand, pulled her to her feet. 'We should avoid talking about my uncle . . . and you should keep your advice to yourself. You hardly know him, and certainly don't know what he's capable of. Curiosity can get you into serious trouble in these parts.'

'So much for true love,' she shot at him, and, jerking her hands away, she stomped off.

When she looked back there was no sight of him. 'Don't keep appearing and disappearing without notice,' she shouted. 'And it's rude to part without saying goodbye.'

He was waiting for her at the turn-off to the road and held out his arms to her.

They closed around her when she went to him, and he spun her round.

'I have to tell you something before you go, Fletcher.'

'Is it that you love me?'

'I can't love you . . . not yet.'

'What's that supposed to mean? You can't control love; it's something you feel.'

She ignored what she knew to be true. 'Your uncle has proposed marriage to me, and I promised to let him know by the end of June. He wants me to provide him with an heir. I've already told him that he's got one in you.'

He pushed her to arms' length. 'How deep are you in?'

'I don't know what you mean.'

'Yes, you do, Miranda. Has my uncle bedded you yet?'

She suddenly remembered Sir James's hands on her body and her cheeks flamed, but mostly from anger towards Fletcher.

When she lashed out at him, he caught her wrist, and although she tried to free it, he held it fast. His eyes looked wounded, but they gazed steadily into hers as if daring her to lie, when he said harshly, 'Answer me.'

'Your uncle has been a perfect gentleman towards both my sister and me. In fact, he spoils Lucy as if she were his own child. Let go of me.'

He removed his grip. 'I believe you. Go ahead and hit me. I deserve it.'

'Yes, you do. I'm angry that a man who professes to love me can think so little of me, and I allowed it to get the better of me. Just at this moment, I don't care whether you believe me or not. I thought it best that you knew what was going on, that's all.'

'Thank you for your honesty. It will help me to plan my campaign. Be warned . . . I'll snatch you from his side at the altar if need be.'

She kissed him, a gently placed caress against the corner of his mouth.

He turned his head, stooped and captured her mouth. 'You haven't seen the last of me, Miranda.'

Thank goodness for that, she thought as he walked away from her.

Miranda felt uneasy again when she reached the road. Her back prickled, as though she was being followed.

Caesar didn't seem to be alarmed, though he gazed back at her a couple of times to wag his tail. He was a nice-natured dog, despite his training to guard, and loved being petted. When she rounded the bend, she drew him back into the shadow of a hedge and waited.

She was surprised when Lucy came into view and she stepped forward, causing her sister to jump. 'What are you doing here? Are you following me?'

Her sister's hands went to her hips and a wounded look exploded on her face. 'I certainly was not. I felt like a walk and I was looking for you. You could have asked me to join you!'

Guilt filled her. 'Sorry, Lucy. You were playing the piano, and I know you don't like being disturbed when you're practising. I thought you'd be writing your book afterwards. Have you made much progress?'

'Not in the writing, though I've finished the first chapter. Now I'm going to make a plan of chapters with scenes in. Making up stories is so interesting.'

There came the sound of a horse, and they both turned. It was Simon Bailey.

Caesar placed himself between herself and the horse and created an impressive rumbling brown growl deep in his throat.

'Quiet, Caesar,' she said and fondled his velvety ear.

Simon doffed his hat. 'Good afternoon, Miss Jarvis. Miss Lucy. A lovely day, isn't it?'

Miranda nodded. 'It certainly is, Mr Bailey.'

'On your way back to Marguerite House, are you?'

'We are.'

He dismounted. 'I'd better escort you. It seems that a trespasser has been seen on the estate. It might have been a smuggler.'

Lucy's eyes began to shine. 'How exciting! Where?'

'Near the cemetery; I've not long come from there.'

Miranda raised an eyebrow, though her mouth dried and her heart began to thump. What if he'd seen her and Fletcher together? 'What was the intruder supposed to be smuggling? Bones?' When he chuckled, she said, 'Does it concern you so very much, Mr Bailey? This is, after all, Sir James's estate. How do you know it's a trespasser?'

'Someone who saw him told me. Anything out of the ordinary that happens on this coast concerns me. That's my job.'

They began to walk.

'Ah yes . . . smugglers and such. I've never actually seen a smuggler.'

'You wouldn't know one if you did see one, but you need look no further than the adjoining estate. They're a murderous lot, and you should keep away from there if you can. Now Sir James has closed the road, it will make it harder for them to convey the smuggled goods through his estate and that route will be blocked.'

Shock rippled through her. 'Are you telling me that Fletcher Taunt is a smuggler? He's Sir James's nephew, and has only just bought the estate.

'But he was on friendly terms with the previous owner, and Silas Asher was an out-and-out scoundrel. I'll say no more.'

Despite declaring he'd say no more, Simon Bailey carried on talking. 'I've been given no reason to believe he is, apart from rumour, which gave me cause to search his company's ship, *Midnight Star*, on a couple of occasions.'

'What did you find?' Lucy asked, her eyes alight with curiosity.

'Unfortunately, there was nothing, Miss Lucy. If there had been, he'd now be languishing in jail. Silas Asher, who previously owned Monksfoot Estate, was the scum of the earth, and so are those who were his partners in crime . . . many of whom are still employed there.'

Lucy asked Simon Bailey the question Miranda would have liked to ask him, except she was reluctant to expose herself to any questioning regarding Fletcher Taunt.

'Sir James can be awfully stern. He'd be cross if you arrested his nephew, though. What would happen to him? Would you give him a good flogging?'

'It would depend on the magistrate. If he was found guilty and

I recommended it, the man could be put to death by hanging or firing squad. It would serve as an example to other miscreants.'

Lucy shuddered. 'That's a horrid suggestion. In all conscience, how could you do such a thing?'

Miranda intervened. 'Mr Bailey, I would suggest you remember that you're speaking to a young woman of impressionable age. I do not want my sister exposed to such information.'

He coloured a little at the reprimand. 'I'm sorry, Miss Jarvis . . . Miss Lucy. Perhaps it will put your minds at rest if I tell you that the usual punishment is transportation to a place where the felon can live an honest and useful life and learn practical skills. If Sir James's nephew happened to be involved, I imagine their relationship would be taken into account before any charges were laid.'

As the house came into view, Miranda said, 'Please don't go to any more trouble, Mr Bailey. We can go the rest of the way unescorted, I think. We have Caesar to look after us, after all.'

'It would only take one bullet to dispose of the dog. In any event, I'm going to see Sir James. We travelled back from Dorchester together and I said I'd report back to him after I'd taken a look around. I expect the intruder has gone by now, don't you, Miss Jarvis?'

'One would hope so.'

'Perhaps it was a ghost in the cemetery. There must be hundreds of them floating about,' Lucy remarked, and Miranda wished her sister would abandon her fascination with the wandering spirits of the dead.

They parted company in the hall. 'I'm looking forward to your birthday party, Miss Jarvis,' Simon Bailey said as they began to climb the stairs. 'I believe Sir James has invited guests from as far away as Southampton.'

And she wouldn't know any of them, and Sir James would expect her to act as host. Not only that. It didn't seem decent to celebrate her birthday when her mother had died so recently.

Miranda almost felt sick at the thought.

Eleven

So Fletcher Taunt was suspected of being a smuggler! A thrill of dismay rattled through Miranda. She couldn't believe it – wouldn't believe it!

She was disappointed when he didn't put in an appearance at the church for the service.

She wondered how many members of the congregation were involved in such a pursuit, and gazed around her. Perhaps it was her imagination, but some of the men were villainous-looking and others had sly faces. Most of them had weathered skin, for they spent most of their days working on the sea or in the fields. Many appeared to be ordinary men and women going about their business. But even in their Sunday clothes, the whole bunch of them began to appear sinister to her.

Obviously, Sir James wasn't one of the villains, though Fletcher had warned her that his uncle wasn't what he appeared. He was an honest, upright gentleman, his head bowed in prayer. His voice was deep and a little husky when he sang the hymns. His forehead knitted in a frown when the rector launched into a rambling sermon and he heaved a huge sigh.

When a small chuckle escaped from her, his glance came her way and he raised an eyebrow. She gazed back at her hands. She couldn't imagine being married to him. He was older than her father had been when he'd died from his fall.

Like most accidents, her father's had been unexpected – his neck broken across a fallen log. At least he hadn't suffered, she thought. Death had been instantaneous and the course of their lives had been changed by it. It seemed so long ago now, and her memory of him was not quite so painful and acute.

The rector's voice droned on for what seemed like forever. Someone at the back of the congregation began to snore loudly.

There were shouts and hoots of laughter, and several faked snoring noises in various tones, so it sounded as though there was a sty full of pigs at the back of the church.

Miranda felt sorry for the rector when his voice tailed off. Looking tired, grey and beaten down by life, he shrugged, mumbled a blessing over them all and walked up the aisle to wait in the porch as his congregation filed out.

His wife followed after, her lips pursed into nag lines. It was as if she was sorry to be married to such a poor creature of a man and was intent on improving him.

The congregation fell quiet when Sir James's party stood and proceeded to leave. Miranda knew that all the glances were directed towards her and Lucy. Her face heated as she wondered what they were thinking. Nothing good, she imagined.

'Thank you, reverend.' Sir James placed his hat on his head.

A pair of weary blue eyes fell on her. 'God bless you.'

'I enjoyed your sermon, reverend,' Miranda lied, because she felt sorry for him; she couldn't actually remember one droning sentence of it.

The eyes sprang open in surprise and he stuttered, 'Why, thank you, young lady. Which part did you like best?'

Moses came into her mind, but before she could recall it clearly, Lucy stepped into the sudden silence. 'I expect it was the bit in the story where the waters parted and the Israelites walked across. I liked that bit, too. It was exciting because I imagined the water closing over to drown them all. I expect the fish got rather a surprise too when they tried to swim across the gap. Did it really happen?'

A smile lit the rector's face at Lucy's enthusiasm, abandoned when his wife snapped, 'It's not your place to question the reverend over the miracles contained in the Bible, young woman.'

Sir James surprised Miranda by saying, 'Do be quiet, Mrs Swift. The question was not addressed to you and it's not your place to criticize my guests. Miss Lucy, Miss Jarvis, the carriage is waiting. Reverend Swift, do visit us for afternoon tea one day next week. Wednesday or Thursday will suit. There's something I wish to discuss with you.'

'Those are my days to be charitable and visit the poor in the parish,' Mrs Swift said. 'May I suggest another day?'

'Yes, I'm aware of that. Never fear. I shall send one of my stable hands to help you. He can carry your things and accompany you.'

Miranda looked at him in surprise, for she hadn't thought him the type of man to be churlish to a woman in public.

Lucy stuck her nose in the air and swished off towards the carriage. Miranda resolved to have words with her sister about her attitude. They were, after all, reliant on the good graces of another, and their position in life was not ideal when the mentor was a relative stranger to them.

'Good-day, reverend.' Sir James ushered her before him, and once they were settled in the carriage, he said. 'It's best not to linger after the service. Too much gossip circulates.'

'I felt sorry for Reverend Swift,' Miranda said.

'Having a shrew for a wife would be wearing for any man. He should grow a backbone and stand up to her. Perhaps you should learn a lesson from it for when you become wives. Always be obedient and agreeable to your husbands, and then you will both live happier lives together.'

The words left her mouth before she could stop them. 'And if I'm not inclined to be either?'

'Bear in mind that he may take a strap to you.' His eyes met hers, dark and unfathomable, and he smiled. 'There are ways to bring someone to heel, especially a woman. They're emotional and self-sacrificial. They love too deeply, and that can be used against them.'

Her skin crawled.

When they arrived home, she was about to go upstairs when Sir James said, 'I understand you ran into Simon Bailey a day or so ago.'

'Lucy and I were on our way home and he came up behind us on the road. He said there was talk of a trespasser, didn't he, Lucy?'

'Yes.' Her sister laughed. 'He talked about horrid things such as hanging and shooting felons. He said it wasn't up to him but to the magistrate. You wouldn't sentence anyone to hang, would you?'

'Such sentences are for learned men to ponder on and decide on, Miss Lucy. The punishment for various crimes is decided upon by parliament. By law, a magistrate has to use them for their proper purpose, without fear or favour.'

'Miranda was cross with Mr Bailey,' Lucy said. 'She told him I wasn't old enough to hear such things.'

'Your sister is right . . . but you should have told me, Miranda. I would have had a word with him.'

'There was no need.'

'What do you make of the man?'

'He seems to be an upright and honest man, though a little awkward in manner. I feel sorry for him.'

'Miranda feels sorry for everyone,' Lucy threw in. 'I'm sure Mr Bailey could improve himself if he tried to be pleasant. I would love to hear his stories of smugglers and piracy on the high seas. How exciting it must be to be a man.'

Sir James smiled. 'When men puff themselves up with pride at their own honesty they seem to lose sight of the fact they're not perfect. Honest men cannot be trusted.'

'Can you be trusted, Sir James?' Lucy asked him.

'Not at all.'

Miranda believed him, even though it was said in a jocular manner. It seemed to her that nobody could be trusted in these parts, not even Fletcher Taunt. 'What are you suggesting Simon Bailey do – commit a crime to feel less about himself?'

'At least it would make him human. None of us is perfect. Tell me. How many lies have you told today?'

Did lying include avoiding giving him a straight answer? 'None that I can think of.'

Lucy scoffed, 'What about the fib you told the reverend about liking his sermon. You couldn't even remember it was about Moses parting the water.'

'I admit, my mind was far away, but that was just to make him feel happy, because he looked so sad. Was the intruder caught, Sir James?'

'No, so I'd rather you stayed within sight of the house for a while. I'm sure there are enough wildflowers in the garden to keep your sketching pencil busy.'

She nodded, and then her blood ran cold as she remembered her sketching block. She'd left it at the cemetery. She hoped he wouldn't ask to see it.

'By the way, the couple who robbed your mother were apprehended. They were caught stealing food in the market place.'

'What will happen to them?'

'They will be tried and will receive the appropriate sentence within the law, no doubt.'

She felt her face drain of colour. 'You won't . . .'

'Their case will be heard by another magistrate. You'll be

expected to identify them and make a witness statement.' He guided her to the chair. 'Sit down. Miss Lucy, see if there are any smelling salts in Miranda's bag.'

The sharp assault of the whiff of salts into her nostrils cleared her head in an instant.

'Come, come, Miranda. There is nothing to worry about.'

'They were hungry, that's all. When Lucy and I were hungry, you allowed me to steal from you without punishment. You fed us and looked after us. I would like to see the same charity afforded to this couple.'

'Your rescue was a moment of weakness on my part, and at times like this I think it would have been wiser to have allowed my dogs to eat you for dinner. I cannot feed and house every waif and stray who crosses my path, though I do help fund a school for orphaned boys that furnishes them with useful disciplines for the future, so I hope that will redeem me in your eyes.' He chuckled at the thought, and then sighed. 'Very well – for the sake of your conscience, I suppose we can drop the charges relating to their crime against you. No doubt the people they stole from in the market place will be less charitable. Your evidence wouldn't have made any difference to the outcome, anyway.'

'Thank you, Sir James.'

He kissed her forehead. 'Go and rest now, Miranda. You too, Miss Lucy. I'll see you both at dinner.'

A few days later, Sir James informed her, 'You might be interested to learn that the couple who robbed your mother's body tried to escape. The man was shot dead, and the woman sentenced to transportation with hard labour. None of your goods were recovered. I expect they sold them. So justice has been served, and you needn't worry about them any more.'

So matter-of-fact, and without any pity for them at all. What kind of man was he?

Sir James usually had guests for dinner at the weekends. Tonight was no exception. There was a local corn merchant called Harold George, and his rather dull wife, and Sir James's legal representative, Andrew Patterson and his wife, Mary, whom they'd met before.

They were assembled in the drawing room when a servant

entered and whispered something to Sir James. He smiled. 'Tell him to come in.'

Nothing could have surprised Miranda more than Fletcher's entrance.

He wore a black evening suit over a burgundy-hued waistcoat threaded through with gold thread. A high-fastening shirt with bow completed his outfit and his dark, crisp curls sprang about his head. He was a handsome, strong-looking man.

Her body became aware of him, of the caress of his glance, the unruly curl of darkness against his ear lobe, the long sweep of his lashes on his lean and hungry-looking face. Desire tore through her like a flood, sending pulses of moisture to lap like an incoming tide at the secretive centre of her. She wanted to run to his side, throw herself into his arms, and kiss him over and over again. She nearly called out his name.

His glance ran over the assembly and then lingered on her for the moment it took for him to smile. He turned to Sir James and inclined his head slightly. 'Uncle . . . you are well?'

'As you see. To what do I owe this honour, Fletcher?'

'I wanted to discuss business, but I see you are about to eat.'

'You've always known the time we dine. In fact, I'd swear you were dressed for the occasion.'

'I was hoping to be invited, since I haven't tasted cooking as good as Nancy's for quite some time.'

Sir James nodded to the servant. 'Set another place for my nephew. You know almost everyone here, don't you, Fletcher?'

'He doesn't know me,' Lucy said and smiled at him. 'How do you do, Mr Taunt. We have your portrait hanging on our bedroom wall, so I feel as though I know you. I'm Lucy Jarvis, and this is my sister, Miranda Jarvis.'

He took Lucy's hand in his and kissed it.

Sir James said, 'You're supposed to wait to be introduced, Miss Lucy.'

Lucy giggled. 'I know, but you were taking such a long time about it that I thought I'd help things along. That's the first time anyone has kissed my hand, Mr Taunt. I shall write it into my story.'

'Miss Jarvis.' Fletcher's mouth brushed lightly across Miranda's knuckles and his eyes engaged hers. 'I'm pleased to meet you. I'd heard my uncle had house guests, so I found an excuse to come and see for myself.'

'What excuse is that, Fletcher? Let me hear it.'

The air was suddenly charged with tension.

'Can it not wait until we're alone?'

'I think not, since it seems to me that we've waited long enough. If we are to reconcile, we must make things clear on where we stand. I'm sure my guests won't mind.'

Miranda wasn't quite sure what was going on, but she'd picked up that Sir James was out to humiliate Fletcher. 'I think I'd rather not be a witness to this.'

'I'd prefer you to stay, my dear, since it won't take long.'

Fletcher drew in a deep breath. 'Two years ago, we had an argument over the *Midnight Star*, which got out of hand. You accused me of cheating at cards, I recall. I was drunk at the time. If I did cheat, it was unintentional, and I've regretted the barrier between us ever since. For that I offer an apology.'

A man of pride and position who was able to offer a public apology with so much grace and aplomb was admirable. At that moment, Fletcher won both Miranda's admiration and her heart.

Sir James patted his nephew on the shoulder. 'Perhaps I was a little hasty at the time. We will sort this out privately between us a little later on and see what can be done to remove this barrier. Let's go in for dinner now, lest the food spoil. Fletcher, you may escort Miss Lucy in.'

Miranda felt a moment of disappointment when she found herself seated as far away from Fletcher as she could be, though he was well in her line of sight. But perhaps it was just as well, she thought; otherwise she might give herself away. Just knowing he was near would make dinner an agony.

After a delicately flavoured leek soup, a saddle of lamb was served with roast turnips, potatoes, and peas with a delicious aroma of wild mint. There was a pudding of custard tart, served with strawberries and cream, and garnished with chocolate flakes.

The ladies were eager to gossip about Fletcher when they returned to the drawing room.

'I'd forgotten how handsome Fletcher Taunt is,' Mary Patterson said, claiming the earliest acquaintance. 'He was such a flirt, and that hasn't changed.'

'And charming,' Mrs George murmured. 'What do you think, Miss Jarvis?'

'Yes, I imagine he is, but we hardly spoke during dinner.'

'Nevertheless, he couldn't take his eyes from you.'

'I don't think that's quite true; if so, I didn't notice.'

Lucy offered, 'He was charming to me. He told me my eyes were pretty, just like Miranda's, and that made my face go all red. Then he said I needn't worry about blushing because it happened to every young lady of my age, and when I'd grown up properly and was used to receiving compliments from men, it would stop. Of course, he was teasing, and that made me blush even more. But he was such fun.'

Mrs George engaged her eyes. 'Do you really have his portrait on your bedroom wall, Miss Jarvis?'

'Yes . . . but the room was used by Sir James's sister, Elizabeth Taunt, and Mr Taunt is a child in it, though he seems to have changed very little.'

'Ah . . . I see. Mr Taunt is very much like Sir James—'

The door opened and the men came in. Into the sudden silence, Sir James said, 'Did I hear my name mentioned?'

'I was just saying how alike you and Mr Taunt are. You look more like father and son than uncle and nephew,' Mrs George twittered.

'Which is a comparison made on previous occasions, Mrs George. There is more than a passing family resemblance, I admit. That would have come through my sister, unless you have another theory to explain it. Goodness knows, many have been bandied about. Isn't that right, Fletcher?'

Mrs George lowered her glance to her hands and, sounding distressed, she murmured, 'I meant no offence.'

Stepping forward, Fletcher relieved the tension by taking her hands in his. 'No offence was taken, Mrs George. My father was the ne'er-do-well Adrian Taunt, who was killed abroad, I'm given to understand.' Lowering his voice, he looked around and whispered loudly. 'The family is littered with villains and my father is just one of them.'

Miranda stepped into the lighter mood he'd created. 'Who are the others you mentioned? Yourself and Sir James excepting, of course, since it wouldn't do to incriminate yourselves.'

That brought laughter from everyone, and it was Sir James who answered, 'I think we'll let sleeping dogs lie on that. Miss Jarvis, I hear you've been sketching flowers. Please fetch your sketching block so we can see them.'

Her heart sank. 'I seem to have mislaid it . . . Besides, my sketches are not very accurate.'

Sir James beckoned to a servant. 'Tell Mrs Pridie to go to Miss Jarvis's room and look for her sketching block.'

Fletcher stopped the progress of the servant. 'You might want to look on the hallstand first. I recall placing my hat on top of a sketching block.'

Within a short time, the servant came back with the block and handed it to Sir James.

Miranda sent Fletcher a smile that thanked him for getting her out of that particular hole. 'You have sharp eyes, Mr Taunt. I seem to be getting absent-minded, and I'm certainly too embarrassed to show anyone my poor sketches.'

'Nonsense,' Sir James said, riffling through the pages. 'This sketch of a briar rose is excellent. And, see, it has a message underneath on a ribbon . . . "Love never dies". For whom was this sentimental message intended?'

It was intended for her, because Miranda hadn't sketched the rose; Fletcher must have.

Now Fletcher gazed over his uncle's shoulder and rescued her again. 'That rose rambles over one of the graves, I believe. The message is inscribed on the headstone, so it must be intended for the person who occupies the grave, which isn't named. It's probably a woman buried there.'

'What makes you think that?'

'The fact that there's a rose planted on the grave. It's a woman's flower with a female name. And up to fairly recently, it's been pruned regularly. Perhaps it was someone of Silas Asher's acquaintance.'

Sir James threw a frown his way. 'I must take a look at this grave and go through the family records. It's more likely someone who disgraced the family and was punished in death by being buried unnamed.'

Lucy's eyes were as round as saucers. 'How wonderfully mysterious! You will tell me when you find out, won't you, Sir James?'

'You're as curious as a cat sometimes, missy. One day that nose might get you into trouble.'

Lucy blushed at the mild reprimand and retreated to her chair.

'There's just one small mistake as far as I can see, Miss Jarvis; it's the wrong time of year for roses to bloom.'

Fletcher took up her defence. 'Miss Jarvis did say her sketches weren't accurate. Obviously, she preferred the plant to look as though it were blooming. It's a pretty little picture, Miss Jarvis.'

'I appreciate your comments, Mr Taunt. Next time I draw, I'll try to please others instead of myself, and be more accurate in my application of pencil to paper. Goodness, what a fuss about a small drawing. What will you make of my poppies, I wonder?'

His eyes engaged hers. Mischief danced in their depths like glimmers of sunshine on the surface of a mossy pool. 'I imagine your poppies will be a delight, Miss Jarvis.'

Sir James smothered his laughter with his handkerchief.

Miranda only just managed to keep hers under control, but she wasn't quite as successful with her blush.

The others crowded round to admire her work, and someone tickled the palm of her hand. She didn't look to see who it was; she didn't need to.

Sir James drew Lucy back into the fold by saying, 'What are you going to entertain us with tonight, Miss Lucy?'

'Some Mozart, I think.'

After the entertainment, the guests drifted off to their allotted rooms. They were staying the night and knew better than to linger when Sir James had already indicated he had business to attend to. Reconciliation seemed to be on the agenda.

Fletcher didn't feel easy about it, as though his absence had created a divide between them that couldn't be breached without a large dollop of hypocrisy to oil it.

Sir James poured them a brandy apiece, and they took a chair on either side of the fireplace and contemplated each other – just like they used to, for old habits died hard, Fletcher thought.

The clock ticked steadily, the leaping flames crackled in the fireplace and the shadows danced on the wall. The brandy was one to be appreciated, smooth when savoured against his tongue.

His uncle broke the silence. 'Now, then, Fletcher, how shall we go about resolving our differences? Do you have anything to redeem yourself in my eyes after cheating me out of my half of the *Midnight Star*?'

'I believe you agreed you may have been hasty over that.'

'I'm willing to be convinced.'

'I destroyed the note you signed that gave me your half of the ship in settlement of your gambling debt.'

'I had no idea you'd done that. Why didn't you tell me then?'

'Because, in your usual bloody-minded way, you locked me out and sent me packing before I could tell you. The ship is still a company asset, and that company is in both our names. Moreover, the money your half of the ship has earned in the past two years is in a separate account in your name. You could have examined the books any time you wished by contacting Sir Oswald. What stopped you?'

'The same issue that stopped you from contacting me; you call it bloody-mindedness and I call it pride. You made it perfectly clear the shipping business would be managed by you alone. I had no intention of going cap-in-hand to consult with Oswald, a man I dislike.'

'But you said you didn't want any part of managing it. The shipping company is doing well, and will do even better in the future. I'm proud of it.'

'Very well, I'll allow you that. Now about the Monksfoot Estate. You stole that from under my nose.'

'I didn't steal it. Silas said he'd never sell it to you. He was fond of the place, and he knew you'd pull it down. He seemed to have some sort of grudge against you, and suggested that he and I might be related.'

'Did he, by God!' James spluttered. 'The arrogance of the man! You look nothing like him. You're a Fenmore through and through.'

'Didn't the Taunt family have some hand in it?'

'We've been through all this before. Let's change the subject. What are your plans for Monksfoot?'

'As well as the seaweed trade, I intend to run the estate as a farm.'

'It's good soil, I admit.'

'Eventually, I'm going to put a stop to the illicit trading in smuggled goods. The authorities are strong now, and are backed up by the navy on occasion. It's too close to home and only a matter of time before they catch up with us.'

'Silas was always a bit flagrant about his business. He liked to flaunt it under the noses of the authorities.'

'There have been running battles. I've got no desire to get a bullet in my back or dance a jig at the end of a rope. That tame customs man of yours has caused me some annoyance, boarding the *Midnight Star*. He's already damaged some sails and the company's reputation.'

'It was not at my urging. Simon Bailey is a law unto himself. He's a hard man to fathom. One day he'll get a bullet in his back.'

'Not from me. The shipping company is a legitimate business that fills both our coffers, and that ship is the only asset.' Fletcher hesitated about mentioning the *Lady Miranda*, and decided not to – not until she was ready for sea and had a cargo lined up. 'I'm worried Bailey will do something stupid that will jeopardize the lives of the crew. The last time he boarded, he held a gun to my head.'

'You should be grateful he didn't pull the trigger.'

'I've told Tom Pepper he's to make sure to keep his activities at a low-key level. I don't want to spend the remainder of my life watching my back.'

'Tom Pepper and his crew will do as he's always done, with or without you. They're all sewer rats and you can't trust any one of them. The trouble with you, Fletcher, is that you've got a conscience.'

'So have you! You know, uncle, we should forget the smuggling and work the land together – in the same way we run the shipping company. You're a much better farmer than I could ever be.'

'It's a thought, and I'll consider it.'

'Tell me about those young women.'

His uncle stared into his glass and smiled. 'I wondered when you'd get round to asking. Miranda is a fetching little thing, isn't she? They have nobody to care for them – except me. I thought I might wed the older one and breed from her. She didn't seem very keen on the idea, so I'm giving her a little time.'

It was dropped into the conversation casually, as though Miranda was a brood mare. Fletcher felt sick. 'What if she decides against it?'

His uncle shrugged. 'If I cannot persuade her, there are other options to explore. I've spent a considerable amount of money on that pair. I look on them as an investment and they owe me.'

Fletcher could only imagine what those options were. 'And the younger girl?'

He shrugged. 'In a year or so, she'll be old enough to wed. Simon Bailey needs a young wife to keep him busy. I'm sure I could supply Lucy with a dowry – not a big one, of course, but enough for Simon to feel grateful towards me. You know . . . that idea of combining the estates is a good one. I'll expect my name to be on the deeds, of course.'

His uncle was still as devious as they came, Fletcher thought, trying not to grin. 'I bought Monksfoot fair and square. I had no idea that Silas intended to leave his estate to me. One day, I'll marry and produce a child or two of my own. I'm not such a fool that I'd jeopardize their futures for your present.'

The brandy in the glass on the table began to ripple, and there was a low rumble followed by an explosion. The boards trembled under their feet. The dogs set up a clamour of barks and the glass in the cabinet tinkled.

'What the hell!'

The first explosion was almost immediately followed by a second. The two gazed at each other, then shot to their feet.

Voices were heard in the hall and then the door was thrust open and Jack Pridie came in. 'I think the new gatehouse and walls have been destroyed, Sir James.'

'The devil they have! Where was the watchman – asleep? Arm the men and get over there. If he survived the explosion, dismiss him.'

Sir James moved to the side table. Taking out a pistol, he cocked it, turned and aimed it at Fletcher's head.

Fletcher's scalp seemed to shrink when his uncle said, 'I'm of a mind to kill you. I was a fool to allow you to advance over the doorstep.'

Andrew Patterson called out, 'You have no reason to believe this was done on Fletcher's orders, Sir James.'

But his uncle wasn't listening to reason and Fletcher had cause to be worried. Sir James was a crack shot, and from this distance he'd probably blow half his head off.

'You have to the count of five to get out of my house. If you set foot on my property again, I'll leave instructions for you to be shot out of hand. One . . .'

'This is not my doing, uncle.'

'Two . . .'

There came a babble of voices from the landing, and Fletcher caught a glimpse of Miranda in the shadows. Her arm was around her sister, her hair a shining cascade about her shoulders, though they were still in their clothes. Both pairs of eyes were as wide as saucers.

'Three . . .'

She did what he prayed she wouldn't: left her sister's side and advanced down the stairs, trying to distract his uncle. 'What's happened? Why are you pointing that gun at Fletcher?'

'Four . . . Get back upstairs, girl,' his uncle said sharply.

'Do as you're told, Miranda,' Fletcher shouted in alarm, but on the count of five she moved between them and threw herself against him. Arm sliding round her, he swung her aside.

'Five!'

Surely his uncle wouldn't be stupid enough to kill him in cold blood, and in front of witnesses? Fletcher cursed, but he knew he was right. At the last moment, Sir James sloped the weapon away from them, his finger still taut against the trigger.

It discharged, and there was a chorus of screams from the small group of ladies assembled on the landing.

'Miranda,' Fletcher whispered and caught her up in his arms as Lucy half tumbled down the stairs to Miranda.

Twelve

It had taken the bullet but an instant to punch a ragged tear in Miranda's sleeve. It had emerged further along the fabric and had lodged in a cushion on the hall seat in an eruption of feathers.

Lucy's shocked screech echoed through the house.

Fletcher relaxed. 'It's all right, Lucy; she's not injured. It's just a faint and your sister is already showing signs of coming round.

I'll bring her up to her room.' He nodded to a wide-eyed maid. 'Ask Mrs Pridie to attend to Miss Jarvis.'

The servant aimed an uneasy glance at Sir James, who said calmly, 'It was an accident; the girl distracted me and the gun went off. Get about your work now.'

'Yes, sir.' She scurried off, as if eager to escape the reach of Sir James's trigger finger as well as relate the goings-on to the rest of the servants.

Lucy exclaimed, 'Oh! Thank goodness,' and she burst into tears as she followed Fletcher and his burden up the stairs.

The room that had once belonged to Fletcher's mother had a fragrance peculiar to females, of perfume and powder and the more floral scents used in the pastille burner.

He lowered his dainty burden to the bed and gazed at the portrait of himself hanging there. He couldn't imagine being so young and smooth-faced. He couldn't recall much about his mother either – couldn't remember ever being close to her. He only remembered snatches of his infancy, and her indifference had kept him at bay.

To make up for it, there had been a nursemaid when he was very young, a woman who'd held him to her breast and tenderly kissed away his hurt. He closed his eyes and took in a deep breath and the familiar, spicy and poignant smell of her seemed to infuse him for just a second before it eluded him again. One day she hadn't been there any more and he'd felt lonely without her.

Miranda made a startled little noise and scrambled upright. 'Are you all right, Fletcher? You're not hurt?' She gazed around the room, bewildered, and her eyes fell on Lucy. 'I remember now.'

Lucy scolded her. 'You gave me such a scare, Miranda. What on earth did you hope to achieve?'

'It was an instinctive moment of decision.'

'It certainly was. Mr Taunt looks as though he's capable of defending himself, though.' Lucy gave a bit of a giggle, though her eyes were still damp. 'You've certainly given everybody something to talk about. I bet Sir James is lathered up with guilt in case he's killed you.'

Fletcher chuckled. His uncle didn't know what guilt was, let alone give in to it. All the same, he liked this younger sister of Miranda's. 'So much for my family reunion.'

'It was enthralling – so passionate and sincere that it brought tears to my eyes. I enjoyed every moment. You bear a strong resemblance to Sir James, Mr Fletcher.'

He hoped the resemblance was physical rather than stemming from nature. 'So I'm given to understand, Miss Lucy.'

Mrs Pridie came in, carrying two glasses of milk. 'Sir James requests that you join him in the hall immediately, Mr Taunt.' She turned to the two young women. 'He's sent up a sleeping draught. He said to take it early so it will calm your nerves.'

Crossly – and Fletcher could almost imagine her stamping her foot as anger replaced any fear she'd felt – Miranda said, 'My nerves are just fine; it's Sir James's nerves that need attention if he pulls a gun on his guests at the slightest provocation. Tell him to drink it himself.'

'I'll leave it on the table in case you feel the need for it later.'

Fletcher exchanged a grin with Mrs Pridie. 'I'll leave her in your good hands, Mrs Pridie. They're much safer than mine. At this moment, I feel like hanging Miss Jarvis here over my knee and smacking that pert little backside of hers.'

It was to his great satisfaction that Miranda blushed before she glared at him, saying, 'Ungrateful wretch! Next time I'll allow him to blow your damn-fool head off.'

'Which would make me feel marginally better than watching you get your damn-fool head blown off.' His smile encompassed them both. 'Thank you for saving my life, Miss Jarvis; I'm indebted to you. You and Miss Lucy must come and visit me at Monksfoot.'

'Hah!' she said, as bristly as a dog with a bone, and Lucy giggled.

'Best you don't go stirring up trouble for yourself, young man,' Mrs Pridie said, clucking her tongue when he gave her a hug and planted a kiss on her cheek. 'You always had more than your fair share of charm, and you'll need all of it to talk yourself back into the good graces of Sir James. Be off with you now.'

When Fletcher went downstairs, his uncle didn't look in the least bit contrite, just disgruntled, for he'd always disliked the calm of his household being disturbed. He was wearing his topcoat. 'I'm willing to believe you're innocent in this matter, Fletcher. I was too hasty.'

Fletcher knew that was probably all the apology he'd get from him, yet he couldn't help but needle him a little. 'I'm relieved to be alive.'

'You know damned well I wouldn't have shot you out of hand. However, over the past two years you haven't done anything to inspire my confidence, either.'

'And neither have I done anything to worsen the situation between us, though there has been provocation that could have resulted in retaliation. Most of the time I was on board the *Midnight Star*, learning as much seamanship as I could absorb to further the business. A man should be aware of the practicalities of sailing a ship if he intends to run a shipping company, and it's a hard life for those on board.'

'A man gets paid an amount equal to the work he puts in. Now, I'm going to see what damage has been done. Put your coat on and come with me. The others are waiting outside with the dogs, and we're all armed. Here, take this pistol, and make sure that female doesn't get in front of it. Has she recovered from her fright?'

'She's as mad as a nest of wasps.'

'Serves her right.' With some irritation, his uncle added, 'Women should keep their noses out of a man's business. Where's that damned dog got to?'

When his master gave three sharp whistles, Caesar came from the house, but he was reluctant and kept looking back and whining.

Sir James cuffed the dog across the nose. Caesar showed his teeth and growled. When struck again, the dog's tail went between his legs and he rolled on his back in the submissive position. A kick in the ribs made him yelp and got him on his feet. 'That female is turning you into a fancy lap dog. I'll have to give you a beating so you can learn who's the boss.'

They went on foot, the moon allowing them enough light to cover the ground safely.

Caesar had slunk off to join his parents. Fletcher felt sorry for the animal. Well trained though he was, he had been guarding Miranda, no doubt by his uncle's orders, and he was now confused by his own instincts.

The night was clear and there was nobody about except for his uncle's workers, who stood in a group. Their voices rumbled as they stood around talking amongst themselves. The light from the lanterns illuminated their faces and gave them a demonic appearance.

There had been considerable damage done to the wall. The

gates were bent and the pillars blown apart so the stones were scattered. Smoke and dust rose into the air.

'Has anyone seen the gatekeeper?'

There was a general shaking of heads.

They turned at the sound of riders, and pistols were displayed. It was Simon Bailey and three of his men.

Bailey said, 'We were riding the coast looking for signs of catchers and heard an explosion. What has happened, Sir James?'

'Someone's demolished the new gate and part of the boundary wall, and the keeper is missing.'

Simon's eyes gleamed in the lantern light. 'We'll keep our eyes open for him.' His gaze ran over the men and stopped on Fletcher. 'Mr Taunt, I noticed your lugger isn't at its mooring. Gone across to Cherbourg, has she?'

Fletcher nearly cursed out loud, and his brain scrambled to come up with anything that sounded remotely plausible. 'Could be. The *Wild Rose* is delivering sacks of seaweed fertilizer for the French farmers, and doing a little fishing on the way back.'

Simon Bailey nodded. 'I'd expect you to keep the fertilizer for your own fields. Still, what do I know about farming? I've heard a rumour that you intend to have Monksfoot Abbey under cultivation as soon as possible.'

'Have you indeed? News travels quickly, and farming wouldn't be part of your duties, surely?'

'It's amazing what can be found hidden in a haystack.'

His uncle didn't even bat an eyelid and astonished him with a display of family unity. 'I was discussing the possibility of combining the two estates earlier with my nephew, just before we heard the explosion. He prefers to be running the shipping side of the business, so any questions regarding agriculture should be directed to me.' His eyes took in the ruined walls and his mouth tightened. 'There's nothing that can be done until morning, so we might as well return to the house, gentlemen.'

Bailey tipped his hat, though he didn't seem inclined to leave. 'I'll ask the master of the revenue cutter to keep a special look out for the *Wild Rose*. He's patrolling the coast tonight, along with one of the Navy cutters. It's going to be right busy out there in the Channel. I wouldn't want them to mistake her for a smuggler when she's going about her lawful business for the Fenmore and

Taunt Shipping Company. That Navy cutter is well armed, as is the revenue boat. She could blow the bows right off the *Wild Rose*, so I hope she's flying the company colours from her mast.'

'Perhaps you'd inform your men that the *Wild Rose* is not a company vessel, but a privately owned one.'

'Is that a fact?' Bailey gazed up at the sky and smiled. 'I love a nice moon, don't you? Silas Asher would be spitting curses at it, were he still alive. He liked a dark night, did Silas. I heard he left you a fortune, Mr Taunt.'

'Could be, Mr Bailey.'

'No good will come of it.'

'As far as I know, it was earned legitimately, and I can think of several good uses to put it to, including charitable.'

'There was blood on Silas Asher's hands when he earned it, and there's blood on the moon tonight. I can almost smell it.'

Fletcher shrugged. 'Be careful Silas's ghost doesn't rise out of the sea to haunt you, then. There's a saying in these parts: "The spirit of those who curse the moon will rise to do the devil's bidding when he calls their name."'

As if on cue, on the outside periphery of the circle of men, a dog opened its throat and howled. It was Nero. The noise rose into the sudden silence and the air around them throbbed. The other two dogs joined in, perfectly harmonized, the howl primitive and unearthly.

Abruptly, the noise stopped and was answered by a flurry of worn-out barks coming from a distance. Silas's old hounds! They still guarded the old man's room, and Fletcher supposed they always would.

The hair on the back of Fletcher's neck prickled. His uncle's lurchers were on the alert, their heads turned towards the noise the elderly dogs had made, their snouts casting the air.

The horses whickered, snorted and fidgeted, unease displayed in their flattened ears, dancing hooves and rolling eyes. The customs men swore as they fought to bring them under control.

Shuffling their feet, the estate workers looked around them, exchanging uneasy glances.

'We'll be off, then,' Simon Bailey said, the bravado in his smile as shallow as it was forced. It was obvious he intended to have the last word when, before moving off, he said, 'Watch out for the devil, gentlemen. He might be wearing a uniform.'

'I've never heard that saying about cursing the moon and invoking the devil,' his uncle remarked when they began the traipse back to the house a little way ahead of the other two men.

Fletcher laughed. 'Nor I, but his reaction to it was rather surprising. It brought me out in a rash of goose bumps, and I almost believed my own words. Bailey made a good comeback.'

'You'd do well to remember that the man's not stupid by any means, and he's ambitious. He has a tendency to play things close to his chest.'

'Do you have someone in his service?'

His uncle smiled. 'I also play things close to my chest – it's safer, and a habit you should cultivate yourself, my boy, since you have a tendency to follow your heart. And don't imagine all is forgiven. You've turned us into rivals by making a fool out of me. I won't forget it in a hurry.'

'We're not rivals. We no longer have the same values, uncle. I grew up accepting yours. It wasn't until I left and began to think for myself that I realized I didn't want to spend my life trying to outwit the law. I want to live my life without having to look over my shoulder all the time.'

'Yet you accepted Silas's ill-gotten gains.'

'Someone had to have it. He seemed to think we're related.'

A thrusting look nearly speared him. 'You won't leave it alone, will you? How would you define that kinship, nephew? Convince me.'

Fletcher shrugged. 'I can't.'

'Exactly. You are what you are, Fletcher: the product of a coupling between my sister and a man called Adrian Taunt.'

'Why is there no record of him?'

'He came from nothing and left nothing of himself behind when he departed . . . except you.'

As usual, Miranda waited until Pridie left and then poured the milk into the garden bed below the window.

'I hope he hasn't put anything in my milk, too.'

'You'll be able to smell it if he has. It's probably Valerian.'

'Have you seen Sir James's dispensary?'

'No.'

'Perhaps he'll show it to us if I ask him.'

They could hear the two women guests engaged in whispered conversation at the landing. Lucy tiptoed over to the door and opened it a fraction.

Mrs George's voice was a low murmur. 'I'm surprised he keeps those young ladies here without a chaperone.'

'Oh, they're not ladies in the true sense of the word; they were destitute when he found them on the road. Their mother had died in childbirth. Goodness knows where they came from. They are educated to a certain degree, and, as you heard, the younger one plays the piano badly, though Sir James always makes us sit through it.'

'I daresay the pair will end up coming to no good.'

Mrs Patterson gave a low laugh. 'There's no fool like an old fool. I'm given to understand that Sir James has already expressed affection for the older girl, and the little minx is encouraging it. We all know what comes of that sort of behaviour.'

When Lucy gasped, Mrs George whispered, 'Did you hear that noise? I'd heard this house was haunted.'

'So had I.'

'I'll give you haunted,' Lucy whispered.

'No don't, Lucy.' Nearly helpless with suppressed laughter as Lucy headed through to the maid's room, the grab Miranda made at her sister's arm was ineffective. Pulling the sheet off the bed, Lucy threw it over her head and opened the door. Giving a low, bloodcurdling moan, she caused the sheet to drift by slowly making a sweep with her arms, then backed into the room and shut the door.

From her vantage point, Miranda clearly saw Mrs Patterson and Mrs George, who were bathed in the moonlight that flooded through the window. The ladies clutched each other and encouraged the other's fear with almost hysterical screams.

Swiftly, Lucy ducked through the maids' room and threw the sheet at the bed. She locked the adjoining door and pulled open the one from their bedroom to the hall, so both of them were clearly seen. 'We heard screams! Has something happened?'

Almost incoherent, Mrs Patterson pointed a quivering finger to the door to the maid's room. 'Did you see that?'

'See what? What on earth's the matter?'

'A . . . s–spector.'

Miranda couldn't help but say, 'The inspector . . . what inspector? Do you mean Simon Bailey, the customs officer?'

'No, I don't mean Simon Bailey. A ghost. It was horrible, with no head. It was floating in the doorway.'

'With blood dripping from a wound in its head,' Mrs George added. She shuddered.

'But Mrs Patterson said it didn't have a head,' Miranda pointed out.

Mrs George glared at the lawyer's wife. 'I distinctly saw a head. It was under the creature's arm.'

'How exciting,' Lucy breathed, 'I do hope it returns so we can see it, too. Don't you, Miranda?'

'Not in particular.' The joke had gone far enough, she thought. 'I think it's time we retired. I doubt if the apparition will return.'

'There it is.' The woman pointed to the stairs, where a light was ascending, and they clutched each other again.

'Goodness, do calm down; it's only Mrs Pridie.'

'Is everything all right? I heard somebody shout,' the housekeeper said as she neared the top.

'The two ladies appear to have seen an apparition.'

Mrs Pridie's lips twitched. 'It was probably a reflection of one of the trees coming through the landing window, and the light and shade reflected in it.'

'Exactly as I thought,' Mrs Patterson said and snorted. 'Ghost indeed, and with its head under his arm, dripping blood! Where is this blood, pray? The floor's quite clean. You must have imbibed too much sherry, Mrs George. Goodnight, ladies.' She turned away, heading for her room.

'I know what I saw,' Mrs George muttered rebelliously.

'I saw something once, too.' Mrs Pridie hesitated and lowered her voice. 'I could have sworn there was a woman standing on the landing, just about where you are now, Mrs George. But, then, I daresay Sir James was right, and it was a curtain blowing in the wind.'

Touching the back of her neck, Mrs George shivered and headed for her room at speed.

Mrs Pridie followed the sisters into their bedroom. Going into the maid's room, she picked up the sheet and, folding it carefully, she placed it in the wardrobe. She smiled at them. 'It seems as though the apparition has lost its robe. I'll pretend I didn't see this if you promise not to do such a silly thing again, Miss Lucy.'

'How did you know it was me, when it might have been Miranda?'

'Your sister is older, and she has more sense, thank goodness. Though you should have stopped her, Miss Jarvis.'

'Miranda couldn't stop me; she was creased up with laughter. I haven't heard her laugh that much for ages. Usually, she creeps around like a worried mouse.'

'It was funny,' Miranda admitted, a smile coming and going, 'especially when you told Mrs George the tale of the ghost on the stair.'

'And who said it was a tale? Sometimes funny things happen that you can't explain, and when you least expect it.'

'Anyway, they said some horrid things about us, so they deserved being given a bit of a scare. Mrs Patterson said Miranda was a minx and I played the piano badly, and that we'd come to no good.'

'And you will if you don't behave yourselves. You must be getting tired, so get ready for bed. I'll come up in a little while to check on you. Sir James said you can have a last cup of punch. I'll bring it up.'

'Mrs Pridie,' Lucy said when she reached the door. 'Where is Sir James's dispensary? Would he show it to us?'

'It's just off the kitchen in the scullery. He might show you, though he keeps it locked.'

'I heard it was down in the cellars, and he kept snakes and spiders down there.'

Mrs Pridie smiled. 'You shouldn't listen to rumours, and I doubt if he'd allow you down there.'

'Have you been in them?'

'No child – and don't you go poking around looking for snakes and stuff.' She laughed. 'Such ideas you get, Miss Lucy. It will be dragons you'll be after seeing next. Those cellars are extensive and you'd soon get lost.'

After Pridie had gone, Lucy gazed at Miranda and offered her a mischievous smile.

'Definitely not!' Miranda said, and she meant it.

Thirteen

The next morning, the house was enclosed in a cloud of mist that had come in from the sea.

Miranda was glad to see the back of Sir James's guests. There had been no mention of ghosts at breakfast, or of untoward events taking place. It was as if the light of day had banished any supernatural thought back into the shadows where it belonged. Both women wore rather sheepish expressions and were over-polite; they avoided looking at each other.

Soon they and their husbands were gone.

Fletcher managed to catch a moment alone with Miranda and briefly kissed her. 'I adore you,' he whispered in her ear.

Sir James called Fletcher and they went off to inspect the ruined walls in daylight. Sir James came back by himself, with the news that the body of the keeper had been found beneath the tumbled stones.

'Will you rebuild the wall?' Miranda asked, her heart beating fast as she rarely enquired as to Sir James's business.

'Do you think I ought to, then?'

'It seems a waste of time, money and life, if somebody's going to keep blowing it up,' Lucy commented.

'Which is the first comment I've heard this morning that makes any sense, though you will learn in time that life is cheap. However, a man must defend his castle against marauders who would take it from him by force. Fletcher was the one most affected by the gate and wall going up. He assured me he knows nothing about what happened, and he's said he's going to question his staff.'

Miranda looked up at him with dismay. 'Surely you don't suspect that your own nephew lied to you.' She remembered what had occurred the evening before and she gazed down at her hands. 'But, then, of course you do, or you wouldn't have tried to kill him.'

Sir James's eyes glistened. 'Fletcher was too sure of himself and I was giving him a fright.'

'Your intention was written clearly in your eyes, Sir James. Fletcher Taunt is a grown man and he deserves to be treated as one.'

'We are none of us perfect, but killing someone is not an easy thing to do when one has raised that someone from babyhood. Believe me, my dear, I'd stop short at murdering my own kin in cold blood.'

Miranda couldn't understand where her sudden burst of rebellion came from. It was as if love was making her reckless. 'It was hardly cold blood; you were in a temper and your blood was definitely on the boil. I was afraid for him.'

'As I saw, and may I say that your blood was a little overheated, too, my dear. It still is. Anyone sitting at the table could see the regard in which Fletcher held you. Trying to avoid each other made it more apparent. How prettily you blushed and responded to him. It was quite obvious you'd met him before. You really shouldn't have lied to me about that, especially considering the present circumstances. It wasn't polite, and I won't be made a fool of.'

'I haven't lied about anything.'

Lucy was wide-eyed. Although young, she had a sharp mind and she didn't like loose ends. She would sift and analyze the conversation and arrange it to fit a circumstance, like a piece in a jigsaw. Now she said artlessly, even while she knew very well what was being alluded to, 'What circumstances are those?'

Miranda had a sudden sense of danger, and knew she had to get away from the house before this developed into a fully fledged argument. It would be one she couldn't win.

'It's none of your business, Lucy. Let's get our coats and hats and go out for walk. This whole conversation is ridiculous.'

Sir James shoved his hands in his pockets and glowered at her. 'I'd prefer it if you stayed indoors.'

She drew in a deep breath and collected together all the calm she possessed. 'Sir James, I'm grateful for the care and protection you have offered us. However, I'd like to point out that we are not your children, and, as we're not being kept prisoners here, we are free to leave your house at any time we wish, are we not? I intend to go out for a walk, with or without your permission. Lucy, please don your coat and bonnet. You complained the other day that I often go out without you. Now is your opportunity to join me.'

She hadn't expected Lucy to take Sir James's side. 'I don't feel like prowling all over the countryside to sketch flowers. Besides, Sir James promised me another riding lesson. You should learn to ride properly yourself.'

'I can ride; I just prefer not to.'

'You've been scared of horses since Pa was thrown and killed. Still, at least that big hairy dog likes you; that's something, I suppose.'

Sir James said curtly, 'There will be no riding lesson today, missy. I have to go into Poole on business. Is there anything you have need of?'

Lucy didn't seem to notice his mood, or, if she did, she ignored it. 'I need some more notebooks to complete my novelette. Forgive Miranda; she's in one of her responsible elder sister moods, and she worries about things too much.'

His mouth softened and he seemed to make an effort. 'Miranda must learn not to argue with her elders and betters. It's an undesirable trait.'

One she might employ more often if it repelled his pursuit of her.

His eyes gazed into hers, slightly narrowed. How handsome and distinguished he was, she thought, and how calculating his expression. She knew then that she would never agree to marry him.

'Am I forgiven, Miranda?'

She nodded, for she didn't dare speak.

'Good. Then that's settled.' He turned to Lucy. 'How many notebooks do you require?'

'At least six – that's not too expensive, is it? You're always so kind and generous but I don't want to take advantage of your unselfish nature.'

'My dear Miss Lucy, I'm sure my purse won't mourn the cost of a few notebooks? You're an industrious little creature, aren't you? I must read this novelette of yours.'

'But not until it's finished, Sir James.'

'Of course not.' He turned to Miranda. 'You do, of course, have the run of my estate. I just ask that you take the dog with you when you go out, since strangers have been seen.'

A grin crept across her face. 'Caesar won't allow me to go out without him. He's appointed himself my guardian.'

'Will you be long in town, Sir James?' Lucy asked him as he was about to leave the room.

'Most of the day, I imagine. Make sure you behave yourself, young lady. No more ghosts.' He gave a short bark of laughter. 'Apparently, the ladies were quite put about.'

'How did you know it was me?'

Miranda avoided his eyes when he said, 'I know everything that goes on in my home.'

'You didn't tell them it was me?' Lucy said with some alarm.

'Of course not. They'd never forgive you if they knew a chit of a girl had made a fool of them. Besides, it's nice to have a bit of a mystery attached to the house. It stops guests from wandering around and sticking their noses into a man's business if they think they might be in danger.'

'Have you ever seen a ghost, Sir James?'

He looked startled by the notion. 'I can't say I have, Miss Lucy. Men's logic is less prone to such fancies in my experience.'

'If you did see one, what would you do?'

'It's a pointless exercise to speculate on something quite so nebulous, my dear.' Then he laughed. 'Don't tell anyone, but were I to see anything remotely ghoulish, I'd probably run like the devil himself was after me. Now, I must away.' He strode out to where his horse waited, mounted it and was soon hidden from their gaze as the mist closed round him.

Miranda slipped on her jacket and bonnet and prepared to follow. She was hoping Fletcher would be waiting at their meeting place, so she didn't press Lucy to join her. She checked her basket, making sure her sketching block and pencils were there. Mrs Pridie had placed in it a large slice of pork pie wrapped in a cloth, two boiled eggs and a little pot containing mustard pickles. There was also some preserved pears and a spoon to eat them with. Water was plentiful and she could scoop it from the stream.

Reclining on a rug, Caesar watched her every movement and sprang to his feet when she headed for the door. He got there before she did, his tail wagging in anticipation.

Lucy had an air of impatience about her, and her eyes were secretive. 'I'm going to get on with my writing while you're out.'

The mist was beginning to thin and the plants were heavily dewed, while the grass was wet beneath her feet. As Miranda left, she looked back and saw her sister standing at the landing window. Lucy waved to her and she blew her a kiss.

The sun came to reveal a day that was fair, the hedgerows clothed in fresh green. Bluebells had begun to spear up through the earth. In a couple of weeks, the landscape would be multi-coloured with May blossoms — orchids, daisies, parsley and cowslips. She promised herself she'd pick some hawthorn blossom on the way home, so the perfume would fill the hall. May was a colourful month once it had settled in.

Fletcher was waiting for her, his smile warm. Somewhere inside her was a matching glow. When he held out his arms to her, she began to run, jumping from tussock to tussock until she flung herself into his arms. He twirled her round, then set her on her feet and kissed her.

'It was hell being so near you last night and not be able to touch you,' he said, running a finger around the curves of her upper lip until it was sensitized beyond bearing. She caught his hand and kissed his palm.

'Your uncle knows I see you. He said he could tell by the way we acted towards each other.'

'His way of thinking is to throw a hook into the pond and see what he can catch.'

'Then I think I may have given us away. We had a falling-out this morning.'

'If he's in the right sort of mood, he enjoys a good argument.'

'I accused him of harbouring an intention to kill you.'

Fletcher gave a slow whistle. 'He wouldn't have liked that. What was his reaction?'

'He denied it. He said you were his only kin and he'd never harm you.' She hugged him tight. 'I was scared that he would. He has nothing to gain by killing you.'

'Except for Monksfoot Abbey. As you pointed out, I might be his only kin, but that applies both ways. He's my only kin, too, and is now heir to an estate he's always coveted.'

'You mean he might kill you to get the Abbey?'

Fletcher looked troubled. 'What's more, he's set his heart on a wife, one young enough to breed from, and one I've singled out for the same purpose.' He gave her a faint smile when she blushed. 'It makes for an interesting situation where we can't really trust each other. Promise me you won't marry my uncle, whatever the circumstances.'

'I can't imagine any circumstance that would make me do that now. But you must remember that he's been so good to Lucy and me, Fletcher. I owe it to him to be honest about this.'

'Just remember your debt to him doesn't cover an obligation to become his wife.' Taking her gently by the shoulders, he gazed into her eyes. 'You don't love him, do you, Miranda? I must know where I stand, because you could quite easily become an unwitting pawn in the game.'

'How can I, when I'm in love with you? This isn't a game to me, and I have no intention of playing you off against each other.'

'Then that's all I need to know. Will you wed me? I'll get a special licence in a week or two, and we can get the reverend to listen to our vows.'

'Yes, Fletcher, I'll marry you.'

'And in the meantime, if you and Lucy ever feel the need to find a place of safety, you can come to Monksfoot . . . especially if my uncle starts behaving erratically.'

'Erratically?'

'If you feel uneasy in his presence or threatened by him, or if he starts muttering to himself. I'll leave word with my housekeeper to admit you any time. Now, what do you have in your basket? It smells delicious.'

'Pork pie.'

'Nancy was always a good cook.'

They seated themselves on the grass, and she laughed when Caesar came to sit with them, pretending not to be interested in the contents of the basket. 'I can see this slice of pie is going to have to stretch a long way. Luckily, I ate a big breakfast.'

While they were eating, she asked, 'Did you talk to your staff about the damage done to your uncle's property?'

'I talked to Tom Pepper, who's my foreman. He said he knows nothing about it, but he'll question the staff. I'm inclined to believe he's telling the truth.'

'Considering the relationship you have with your uncle, who else could have done it?'

He shrugged. 'It could have been anyone who used that right of way through my uncle's land. Many people use it, besides my workers, though I admit that they would be the most likely suspects. Then there are traders, gypsies, soldiers and customs officers.'

'Surely you don't suspect Simon Bailey?'

'He and his men were in the area.'

'But why would he?'

'To make it appear as though I was responsible for the deed. But, then, my uncle could have arranged the whole thing, and for the same purpose.'

She gazed at him, grinning. 'I think my head is about to start aching from all the intrigue.'

'Then I ought to kiss it better.' His lips were a soft caress against her forehead . . . then her mouth . . . then the sensitive skin inside of her wrist, before his palms slid up over her breasts.

She allowed that liberty because she needed to know that he wanted her as much as she wanted him, and as she had no mother to advise her now, she must trust her own judgement in this matter.

And her judgement let her down, for the more she allowed him, the more she wanted, until her body took over with its own needs and his touch knew exactly where she needed it.

He gazed down at her, his eyes dark with the passion he felt. 'Do you want us to stop, my love?'

'No . . . I want to be yours in every way, Fletcher. I want to die in your arms.'

He was pressed against her, member rigid, and she could hardly wait. Pulling the flap of his trousers down, she took him between her hands when he sprang free.

Giving a groan, he stilled her hands and whispered, 'I can't . . . ruin you.'

'Yes . . . you can. I want you to be yours completely.'

'No, my love. I'll satisfy what I've made you feel, and I'll teach you to satisfy what you've woken in me. But I won't take your innocence completely until we're man and wife.'

And that itself was a revelation on that long afternoon of delight.

Back at the house, Lucy had made her way down the steps to the cellars. She had taken a lantern and stopped to light it from another illuminating the stairs. Placing it on the table, she looked around her. The walls were lime-washed, but displayed an occasional patch of mould where damp had invaded. Racks of bottles were neatly displayed, and kegs of brandy lay in their cradles or stood on end. There was a wooden table, pails and crates of bottles, stoppers and labels. There was another door, but it was locked.

It was disappointing really. Lucy didn't know what she'd expected . . . and the whereabouts of Sir James's legendary dispensary was a disappointment, because she'd convinced herself it was in the cellars.'

Just as she turned back, she heard two men talking from behind the far door. She placed her ear against the panel.

'The master wants the cellars cleared next Saturday, when he's entertaining. There's a big consignment coming in. Every man and his dog will be at the party. That tea can go to the merchant's agent while the party's going on. Give it to that skinny stable lad to take; tell him it's seaweed fertilizer. He hasn't got any relatives and he doesn't know anything, so it doesn't matter if he's caught. And that keg of over-proof spirit can be mixed with water and decanted into bottles before the end of the week.'

Smugglers! A thrill ran through Lucy and she took a hasty step backwards, gasping when she knocked a funnel to the ground with a metallic clatter.

'What was that?'

'A rat, I expect, unless that big old python is on the prowl.'

The other man gave an uncertain laugh. 'He wouldn't be this far from his lair. John Whittle told me the master threw a couple of live rabbits in there yesterday. He said he heard them jumping about for a while, knocking things over in a bit of a panic.'

'He takes venom from the adders to add to medicine, I heard. An odd pastime, if you ask me.'

'Aye, well, best you keep your thoughts on it to yourself. Besides, the master makes tales up to scare people and keep them out of the cellars. I've been working for him for nigh on fifteen years, and I've never set eyes on a python. I reckon it's a rumour.'

A chill ran through Lucy and she shuddered at the thought of Sir James keeping adders in his cellars! But what was a python?

'Pass me the key, Rudd; I'll take a look. It might be one of the servants helping themselves to a bottle of brandy.'

Turning, Lucy fled, imagining an army of adders hanging off her skirt, their poisonous fangs within an inch of her calves. She gained the hall and, heart thumping, closed the door behind her. Then she remembered she'd left the lamp down there. There was nothing she could do about it now. She sprinted up the stairs two at a time and safely reached her bedroom without being observed.

It took a couple of minutes for her breathing to become normal. Taking up a pencil, she flicked open her notebook and busied herself with writing. Before too long, Mrs Pridie knocked at the door. 'I've brought you some refreshment, Miss Lucy.'

'Thank you; I am a bit thirsty. I've been getting on with my novel. Sir James said he wants to read it when I've finished. It's about a woman called Ruby Johnson, who is killed by a man who stole her baby . . . and she comes back to haunt him and get her revenge.'

Pridie smiled. 'Goodness, it sounds quite dramatic.'

'It is. Sometimes Ruby Johnson gets in my head and I can see her clearly, as though she's alive and I'm standing inside her.'

'That must be uncomfortable.' Sounding uninterested, as most people did when she began to chatter about her novel, and probably because she couldn't read very well, Mrs Pridie gazed around the room. 'Hasn't Miss Jarvis returned yet?'

'I haven't seen her, but I haven't looked. Her coat and bonnet would be on the hallstand if she had. You know what Miranda is like; she forgets the time of day. Cook put some food in her basket in case she gets hungry, and she has Caesar with her, so she won't come to any harm. I wish one of the dogs liked me. Perhaps I'll get a kitten from somewhere. They're such sweet little creatures.'

'Happen the dogs might attack it. They don't take too kindly to cats. We took in a litter of cats once; the master brought them home and they kept on having litters. The dogs chased after them and caused all sorts of mayhem. Sir James took them down to the cellars to chase the rats away, and we haven't seen them since. If you ask me, those dogs went down after them. A kitten would be little more than a snack to a dog.'

'Would they eat a rabbit?'

'Reckon so, if they could catch one, but rabbits are fast.'

'What about adders? Would they eat rabbits and kittens?' Lucy said, feeling sorry for them.

'I expect they'd eat mice.'

'Poor mice.' Lucy smiled at the woman. 'Are there many snakes in the countryside, do you suppose?'

'Goodness, how would I know?' Mrs Pridie said a trifle

impatiently, and then she smiled as she remembered something. 'I only saw a snake once; it came into the kitchen. There was Nancy, and there was me, and both of us standing on the table with our skirts hitched up and yelling fit to bust. Sir James came in and he looked at the creature, then he looked at us doing a jig, and he laughed and said he'd never seen anything so funny in his whole life. He said it was a grass snake and it wouldn't have hurt us. He knows a lot about snakes and things, does Sir James. He likes studying them. He said snakes keep themselves hidden and are a bit private, on account of the fact that nobody likes them.'

She chuckled when Lucy began to giggle. 'We must've looked like a couple of lunatics dancing on the table-top . . . and don't you go putting that in that novel of yours, young lady, else I'll never speak to you again. Well, I must be off. Don't forget to drink your tea before it gets cold, and eat your pie.'

After Mrs Pridie left, Lucy went down to the library and gazed around the books. She didn't know where to start, and turned to go back up again. She would ask the rector when he came to take afternoon tea with them tomorrow. He was a learned man and would know what a python was.

Before Reverend Swift arrived, Sir James had called Lucy and Miranda into his study.

'I've got to go out for a while. I've told the rector to bring the designs for the new church window with him and tell me which one he wants. It's been six months and it's about time he made up his mind. There is a problem in that his wife keeps interfering. Persuade him to choose the Saint George one if you can. It's the best and most suitable. I wish I hadn't given him a choice in the first place.'

'Why don't you just tell him you want Saint George?'

'Every time I do, his wife persuades him differently.'

Now, Lucy brought the conversation round to Saint George by asking the rector what a python was.

'A python? Goodness, why would a young lady like you want to know about snakes?'

She shrugged. 'I heard the word mentioned, and I didn't know what it meant. I thought it might have been a sort of fire-breathing dragon that toasted people before it ate them.'

'You're not far off, my dear, except a python is real, whereas a dragon is a mythical beast.'

'Thank goodness. I'd hate to meet one accidentally and be toasted to a crisp. Do tell me all about pythons.'

'Allow me a minute or so to gather my thoughts together,' he said and tucked into a slice of ginger cake. After eating it with every sign of enjoyment, he said, 'Now let me think – what do I know about pythons? To start with, it's a snake . . . pythons come in all sizes from small to large, and are not poisonous, and they lay eggs.'

'Like chickens.'

'I suppose you could say that.'

'Even the male pythons?'

The rector went slightly pink. 'No, not the males.' He hurried on. 'As soon as they hatch, the baby pythons have to fend for themselves.

'What do they eat?'

'Depending on their size, other animals. They coil themselves round their prey to crush them and then swallow them whole – I believe the larger pythons could swallow a whole deer – after which they sleep for a week or so to digest them.'

'Ugh! How disgusting,' Miranda said, though she was as fascinated as Lucy seemed to be and found the rector's conversation more stimulating than his sermons. But Lucy was never this thorough in her questioning unless there was a purpose behind it, and she was beginning to get an inkling of what it was. 'Do we need to dissect the habits of a snake?'

'Sorry, Miranda. Can I just ask one more question? I thought snakes were cold-blooded and needed warmth to give them energy. Can they live underground?'

She adroitly avoided the sharp glance Miranda gave her.

'If there was a sufficient amount of warmth each day, and access to live prey, then I would imagine they could. But I'm not an expert. I learned all this from a missionary who worked in the tropics and had seen one. Most pythons, especially the larger ones, live in warm climates. I've heard of a Burmese Python that grew to twenty feet in length.'

They both gasped at the thought of a snake being so long.

'They're very strong, apparently. On the other end of the scale, we have the grass snake in England, which is harmless.'

'So not likely to eat a human.'

'Dear me, no . . . at least, not in England.'

'Thank goodness, for I'd hate one to swallow me. I'd rather do the opposite and have it wriggling around inside me.'

'Don't be so gruesome, Lucy. You'll have me dancing on the table before too long.'

Remembering Mrs Pridie's tale, which Lucy had related to Miranda with much amusement, they exchanged a glance and laughed.

The door opened and Sir James entered. He gazed from one to the other, smiling. 'You all sound rather lively, so I thought I'd join you for a while. I'm pleased to hear that my young ladies are entertaining you so well, reverend.'

Miranda gazed at him, wondering what his reaction would be if he knew how intimate she'd become with his nephew. 'We were talking about snakes, Sir James.'

An eyebrow rose and his eyelids flickered. 'That's a strange subject. Why snakes?'

Quickly, Lucy answered, astonishing Miranda. 'Why not snakes? Mrs Pridie told us an amusing tale about a grass snake coming into the kitchen, which I was just about to relate to the reverend. She and Nancy thought it was dangerous and they climbed on the table and you had to rescue them. Is it true? We must hear your side of it.'

'It's quite true. It must be the funniest thing I've ever seen.' Sir James laughed as he launched into his own version of the event.

When he finished, Miranda turned to the rector. 'You must eat another piece of cake, reverend, since Nancy made it especially for you.'

'I must admit I'm fond of ginger cake.' He patted his stomach with regret. 'I've already eaten one slice.'

'We won't tell anyone if you eat another. Would you like a second cup of tea to go with it? What about you, Sir James? Shall I fetch you a cup and saucer? After we've eaten, we're going to help the reverend choose a design for the new church window, since he can't make up his mind. Why don't you join us?'

Sir James had a pained look on his face. 'No, thank you, Miranda. I wouldn't want to influence the reverend in any way. I only dropped in for a few moments to make sure your guest was being looked after.'

He lied wonderfully well, she thought. He'd probably been listening at the keyhole.

'The young ladies are delightful hosts,' the rector said. 'They make me feel quite young. I can't remember the last time I enjoyed myself so well.'

'And he hasn't tried to save our souls once. You must invite the reverend and Mrs Swift to Miranda's birthday supper, Sir James.'

'I already have.' Inclining his head, Sir James left the room.

They spent half an hour gazing at the designs. 'I've chosen that one because my wife likes it,' the cleric said, unrolling one dotted with woolly sheep. 'She said it reminds her of lambs waiting to go to heaven.'

Cocking her head to one side, Miranda said, 'It's a lovely design, but it hasn't got much colour, since there is a lot of white and pale green. Also, I've never seen a lamb with cherubic wings flying about the sky.'

Lucy giggled. 'Poor little lambs. They're so innocent and docile, and we're cruel to eat them. Do you think they go to a different heaven to us?'

'I hadn't really considered it.'

'You should pick that design of Saint George killing the dragon. It's so colourful and dramatic. You can just imagine it with the sun streaming though all those colours. Besides, Saint George looks a bit like you, reverend – a knight in shining armour bravely slaying the dragon. Don't you think so, Miranda?'

Miranda nearly choked on her tea. There couldn't be anyone who looked less like Saint George than Reverend Swift. 'Yes . . . I suppose he does.'

The rector looked slightly bemused. 'My wife considered that design to be too expensive.'

'Good gracious, it's not as though Mrs Swift has to pay for it. Sir James offered you the designs to choose from, and that was one of them, so the cost won't bother him.'

'Do you really think so?'

'I really do. Before you go, you must be honest and tell Sir James you like Saint George best. In the strictest confidence, he was admiring it just the other day and said he hoped you picked that one, so I'm sure he'll be delighted.'

'I don't know what my wife will say.'

Miranda gently administrated the *coup de grâce*. 'I doubt if Mrs Swift will object to the symbolism of the fight of good over evil. After all, Saint George is the patron saint of England, a martyr who died defending Christianity.'

'I don't think Mrs Swift considered that. Yes . . . I will choose that one.'

It was a little while before the rector finally took his leave, and he was smiling happily because they had all endorsed his choice of window.

'I shall send a messenger to inform the window-maker at once, and before you change your mind again,' Sir James said drily.

They said goodbye to the rector in the hall. 'You must visit us again,' Miranda told him. 'We enjoyed your company.'

'Watch out for serpents,' Lucy said softly as he strode off, and shivered as she turned to her sister. 'I feel guilty about fooling him, don't you?'

'I don't, because it's a better window, and it's one he liked. So did Sir James. The reverend is a sweet, gentle man, and his wife is beastly to him.'

'For a moment, I thought you were going to say the dragon looked like her.'

They began to laugh.

When they were upstairs, Lucy asked Miranda, 'Why did you lie to Sir James?'

'I didn't exactly lie. I was afraid you'd tell him you'd been down to the cellars . . . You have, haven't you?'

Miranda could always tell when Lucy had done something she shouldn't have. 'I only went a little way in. It was quite boring, with bottles in racks. There was only one interior door that I could see, and that was locked from the other side. Why shouldn't I tell him? He likes me and he wouldn't be cross for long.'

'Because he doesn't want us down there; he's already said so. It's dangerous.'

Lucy began to laugh. 'You don't really think there's a giant python down there, do you? It's just a rumour to keep people out. I overheard two men talking about it before I had to make my escape.'

'Then you must ask yourself this, Lucy: if Sir James has got nothing to hide, why does he want to keep us out? And where does that cellar go if it locks from the other side? There must be another entrance. Use caution, Lucy.'

'Goodness, haven't you realized yet? It's because Sir James is a smuggler and he keeps all his contraband down there. Isn't that exciting!'

Fourteen

Exciting, it wasn't. If it was true, highly dangerous was what it was. Smugglers wouldn't hesitate to kill to protect their trade. It involved men from all walks of life, Miranda's father had once told her. They'd kill anyone who stood in the way of their illegal profit – men, women or children.

Miranda didn't know whether to believe her sister or not. Lucy was highly imaginative. Sir James seemed such an honest and upright man, with a position to uphold, as well as being a magistrate. But he was possessive. He'd referred to them as *his* young ladies when talking to the rector, something she hadn't overlooked.

And then there was the explosion.

Fletcher's theories as to that had been quite plausible.

But Simon Bailey? Surely he wouldn't mix socially with known criminals – or blow their property up. He had a brash sort of courage, which she'd come to admire, despite not being sure whether she liked him or not.

The trouble was, Miranda didn't *want* to believe it. If Sir James was a smuggler, she couldn't help but wonder if Fletcher was involved, too. She hoped not. She knew she loved Fletcher, but she didn't want to be tied to a criminal who lived on his wits, and who attracted the attention of men like Simon Bailey, with the might of the law behind them.

Fletcher had told her that his heart was in shipping rather than farming. He wanted his uncle to run the farming side while he concentrated on the shipping. Had he been lying? He'd grown up here; surely he'd know if his uncle was involved in illicit trading. To be fair, he had warned her not to trust Sir James.

And what if he used the shipping company as a front? She had heard that slaves were shipped from place to place, the unfortunate creatures treated like cattle.

'Besides the *Midnight Star*, I have another ship,' he'd told her. 'She's in a bit of a state, but is being refitted. I've named her after you, but I'd rather it was kept secret between us for the time being.'

'Then why are you telling me . . . and why must it be kept a secret when you're in a partnership with your uncle?'

'There are reasons I'd rather not disclose . . . not even to you, though I know I can trust you. My intention is to distance myself from my uncle. I've named the new addition *Lady Miranda*, after you.'

'Oh, Fletcher.'

'*Oh, Fletcher.*' He'd mimicked her in the same way that last time, when she'd laid abandoned in the grass with him that day. And when she'd kissed the amused little quirk at the side of his mouth, he'd added, his voice almost a caress, 'I really didn't want the complication of love in my life; now I'll never be able to live without you. As for the new ship, she needs a great deal of money spent on her before she's able to start earning her keep.'

The next day the servants were scurrying around, making rooms ready for overnight guests. They lifted rugs from the hall floor to create a smooth area for dancing. On hands and knees, they washed away the dust. Chairs were brought down from the attics, and traders' carts arrived laden with goods and departed empty. Tables were set out with cutlery, bottles brought up from the cellars. Brandy and French champagne.

The terrace was decorated with coloured pots containing candles, and there would be a servant dispensing punch from a crystal bowl, and a little grotto with a gyspy telling fortunes for those who believed in such things.

'The moon will be full that night,' Sir James told Miranda, and she believed him, because the weather wouldn't dare be so contrary as to produce clouds when Sir James wanted moonlight.

'And at ten o'clock there will be a firework display, just for you, Miranda.'

Her heart sank; by going to such trouble and expense, he was telling everybody exactly what his intentions were towards her.

Her sister's eyes flew open and she breathed, 'I've never seen fireworks.'

Lucy was in a ferment of excitement the next day, when parcels were delivered after breakfast and carried up the stairs to their room.

'It's a new gown each. Something special to wear for the party,' Sir James said.

Miranda's spirits dropped. The gowns he'd already bought them were sufficient for the occasion, and pretty enough to grace any drawing room. 'You're too generous, Sir James.'

'You don't sound happy about my little surprise, Miranda. It gives me great pleasure.'

He was a spider spinning strands of silk to capture her and draw her into his web. If she allowed it, he would tie her up tightly and slowly suck the life from her. He'd never allow her to escape. But she would never forget Fletcher.

And what if she didn't allow it? She didn't want to speculate on that.

'As I said, you are too generous. You have provided us with enough since we've been living here, and I'm . . . grateful. There is no way I can adequately repay you.'

'We shall see,' he said, and with such confidence that she felt a moment or two of unease.

He had not mentioned marriage since that first surprising moment of proposal. In fact, his behaviour towards her had been exemplary. Yet she was aware of that stated intention, because with it came an expectation, a tincture of possessiveness that went further than host and guest. She'd rather have chosen her own gown to wear, but she would wear the one Sir James had bought her for the purpose, because, after what had happened the last time, she was aware that such a scene could easily happen again if she thwarted him in this.

And even while her mouth yearned for and accepted the caresses of Fletcher, she felt under an obligation to her host.

To tell the truth, she was scared – scared that Sir James might catch her, and scared she might not see Fletcher again because of it. She was even more scared that she *would* see Fletcher – see him every day of her life thereafter, and observe the hurt in his eyes because she'd chosen his uncle over him. If she married Sir James, she would love Fletcher for ever, and never be able to express or acknowledge that love, while knowing he was as miserable as she.

No, she could not – *would not* – marry Sir James. Nothing he could do would change her mind about that.

The boxes were clearly marked with their names. Sir James had excellent taste, Miranda thought, as they readied themselves with the help of the maid, Anna.

Lucy wore white chiffon embroidered with blue blossoms over pale blue taffeta. It was just the thing for a young lady on the brink of womanhood. She rustled when she walked, which delighted her. Posies of blue flowers were attached to her hair and a matching posy secured by long ribbons to her wrist.

In similar fashion, but off the shoulders and with little cap sleeves, Miranda wore silk in a dark rose-pink. The hems of the double flounces were quite plain, but the pointed and boned bodice was embroidered with gold thread, pearls, and pink and white silk rosebuds that matched the flowery concoction attached to the nape of her neck.

Miranda felt graceful and feminine as she and Lucy went down the stairs together. The little pads sewn into the upper lining of the bodice gave her a shape that wasn't quite natural to her, but they, along with the stiff bone inserts, kept her bodice nicely in place and prevented it from slipping down her arms.

Sir James was waiting for her with a gift. 'Happy birthday, Miranda, and may I say that you both look exquisite.'

There was nothing of the turkey cock about Sir James. He wore sober black, his only adornment a diamond pin in his cravat.

Lucy beamed happily at the compliment, while Miranda wondered whether he was actually congratulating them or himself on his choice of clothes for them.

She chided herself when he placed a circlet of creamy pearls around her neck, which until then had been cool and bare. The gift felt like a manacle.

'You look beautiful,' he whispered, his fingers a caress against her skin, and he prepared to escort her into the drawing room – his arm tucked into hers, as though they were a married couple – leaving Lucy to follow. He was giving a false impression to the other guests, and there was nothing she could do about it.

Her sister would be mortified with embarrassment at being overlooked.

Miranda turned and tugged Lucy's hand. She pulled her against her side and slipped her free arm about her waist.

Fletcher stepped out of the crowd to rescue her sister. 'Ah, there you are, Miss Lucy. How lovely you look. Allow me to escort you in and claim the first dance after supper.' He offered his arm to her.

For a second, Miranda's eyes tangled with Fletcher's and she felt pleasantly scorched in an aware sort of way. He looked quite the dandy in a burgundy-coloured cutaway coat over pale grey trousers, the sleeves fashionably tight and buttoned against the muscular wrists. Fashioned from silver brocade, his waistcoat was topped by a matching cravat secured with a ruby.

Her breath left her body slowly when he smiled. He looked so very elegant, something to savour. He gave a little bow. 'I hope your birthday is enjoyable, Miss Jarvis. You look lovely.'

'So do you, Mr Taunt. Thank you for the gift.' He had dropped in earlier on his way to Poole and left a musical box of enamelled silver for her dressing table. When the music began to play, a door sprang open and a couple began to dance, their arms around each other. As soon as the mechanism ran down, they would spring back from where they'd come from, until the next time she wound it.

When Fletcher chuckled, and said, 'I've never been called lovely before,' Sir James's hand tightened on her arm.

'Shall we go in?'

Fletcher led Lucy in first and, after a short pause, Sir James followed.

They walked into a perfumed atmosphere, a humid bouquet of different flower scents. The mixture tickled her throat as Sir James presented her.

Miranda felt desperate. She didn't want to be here amongst these people, whose conjecture about her relationship with Sir James was so plainly written on their faces. She didn't quite know how to say no to him. He talked her out of things or into things and dismissed any thought she might have to the contrary.

These people hadn't gathered to celebrate her birthday. Why should they do such a thing when they didn't even know her? There were here out of curiosity, to discover if the rumours they'd heard were true.

She could see it in their faces – the women with their slight airs of malice and superiority, whispering behind their fans. The men were speculative, their eyes darting like wasps from her breasts, to her waist, caught there by the belling of her skirt, as if their eyes could undo the hooks securing it to her bodice. There their gaze would linger for a moment or two, as if they could see through it, before rising to her shoulders and face again. Then came the smile – the one that congratulated Sir James on his taste. She wanted to squirm.

'Lucky dog, Sir James,' one of them said quite openly, all the while kissing her hand. She felt like slapping him. Sir James's hand tightened on her wrist as if he sensed her urge.

Then she wanted to laugh. Fletcher had kissed every part of her. She was his – she would always be his.

The torture of introductions seemed to be everlasting, but the atmosphere lightened when it was over and the music began to play. At last! She was able to relax her mouth, which had set in a rigid social smile that had caused her jaw to ache.

She danced the first dance with Sir James. It was for show, and as soon as they'd finished, he left her with Sarah Tibbets, who stared down her long nose at her and didn't say a word. He went off to join a group of prosperous-looking men.

Miranda gazed around for Lucy and saw her in animated conversation with a pretty woman. She couldn't remember her name – Susanna, perhaps. She was here with her brother, a rather weedy young man who looked scholarly and was staring at Lucy as if transfixed, with his mouth hanging open.

She was about to go and join them when Fletcher rescued her by swinging her out into the hall where the dancing was taking place. The small orchestra Sir James had hired took up the entrance to the left side of the staircase, leaving the right side for the guests to use as seats to observe the dancing from if they wished

'You handled the introductions well.'

'I hated being on show. I felt as though I was on trial and they were the judges. But they'd already reached a verdict before they met me. I could see it in their faces.'

'Most of the people here have nothing to be proud of. Some are on the take or involved in whatever will bring them in money, whether honest or not. Mostly, they are all front and no substance.'

He sent Simon Bailey a wry smile, which Simon returned. It was the smile of two men who would have been friends if they were not standing on opposite sides of the fence.

'You like him, don't you?'

'He has guts. He'd be a good man to have on your side.'

'I have you on my side. I do . . . don't I, Fletcher? I'm beginning to see and hear things I don't like much, and I don't feel as if there's anyone I can trust except the reverend. He's so sweet and innocent, like a child.'

His eyelids flickered. 'Better you keep your eyes closed, trust nobody and say nothing, Miranda mine.'

'That's what Mrs Pridie said when she said I can trust her. Are you honest, Fletcher?'

He observed her, his eyes dark pools. 'Poor little Miranda, you landed yourself and your sister in a pot of boiling broth when you tried to steal a loaf from my uncle. Have I done anything to make you think I might not be honest?'

'No . . . but are you?' she insisted.

'Not entirely, but I do my best. I'd never willingly hurt man or beast, never cheat or steal, though sometimes I lie. I adore you, which must lean a little towards my favour, and I hasten to add that I'm being truthful about that. I'm also likeable and have a great deal of charm, don't you think?'

She gazed up at him and laughed. 'Yes, I think you possess an amazing amount of charm . . . now you've seen fit to point it out.'

He laughed. 'Better we don't stand here talking all night, since it draws the attention. Shall we do something entirely scandalous – dance the waltz?'

'And that won't attract attention?'

He grinned, 'It might annoy some of the stuffed shirts.'

'You know the steps?'

'Certainly. On my last voyage aboard the *Midnight Star*, we had a passenger who knew all the dances and taught them to the other passengers, myself included.'

She didn't fail to notice his grin, and when she grinned in return, he shrugged. 'The lady was married and her husband was aboard. He wasn't fond of dancing.'

'Lucy and I learned how to waltz from watching our parents dance. They were so full of life; it seems such a long time ago now. Lucy is very much like our mother.'

'It sounds as though your parents enjoyed their short lives together. Be happy for that, Miranda. Remember the good times, because grieving won't bring them back.' He caught the eye of the orchestra leader and traced a W in the air with his finger. The man nodded.

Fletcher swung her out on to the floor. The music attracted young and old, and the pair found themselves surrounded by onlookers. For the few minutes that they danced together alone, Miranda imagined they were the dancing couple on the musical box he'd given her. Gradually, others found the courage to risk censure and joined in. Miranda saw Lucy being whirled around by the reverend, who seemed to be enjoying himself.

Mrs Swift stood alone, staring at them, a sour look on her face. Miranda suddenly felt sorry for the woman. It must be awful to be so permanently angry.

When she smiled at her, the woman managed to return it before she turned her head away.

Looking as smug as could be, Sarah Tibbets sailed past in the arms of Sir James. They danced well together. Little did Sarah know that Miranda wasn't a rival for the attention of Sir James.

Soon, the gasps and murmurs became laughter, and the hall was a whirling kaleidoscope of colour.

Fletcher drew Miranda closer and whispered in her ear, 'Let's go out on to the terrace. I'll fetch you some punch.'

'Will you do something for me first?' she asked when he returned. 'Anything.'

'Dance with Mrs Swift. She looks so miserable.'

There was a moment of heavy silence before he spluttered, 'She *is* so miserable.'

'I know, but I expect she has reason to be. Do it for me.'

He heaved a heavy sigh and then laughed. 'All right . . . I'll meet you on the terrace afterwards.' He handed her the punch.

It was quiet on the terrace, for the French windows hadn't been opened yet. Most of the guests were enjoying the spectacle of the dancing, but the music filtered through the air. She placed the cups of punch on the low wall and watched the dancers.

The air was cool but not cold, and the coloured lights were confections that looked pretty enough to eat. The moon was high in the sky and sailing along, though she supposed it was the occasional clouds that were doing the sailing.

As she sipped at her punch, she couldn't resist peeking through the open doorway. Somehow, Fletcher had persuaded Mrs Swift on to the floor and they were slowly circling around, while Fletcher taught her the steps. Her lips were pursed into a tight smile, as though she was afraid to allow it to relax into laughter.

Before too long she was dancing easily, and James handed her over to her husband just before the dance ended and went waltzing off with Lucy. There was an animated buzz in the room now. The orchestra leader announced a quadrille and the dancers organized themselves for the event. Lucy was talking to a rather elegant woman and the man with her. Miranda couldn't remember being introduced to them; they must have arrived late. Lucy looked as though she was enjoying the party.

Fletcher was making his way through the crowd, stopping to exchange a few words or smiling at people.

Eventually, he joined her and kissed her forehead.

Miranda finished her punch in a couple of gulps and gave a little shudder. It was deliciously sweet and had a crisp, fruity undertone that was warm, yet it slaked her thirst and left her tongue feeling clean. 'What's in this?'

He picked up a cup and smelled it. 'Hmm . . . it's one of my uncle's cure-all spice and herb recipes. He keeps the basic condensed mixture in an oak keg in the wine cellar and dilutes it according to the purpose he needs it for.' Taking a sip, he rolled it about his mouth and then swallowed it. 'It's got brandy in it as well as ginger, herbs and fruit juices diluted with water.'

'He should bottle it and sell it. It tastes like wine, only it's sweeter and crisper.'

Fletcher chuckled. 'He probably does bottle and sell it. My uncle is an enterprising man. It's a perfect brew to use in fruit punch. It has rather a strange effect on me, though. I have a sudden urge to kiss you.'

She laughed and moved closer. 'I have the same urge, Fletcher.' Putting the cup aside, she slid into his arms and sought his mouth with her own.

She couldn't believe she was so in love with this man – and that he loved her in return. When the kiss ended, he looked down at her, his eyes gleaming with reflected starlight. 'I have the licence and Reverend Swift has agreed to wed us in private. We can make our vows tomorrow at eleven. He has also agreed to keep the matter a secret.'

Although she had no qualms about a hasty marriage union with Fletcher, Miranda was beset by uneasiness and felt guilty about deceiving his uncle. 'Sir James will be angry when he finds out.'

'By which time you'll be my wife and he won't be able to prevent it.'

'Even if he knew, how could he prevent it?'

He ran his finger down her nose. 'Believe me, this is the best way. He is unpredictable, and at least you won't have to face him alone, my love.'

They moved apart when they heard footsteps.

Sir James appeared and gazed from one to another. 'Ah, the pair of you are out here . . . You have not danced with your host yet, Miranda.'

She could barely meet his eyes. 'I needed to quench my thirst and Fletcher brought me some punch. He said you made it yourself and we were discussing the quality of it. It's quite delicious.'

'It has many uses, depending on its strength.' He held out his hand to her. 'Come, my dear. It's not a wise policy to ignore either your guests or your host so completely.'

Reminded of her manners, she smiled at Fletcher, trying to hide her regret. 'You will excuse me, won't you?'

'Only under protest,' he said and kissed her hand.

'Oh, by the way, if you see the reverend anywhere, kindly tell him his wife is looking for him.'

'It depends how happy he looks.'

Sir James laughed, saying drily, 'Extremely, I should imagine, since he was last seen heading towards the coast with a bottle of my best brandy under his arm. I doubt if he'll get very far.' Tucking Miranda's arm into his, he led her back inside.

Fifteen

Beyond the bay, the crew of the revenue cutter turned the ship about and headed for the harbour at Poole, satisfied they'd find no smugglers abroad on this bright night. There had been a French fishing boat that had strayed too close to the coast earlier. She'd carried no contraband but a mess of fish, and they'd flung a few common curses at each other, exchanging insults.

'*Fils de salops!*'

'Bugger off, frogs.'

'*Nique ta mere! Englishman!*'

'You leave my mother out of it . . . she's still a virgin.'

If the officers hadn't been so preoccupied with the sport, and had looked up before the French fishing boat came between them and the shore, they would have seen a man crawl from the water.

As it was, the cutter was showered with stinking fish guts until the crew trained their gun on the Frenchies. The fishermen understood that gesture in any language, and had turned tail and sailed off, the crew singing *La Marseillaise* at the top of their voices.

Shortly after both ships disappeared from sight, the *Wild Rose* came over the horizon. She was heavy in the water. The men would place the goods in various hiding places – under the floor in the drying sheds, the inn, under the altar in the church or hidden in tombs and haystacks – from where they'd be distributed.

Fletcher Taunt would turn a blind eye, because although he'd inherited Silas's estate, he had no power to enforce his will against that of his uncle single-handedly. His workers owed him no loyalty. Tom Pepper ran things, as he always had, hand in glove with Sir James.

Another firework bloomed and a reflection of red flames danced on the surface of a stranger's eyes. The man was dressed like a monk and gazing down at him. 'Do you need help?' When he pushed back his cowl, his unruly shoulder-length hair was damp.

'Do you have some?'

'I might.'

Reverend Swift peered at the man. 'You're no ghost, but you look familiar. I think we've met before. What's your name?'

The figure chuckled. 'We haven't met before . . . and it's a cursed name.'

The moon sought out the pits and scars, bringing them into relief so he looked as though his face had been carved from shining stone. One side of the face was paralyzed. But the other side was strong and mobile when he talked.

The reverend recognized him then. Laughter rattled out of him

like the last gusts of a banshee retreating back into its den. 'Well,
I'll be damned. *Adrian Taunt.*'

'You know my name?'

'It's whispered in the shadows. I understood you to be dead.'

The man chuckled. 'I *am* dead. What you see before you is my
wretched remains. Now I must go. They'll be bringing the contraband ashore soon.'

'They will fill the church vaults with it and desecrate the souls
of the dead.'

'Better that than to corrupt the souls of the living.'

'Would you have your own child drawn into that corruption?
You're a man of the cloth. Forget your revenge.'

The eyes glittered. 'Ah yes . . . my son. So far, he's allowed him
to live.'

'Sir James loves him.'

'My half-brother is incapable of love. All he craves is power.'

'Then help me put a stop to what's going on here. Help me back
to the church. I urgently need to write a letter . . . two, in fact.'

'Nothing will stop me from taking my revenge.'

'I know.' The reverend wished he was going to be around to
witness it.

He was in a jovial mood. His wife hadn't bothered him all
evening. The brandy provided by his host was powerful, better
than he'd hoped for or deserved, and the sky was so clear he could
almost see right into heaven.

Now he had to expose his conscience before his maker – and
not for the first time.

He sat amongst the long-dead with his back against a tombstone.
'I'm sorely troubled, Lord,' he said, taking a fortifying swig from the
bottle, because talking to God took courage – something he was often
short of. 'And you send me a monk who is as troubled as I am.'

'Tell me what troubles you,' the monk said.

'I know He sent me here to save the souls of the sinners, but
unfortunately the opposite seems to have happened and the sinners
have captured my soul. I'm powerless to stop it. What have I done
to deserve such misfortune?'

The reverend smiled as he remembered the Jarvis girls, so sweet
and innocent. The older one was shining and doe-eyed with love.
He'd watched her with young Fletcher on the terrace together,

experienced the sweet lust in the kiss they'd exchanged. Such a long time since he'd experienced that – if he ever had. He couldn't remember.

He'd promised Fletcher Taunt that he'd sanctify their marriage vows on the morrow. But James Fenmore wanted the girl too, and he usually got his own way.

'Not this time,' he whispered. Sir James couldn't have his own way on this, since he wouldn't learn of the marriage until after it had taken place.

'Those that God hath joined let no man put asunder,' he called out, and began to laugh. 'Though if by chance you saw fit to silence Mrs Swift's harping – by making me deaf perhaps, since I wouldn't wish any affliction on her – it would indeed be a blessing.'

'Your wife is a good woman. Like most women, she wanted a hero.'

'There are no heroes in this cursed place.'

Someone had lit a candle in a lantern. Odd how he'd never seen it earlier. It was as though they knew he would be here, examining his sins with this monk, like a good wife hanging washing on a hedge to dry and checking the whiteness for stains.

The moon climbed slowly up out of the sea. It was round and perfect and almost white, resembling the crumbly cheese produced in the district. In front of it was the menacing shadow, a cutter cleaving the moon in half and hunting for prey.

Perhaps God had lit the lantern so he wouldn't feel quite alone with the darkness of his mind.

He winced when pain rippled through his stomach. Another drink would cure it. This was good brandy. The spirit had been created by vines harvested in France. Grapes had been crushed underfoot by peasant maids, their skin as brown as earth, their laughs husky. The wine was like a torrent of melted rubies gushing from the gutters, the fruit musky and ripe. The grapes split open to the pressure of feet stomping on the flesh to release their promise in a torrent of fertility.

He remembered the perspiration, and the summer of the grapes, of the wine cloudy and running like blood, and the girl, her eyes wide and scared and her tears flowing, the centre of her warm, moist and reluctant. Most of all, he remembered the anguish of the little cry she gave. He couldn't remember her name. Something short and biblical, perhaps . . . He'd promised to go back for her.

That was when his elder brother had died, and he'd been called home from his tour abroad to step into his shoes and embrace a living in the church.

'One doesn't wed peasant girls, however pretty,' his father had told him. 'You must forget her. We'll find you a good woman who can bring a dowry with her and calm your bodily devils.'

The stranger who'd been shivering in his arms on their wedding night had not been his French peasant, and he'd prayed that he'd be able to perform the act that would make them one and produce a child.

Neither had come about and he'd sought his manly solace with the young women who thronged in the shadows. But people talked, and there had been a scandal. He'd been sent here and had found himself in the middle of a devil's brew of thieves. What was worse, Sir James had discovered his weakness. He'd been thankful there had been no temptation in this quiet parish – until Lucy Jarvis came along!

Lucy reminded him of the peasant. Oh, she was finer-skinned and dainty, like a little pony that pranced with the joy of living. She had skin that glowed like satin in the candlelight. She'd come into the church once, and he'd watched from behind a curtain as she'd copied memorials into a book. Goodness knows what she was looking for. She'd danced up the aisle, spinning around, her arms wide and her laughter ringing in his ears as though she were performing for God himself.

The urge had come upon him and he'd remembered his youth and wanted to take her tender innocence, crush her and split her asunder like the grapes under a summer sun.

She'd teased him. 'God, how she teases me,' he whispered and his tears began to flow. 'Lord, help me to overcome this affliction. It was wrong of me to fall in love again, and with a girl so young.'

'Did you corrupt her?'

He's forgotten about the monk . . . his confessor.

He lifted the brandy to his mouth and took a good swallow. It was good brandy, and there was very little of it left. 'She's like a day in spring. But no. I've resisted the urge.'

From the corner of his eye, he saw a movement in the shadows and hoped it wasn't his wife. 'Who's there?'

There was no sound. He'd imagined it, as he'd imagined the monk. Another pain rippled across his stomach. It was stronger than the last one. Perspiration coated his body, though the night was cool and he felt sick. Swallowing the rest of the brandy down, he groaned and doubled up, cuddling the bottle against his pain.

When the pain passed, he tried to rise. Feeling dizzy, he hastily sat down again. Fear flooded through him when he saw that the bent, shadowy figure had returned. 'Who is it?'

A firework thrust up through the sky to the left of him and he automatically turned his head as it exploded. How pretty and enticing heaven was – so large, shining and . . . peaceful. It didn't need any human embellishment.

Catching a glimpse of a face partly disguised by a cowl, and a body twisted and bent, the reverend experienced so much fear that he nearly screamed out loud. There had been talk of a spectre that haunted the night over the past couple of years. The locals said he'd returned to claim Monksfoot Abbey. The monk's skin was scarred, his mouth puckered, and he walked with a limping gait. 'Are you a spirit sent from hell?'

The voice was strong and deep. 'I might well be.'

The reverend's limbs were fatigued, and he trembled as pain slid like a fiery worm from his gut into his chest and settled there. It pressed against his heart so he could hardly breathe, and he placed his hand against it. 'I've drunk too much and I'm in pain. I'm seeing things.'

'It depends on what you're seeing.' The stranger's face was bathed in moonlight now and he made so move to disguise himself.

'Are you *Him*?'

The man shrugged.

He told the apparition. 'I think I'm dying.'

'We're all dying.' The stranger took up the bottle, sniffed it, and then placed his tongue against the neck. There was no pity in his eyes, but the smile he gave told the reverend that the man had suffered. 'Have you had the pain long?'

'Several weeks.'

'It's arsenic poisoning. You must have done something to annoy the lord of the manor.'

No ghost this. The reverend could feel his warmth, despite the damp state of him.

'I'll offer you the same parting words he left me with,' the monk said bitterly, setting the bottle aside so it leaned drunkenly against a tombstone. 'God will look after you. And God did. He allowed us both to live – him in prosperity and comfort, and me in ignorance and poverty. Lately, though, God has given me enough strength so I can take my revenge. That's the only message I bring with me. Those who are innocent need not fear.'

This man had a name that could not be uttered out loud on fear of death, and an existence that had been reduced to rumour. This was a man who'd been sent into the wilderness – a man who was dead!

Which was more than would be afforded the monk, especially when Sir James learned that he'd survived. From what he'd heard whispered by his parishioners, Sir James had already killed the man once. Now the spirit of him had hunted him down, and soon he would be dead. The reverend shivered. Could a man die more than once?

As for his own fate, he had made the mistake of telling Sir James of his weakness, and Sir James had seen into his soul and used it to make him his servant.

He sighed. Such a teasing little female, Lucy was, and now he'd never know the delights of loving her, even from afar – only the agony of knowing she could never be his.

He *had* raised the ire of the lord of the manor, but not over the youthful Lucy Jarvis. The man was quite capable of brutalizing her himself and then selling her to some flesh peddler.

Arsenic took time to kill its victim. He wondered: was it his wife who'd told Sir James about the impending union between Fletcher Taunt and Miranda Jarvis?

She could have learned of it by several means. She might have looked in his appointment book and put two and two together, or found the bishop's licence.

Was it his wife who'd noticed his regard for Lucy? He remembered the rat poison given to his wife by Sir James for the demise of the church rodents. That would have contained arsenic.

As for the situation regarding Sir James, since Fletcher Taunt had returned home, he'd had an uneasy feeling that history was about to repeat itself. The pity of it was he wouldn't live long enough to find out.

Despite having had a late night, Miranda rose when the clock struck ten. But Lucy had been up earlier, for her side of the bed was empty. The journals her sister was writing her novel in were scattered over the table, along with her pencils. The diary, old and faded, its spine ragged, was still under her pillow, where Lucy kept it hidden out of sight, when she wasn't working from it.

Fighting off the urge to go back to bed, for her head was thumping, Miranda picked the books up and placed them neatly in the cupboard. Lucy wouldn't like it if they were left open for anyone else to read. She frowned, surprised that they'd been left on the table because her sister had become almost secretive about her writing.

She dressed in her favourite blue brocade, her stomach being attacked by butterflies. Soon she would be Mrs Fletcher Taunt. She nearly tripped over Caesar who lay across the outside of the doorway. He stood and stretched, then wagged his tail and whined.

'All right, you can come.'

There was no sign of Sir James in the dining room. Mrs Pridie smiled at her. 'Ah, there you are, dear. I thought you were going to sleep all day.'

'But the clock says it is only ten o'clock.'

'It must need winding, since it's eleven. What would you like for breakfast, miss?'

'*Eleven!*' Fletcher would think she wasn't coming. 'I don't want any breakfast, Mrs Pridie. I'm not really hungry. Is Sir James about?'

'He hasn't come down yet. Neither has your sister.'

'Lucy must have gone out earlier then, because she wasn't there when I woke. I'll look for her while I'm out.'

'He likes to know where you are, miss.'

Not after today, she thought. In half an hour she'd be Mrs Taunt and no longer answerable to anyone except Fletcher.

'Tell him I've gone out for a walk.' Snatching up her bonnet, she set off at a fast walk, the dog darting this way and that. After a few deep breaths of fresh air, her headache settled into something more manageable.

Had Miranda thought to look back, she would have seen Sir James standing at his window, watching her go, a faint smile playing around his lips. It wasn't until the house was out of sight that she picked up her skirt and began to run. Thinking it was a game, Caesar pranced alongside her, his bark urging her on.

She was panting for breath when she reached the church, and warmth filled her when she saw Fletcher's horse. She took a moment or two to recover, and then she entered the church. Caesar followed, his nose casting at the musty smell that was unfamiliar to him.

Fletcher's face lit up. 'I was just about to come looking for you.'

Throwing herself into his outstretched arms, she held him tight and said against his ear, 'I was late. The clock had stopped and I thought you might have gone home.'

'The reverend isn't here yet; he must have overslept.' He blew a soft kiss into her hair.

They waited for ten minutes, and then Caesar's ears pricked up and he began to growl, pressing close to her leg.

There came a faint noise from behind the pulpit. The growl became a warning bark and Caesar's hackles spiked. Fletcher's hand closed around his collar.

'Hush, Caesar, it's only Reverend Swift.' Miranda placed a hand over his snout like Sir James did. They turned, smiling – a smile that changed to bewilderment.

A monk in a faded brown robe stood there, his face hidden by a cowl. His back was bent. Offering his fist to the dog, he spoke softly to him. 'Good boy . . . you remember me, don't you . . . we're old friends.'

Quivering, his tail going into a cautious wag, the dog reached forward, and when Fletcher let go of his collar, his tongue investigated the curled fist. The monk opened it to reveal a small delicacy of dried meat inside.

'Sir James doesn't like strangers feeding his dogs,' Miranda said.

'Oh . . . we're not strangers. We met the last time I visited, and the time before. The reverend sends his regrets, but he's been called away and is unable to be here. He intended to leave you a message, but he didn't have time. He asked me to tell you he was sorry he couldn't stay long enough to make you man and wife, and he hopes you'll be happy.' The hand the man offered in friendship was shiny with scars.

Fletcher ignored it and moved in front of Miranda. 'Who are you? Are you acting on behalf of my uncle? Remove your cowl so I can see your face.'

A sigh left the monk's mouth, but he did as he was asked. His eyes blazed darkly from a face that was barely recognizable as a face on one side, and there were tears in them. His hair was heavily threaded through with grey.

Miranda gave a cry of distress, and she saw the Fenmore resemblance, even though she'd never set eyes on the man before. 'Oh, you poor man,' she said involuntarily, and she turned to gaze at Fletcher.

'Where's the reverend?' Fletcher said. 'What have you done with him?'

'He's dead.'

Miranda drew in an anguished breath. 'He was so happy at my birthday supper. How did he die?'

'Somebody poisoned him.'

'You?' Fletcher asked.

'Why should I kill him when he's done me no harm?'

Miranda pulled at Fletcher's sleeve and whispered, 'Look at him, Fletcher.'

'I am looking at him. How did you get your injuries?'

'Somebody pushed my face into the ashes of a fire. Then I was thrown over a cliff, which broke my legs and one of my arms. After that, I was taken out to sea, hit on the head and thrown overboard.'

'That sounds like a tale told by sailors at the inn.'

'There's more, so please hear me out before you condemn me for a liar. By some miracle, a French fishing boat dragged me up in their net, barely alive. My skull was cracked and I had no memory. An order of Franciscan friars took me in and nursed me back to health. I stayed with them. It's only in the past two years that my recall of my past life and identity has returned, but in snatches.'

She pulled his sleeve again. 'Fletcher . . . look past the scars on his face.'

Miranda saw the moment when recognition was followed by

uncertainty, then disbelief. The colour in Fletcher's face seemed to drain away. 'Who are you? What are you doing here?'

'I think you know who I am, and I'm here to right a wrong.'

There were footsteps on the gravel outside and a shadow blocked the door.

As they turned, their combined bodies shielded the monk, who hastily whispered, 'Say nothing. Don't look for me. I'll find you.' He melted away as silently as a shadow.

'Have you seen my husband anywhere?' Mrs Swift said, and she looked so worried that Miranda felt sorry for her.

Fletcher and Miranda exchanged a glance, and then Fletcher gently squeezed Miranda's hand. 'No, I'm afraid we haven't.'

'Nor I.'

'How did you get into the church?'

'The door was open, and the key is still in the door. I came to meet the reverend. He'd asked me to read a lesson next month.'

Her expression was unbelieving. 'And you, Miss Jarvis. Are you reading a lesson too? I find that hard to believe.'

Flags of heat settled on her cheeks. 'Do you now? Why is that?'

'Because I know he intends to wed the pair of you this morning.' Her lips settled into a thin line that represented a smile, and her eyes darted from one to the other. 'Well, what have you got to say to that?'

'Have you told anyone else?'

'No, Miss Jarvis. I may be a shrew but I'm not a fool, though I imagine Sir James might be interested in the fact that his *guest* and his nephew rather conveniently happened to be alone together in the church at the same time.'

Fletcher shrugged. 'Then I suggest you scuttle off and inform him . . . and far from being convenient, the opposite applies. My appointment with your husband was for nearly an hour ago.' He turned to her, shades of bewilderment still layered in his eyes.

'What's your excuse for such unseemly behaviour, Miss Jarvis?'

Miranda found a convenient lie. 'Despite not feeling inclined to satisfy your curiosity, Mrs Swift, I happen to be looking for my sister. I saw the horse outside and the door was open so I came in.'

'Ah yes . . . your sister is a rather precocious little creature, but that's another subject altogether. Are you telling me you didn't know who that horse outside belonged to?'

Fletcher shrugged. 'I doubt if Miss Jarvis knows who owns every horse in the district. I doubt if you do, either. It happens to be my horse. Now, can we end this inquisition, Mrs Swift? Would you like me to help you find your husband? Considering that the door was open, he may have tripped and fallen. I've called out a couple of times, to no avail.'

They found the reverend in the choir stall, stretched out tidily with his head on a kneeling pad and his hands clasped over his stomach. An empty brandy bottle was cradled in the crook of one elbow. His wife plucked the bottle from him and stared at it in disgust before setting it aside. 'Sir James's coachman sends this over for him. My husband is weak and can't resist it.'

He looked as though he was sleeping, until his wife gave him a vigorous shake and said firmly, 'Wake up at once, Ambrose.' Then his head rolled to one side and his mouth fell open, displaying his teeth, so he appeared to be smiling.

Miranda gave a little gasp and said, for the second time that day, 'The poor man.'

Fletcher went through the conventions, placing his ear against the man's chest to see if he had a heartbeat. He examined the greenish tinge of his fingernails, an indication of arsenic poisoning, or so his uncle had told him when he'd been small. He said, 'The reverend looks peaceful and I think he may have died in his sleep. I'll go and fetch the doctor, shall I?'

He was fixed by a stare. 'Why would he need a doctor?'

'To certify that the manner of his death was from natural causes.'

'What else would it be − a criminal act?'

That's exactly what Fletcher thought it was. However, the doctor was in the pay of his uncle, and nearly every death that wasn't obviously accidental was recorded to be as being from natural causes.

Miranda said, 'I'll inform Sir James when I get back. He will know what to do.'

He didn't want her to go off before he had time to speak to her. 'If you'd care to wait a few moments, I'll escort you, Miss Jarvis. It's on my way.'

'There's no need. It's not too far to go unaccompanied, especially if I go via the copse. Good-day, Mrs Swift. Please accept my condolences on the death of your husband. Mr Taunt.' She inclined her head to him.

Miranda didn't look at either of them again, but whistled for the dog when she reached the porch. For a moment, she was silhouetted against the sunshine.

Fletcher was left with the impression of her in his eyes for a few seconds after she'd gone, and hoped he'd read her message correctly.

His mind wandered back to the monk. It was a complication he didn't want to think about. His first thought had been that the man was his father, Adrian Taunt. But how could he be? From what Fletcher had seen of his face, the resemblance to his uncle and himself was very strong. But that would make his mother a sister to both of the men. Surely his mother . . . Fletcher felt sick at the thought. Yet the fact remained; the question of who his father was brought only evasion.

Damn it, he didn't need this much complication in his life.

Sixteen

Miranda waited for Fletcher in the copse. When he reached her, he took her face between his hands, his middle finger settling in the little pockets behind her ears. He caressed the sides of her mouth with his thumbs, as gentle as a butterfly, and then his mouth settled on hers in a long and loving kiss.

She needed this tenderness from him, like she needed air to breathe.

'What do you make of the monk?' she asked when he released her, absorbing his smile that told her that he loved her, without needing words.

'I've not had time to think it through, but what I saw rattled me. Despite his injuries, it's obvious the man is kin to the Fenmore family. He and my uncle are about the same age, so must be brothers or cousins. My uncle has never mentioned other relatives beside my mother. Yet before he died, Silas Asher told me I was related to him . . . and I wondered if he was my father. I just don't know what to think now.'

'The monk didn't give a name.'

'Perhaps I'll ask him if I see him again.'

She uttered the almost unspeakable. 'What if he tells you his name is Adrian Taunt?'

'That rather depends on where he fits in the family.'

She hugged him tight, and he rested his chin on her head. 'What will we do, Fletcher? I can feel all this tension around us. I'm scared, but I don't know why, and I don't know whom I can trust.'

He shrugged. 'Perhaps we'll sail away on the *Lady Miranda* and never return.'

'And perhaps we won't.'

Caesar cast with his nose in the air and barked when he saw Roma and Nero coming from the stable, followed by Sir James on his horse.

'I must go, else he'll soon be close enough to spot us.'

'Does that matter?'

'I'm scared he might do something to hurt you, after that last time, when he nearly lost control of himself.'

'Do nothing to raise my uncle's suspicion, my love. I'll meet you and Lucy at midnight under the horse chestnut tree and take you back to Monksfoot, where you'll be safe.'

When she nodded, he kissed her, a long and lingering kiss that was altogether delicious. 'You should have been Mrs Taunt by now, but another opportunity will present itself,' he said, and was gone.

Miranda started off, hurrying across a meadow knee-high in grass, and threaded through with a happy blending of brightly hued flowers. It was too nice a day to die in – though the reverend hadn't looked too bothered by it – and it was too honest a day to try to deceive someone. But lying and evasion seemed part of life here, and deceive she did.

Spotting her, Sir James cantered towards her and circled her with his horse. 'My dear, you must slow down.' He gazed at the copse, his eyes narrowing as if he could see into the interior. 'You're out of breath; is someone chasing you?'

The tears that filled her eyes were genuine. 'I've just come from the church. The reverend is dead. We found him in the choir stall.'

'We?'

'Mrs Swift and Fletcher . . . and me.'

'Fletcher?'

'He had an appointment with the reverend, I believe.'

'And what were you doing at the church?'

'I was passing, when I saw a horse and stopped to pass the time of day.'

'You stopped to pass the time of day with the horse?'

She wished he would stop parroting everything. She said, her tone barely civil, 'Of course not; I was with Fletcher. He's gone to fetch a doctor and to inform the undertaker. I said I'd come and tell you, because I didn't know what else to do.'

'And Mrs Swift?'

'She's still at the church with her husband's body. She didn't seem to want to be comforted.'

'Ah yes, of course . . . she's one of those tedious females with strong opinions that they're not afraid to inflict on everyone else. The reverend should have thrashed her a couple of times to bring her to heel. But, then, he was a weak excuse for a man.'

'He was a nice man, and I liked him, and may I point out that Mrs Swift isn't a dog.'

'She's the female equivalent, and in more ways than one,' he grumbled. 'Was the reverend dead when you found him?'

'I imagine so. Fletcher listened for a heartbeat and said there wasn't one.'

'Thank you, my dear. I shall go to the church and sit with Mrs Swift and play my part while she waits for the doctor to come. She must make arrangements to vacate the vicarage, since we'll have to find a new cleric to fill the position.'

Miranda remembered what had happened to her mother after being placed in the same position. Well, almost the same; at least Mrs Swift wasn't with child. 'But surely not straight away, Sir James.'

'Indeed not, but as soon as is humanly possible. She has a sister in Hampshire she can stay with, I believe. I'll provide the use of my carriage to convey her there after the funeral. I'll also inform the bishop of Reverend Swift's demise and he can suggest someone suitable to replace him. He can also do the honours at the funeral.'

Tipping his hat with his cane, he rode off towards the church, the dogs tracking the scents in the meadow from left to right and back again. How cold-blooded Sir James was, despite his charm, she thought. Caesar gazed back at her, then decided the romp with his parents was more inviting.

When she got back to the house, she expected to see Lucy, but there was no sign of her.

Mrs Pridie hadn't seen her, either. 'She might have gone visiting. She was on friendly terms with that young woman and her brother last night. They stayed the night and left as soon as it was light. They live in Southampton, I believe.'

'Southampton is miles away, and she hasn't taken any of her clothes. She would have told me, or at least left me a note.'

'Perhaps she has; have you looked for one?'

Miranda remembered the scattered exercise books. 'No, I haven't had time, but I will.'

Mrs Pridie placed a hand on her arm. 'You look distressed, Miss Jarvis. Has something happened to upset you?'

Miranda remembered the deceased. 'Reverend Swift has died. I've just come from the church. I ran into Sir James on the way.'

Breath hissed from the woman, and she said, almost to herself. 'So it's begun.'

'What's begun?'

'Nothing you should concern yourself with. I'm just an old woman talking to herself. The reverend seemed to enjoy the party last night. He paid your sister a lot of attention. I was going to tell you to be careful in that regard.'

'But the reverend is . . . *was* old enough to be our grandfather.'

'They say that there's no fool like an old fool. But there . . . It was only a rumour and best to let it lie now he's gone, may he rest in peace.'

'You mean—'

'I don't mean anything, Miss Jarvis, since it does no good to speak ill of the dead – none at all. Forget I spoke. Besides, the least you know, the better off you'll be. Would you like me to bring you up some tea, and something to eat? Some toasted muffins perhaps, since you went out without breakfast.'

'Thank you, Mrs Pridie.'

Frustrated with always being fed hints and snippets, Miranda went up to her room. She tidied her hair, braiding it, then stared into the mirror. The maid hadn't been up to make the bed yet – not surprising, since they'd probably spent all night cleaning the house after the party. She made it herself, and then picked up the two dirty glasses from the table. Punch! She recalled that Sir James had sent them up a glass after they'd gone to bed. She'd been so tired she could hardly stand. She tipped the glass so the dregs ran up to the lip, and tasted it, her tongue sifting through its strong fruity flavours to isolate those she knew. It contained laudanum, as well as valerian. Her mother had told them that such remedies became a habit. No wonder she'd woken with a headache.

There were a number of gifts for her, left there mostly from people she'd already met. She unwrapped them.

Mr Bailey and his sister had presented her with some silk gloves. The Pattersons' gift was a pretty silver trinket box. And there was a sweet little Bible with a lustrous mother-of-pearl cover. It didn't take much to guess who'd given her that. She opened the package from Fletcher to discover a tasselled silk and ivory fan. Loving it, she spread it open and found a ship in full sail painted on the silk. *Lady Miranda* was embroidered on the hull. She must remember to write and thank everyone.

After Mrs Pridie had gone, she took out Lucy's novel to see if there was any message from her. There was nothing except the story she was writing.

The journal itself was faded and ripped. The writing was legible, but the words badly spelled. It was nothing like Lucy's neat writing and the writing had a childish feel.

The journal of R.J.

Lucy had called her Ruby Johnson in the novel.

> My cousin S was furious when he learned that the baron had taken my innocence in London. They had words. S told me that I'm little more than a lightskirt. I like the baron. Despite everything, he is kind and gentle with me – he said he loves me and will make me his wife, since no other woman will have him. When I told him I wasn't good enough for him, he said it was nonsense and I will learn to be a countess and our baby will inherit if it turns out to be a boy.

She continued reading a little further on.

We have arrived in Dorset. The journey was wearying. Today, A told his half-brother about the coming child. I could hear them shouting at each other. J has a son who is almost a year old, and he told the baron that I'd given my favours to anyone who wanted them, and the child I was carrying could have been fathered by anyone, even S, or himself. Truly, the man is evil. It was a pack of lies to blacken my name. I was scared he might harm me, so my mistress locked the door to the maid's room. She said J was envious of the baron because he was born of their father's first wife and took precedence.

Goodness, she should have read this journal herself before allowing Lucy to read it. It was too late now. She felt compelled to read on.

My heart is broken. J came to see me. He tells me that the baron threw himself over the cliff on to the rocks below in a fit of melancholy, and had died. If it weren't for the infant, I would follow him into his watery grave. From my window I could see the crew of the *Wild Rose* searching for his body, and I wished I were there with him, dying in his arms.

Miranda's hair prickled. If this was a journal, the events recorded in it were probably true.

The infant I am carrying has caused them unease. I heard the new baron arguing with my mistress. She said that if I had been wed to A and the child was a boy, he would inherit the title. J shouted out that he had a son who was legitimate and who would succeed him. She cried out as though he'd hit her. Afterwards she told me the child would not be harmed, and she was thinking of a solution to the problem.

No wonder Lucy had been so excited by the story. Miranda shoved the journal under her cushion and sat on it when she heard a knock on the door. Pulling a piece of loose paper toward her she hurriedly wrote on it.

Dear Mr Bailey and Mrs Tibbets.

It was Mrs Pridie with her tray of refreshment.

'I'm writing thank-you letters,' Miranda said brightly – and unnecessarily, for the woman's gaze was on the paper as she lowered the tray to the table.

'That's thoughtful of you. Sir James likes good manners. There are some embossed cards especially made for the purpose. They have the Fenmore crest on them.'

'You seem to forget that I'm not a part of the family.'

'Aye, that I did.' Mrs Pridie's eyelids flickered as she began to pour out the tea. 'There's some notepaper that's kept for guests to use. It's in the bureau in the morning room. You can write your letters there and leave them on the hall table. Sir James will take them in when he next goes to the assizes, and will give them to a messenger to deliver.'

Miranda looked at the woman as she picked up the dirty glasses. 'There was laudanum in our drinks last night, as well as valerian. Why?'

'Sir James thought you were too excited to sleep. He gave me a measured amount to mix in with your drink.'

'You told us we could trust you, Mrs Pridie. Now I discover that I can't.'

'You can trust me, which doesn't mean to say I can help you if you get yourself into trouble. Heed what I have to say and you won't; otherwise you might go from one spider's web into another.'

'So if I told you a confidence, you would keep it to yourself, then.' She nodded.

'I'm in love with Fletcher Taunt and he loves me.'

Pridie gave her a broad smile. 'As if I couldn't see it in your eyes every time the pair of you looked at each other.'

'We were to be wed this morning. Only the reverend died before we got there. He'd been drinking, for he had an empty brandy bottle with him. And he had his head on a kneeling pad and looked as though he was sound asleep and freed of all his cares. I wondered—'

A name exploded into her mind . . . *Adrian Taunt*. Was that the A in the journal? The characters' initials began to slot into place. The journal pressed against her buttocks, the pages swollen with Fenmore secrets that had found a way to escape. Her sister had provided them with the means to.

Pridie put a finger over her lips when a noise came from the door. It swung open on its hinges. Beyond the opening, the corridor was dim and quiet, until a large cracking noise made them both jump.

'Who's there?' Pridie said loudly, though her voice wavered a little. When there was no answer, she reassured them both, 'It's just the house settling, I reckon.'

'Perhaps there's some truth in the rumour of this part of the house being haunted.'

Pridie shut the door firmly. 'I've lived in this house long enough not to believe in such nonsense. It's just a draught – the wind is getting up outside. I think we're in for a storm before too long. Now, I can't hang about here talking. I must go and get on with some work.'

Miranda waited until she reached the door, then said, as casually as she could, 'Mrs Pridie, did Sir James have a brother or a cousin who had the title before him?'

'Dear God!' Her back straightened and she turned, alarm in her eyes. 'Don't you ever mention that to Sir James!'

'Why not? Was that who Adrian Taunt was?'

'For your own good, don't meddle in something that doesn't concern you.' Mrs Pridie departed, her feathers clearly ruffled.

Curling up on the bed with the journal, Miranda began to read it again, to get events clear in her mind. Everything slotted into place. She must warn Lucy to hide the journal when she returned.

She gazed into space for a moment and frowned. Where exactly was her sister?

Seventeen

After Fletcher dispatched the doctor and the undertaker to the church, he visited Oswald Avery in his office and handed him a package. 'I was asked to deliver this to you, Oswald.'

Oswald turned it over. 'Who's it from?'

'It was handed to me by a monk, on behalf of Reverend Swift, who has unfortunately died.'

Oswald's smile still lingered when he shifted his gaze from the package to Fletcher, but his eyes were cautious. 'A monk, you say . . . Are you serious? There have always been apparitions sighted at Monksfoot, but I didn't think you'd be susceptible to such vagaries of the imagination.'

'This monk was as real as you and me. He wasn't an apparition, and neither was he an ordinary monk.'

'Is there anything ordinary about being a monk?' Oswald turned the package over and closely examined the seal. His eyes narrowed and he murmured, 'That's odd.'

'What is?'

'It appears that the Fenmore seal has been used, though it has some cracks and scratches across it.'

'The seal is bigger than that.'

'This would have been in a ring. There was talk . . .' He shook his head. 'I overheard my parents talking . . . Parents are often unthinking in front of children and don't understand how much can be absorbed.'

Suspecting he was getting nearer to the truth of his existence, Fletcher drew in a careful breath. 'What talk? For God's sake, Oswald, stop taking me around in circles.'

Oswald shrugged. 'I'd heard that Sir James had a half-brother, one born of his father's first wife. He was not very robust, though he grew up to inherit the title.'

'What happened to him?'

'Oswald shrugged. He died before you and I were born, I believe. I expect he was buried without fuss in the family cemetery and promptly forgotten. Now, let me open this missive. I must admit I'm intrigued. I can't think what the Reverend Swift would want with me, since we've never had any dealings.'

'You have a reputation of being honest . . . for most of the time, anyway.'

To that Oswald grinned. 'I'm only as honest as any other honest man in the district. Perhaps it's the reverend's last will and testament, though he didn't look as though he had much to leave. Let me open it and find out.' He inserted his thumb under the wax seal, breaking it.

'I think he might be my father, Adrian Taunt.'

Oswald's eyes flew open, and then he laughed. 'Who – the reverend? That's preposterous. A couple of months ago you thought Silas might be your father.'

'Only because he hinted that we were related and had left me his fortune.'

'Did Silas say how you were related?'

'He closed up like a clam when I pushed him about it. But I'm talking about the monk now.' Fletcher twisted in his chair. 'His face was badly scarred on one side where he'd been pushed into a fire, and he was thrown over a cliff. Both legs were fractured and one healed shorter than the other, so he also has a slightly crooked spine. He walks with a limp.'

Oswald winced. 'I'm surprised he survived that sort of ordeal.'

'I haven't finished yet. His tale was that he was taken out to sea and hit on the head before being thrown overboard and left to drown. Some French fishermen hauled him up in their net – probably thinking he was contraband. He had no memory and they handed him over to an order of friars who nursed him back to health. His memory returned two years ago.'

'You believe him?'

'I believe he's a Fenmore. It was Miranda who saw the resemblance.'

Oswald sighed and exposed the missive from the reverend. There were three pages of loosely spaced writing. 'It starts off: *My name is Ambrose John Swift. I am dying. My wish has long been to clear my conscience before my Lord . . .*' Oswald fell silent while he read the rest.

'Well, what does he have to say for himself?' Fletcher asked when Oswald finally looked at him.

'It's partly the confession of a troubled soul. I cannot divulge the contents of this document because not only is it a deathbed declaration, it's also a sworn document. Therefore I must obey the law and hand it to the proper authorities. They will investigate the claims made in this. I will allow you this, Fletcher, but I think it will bring you no joy.' He turned the paper round.

There was a currently dated signature beneath that of the reverend, and a legal-sounding statement.

To whom it may concern. This is to affirm that I, Sir Adrian Taunton Fenmore, Baronet, Justice of Assizes, lately living in France, witnessed the death of the above servant of the church, and certify that the enclosed statement was sworn before me this day on his deathbed.

The breath left Fletcher's lungs in harsh little jumps. Oswald was right; it did bring him no joy. 'This has come as a shock, because I didn't want to believe the monk. It has turned any thought of reconciliation with my uncle on its head. Sir James has always been my kin, and although I overlooked most of his cruelties, I looked up to him and admired him.'

'My dear Fletcher, you have always had a forgiving nature, and a boy needs a father's love. Sir James filled that role. If you had no consideration of the welfare of others, you would have never found a convenient excuse to come back here, but would have dismantled your business dealings, as I urged you to at the time.'

'You were right, Oswald. I don't know what will eventuate from this, but it sounds very much like a challenge and it smacks of revenge. And I'm standing in the middle of it. Certainly, it will cause maximum damage. And if the monk is the Adrian Taunt who fathered me – as he appears to be – then my mother must have . . . Damn it, Oswald, I can't even say it. He was her half-brother. How can I have any respect for a man like that?' He shook his head, still unable to believe such a thing. 'He didn't strike me as being a weakling, though he was certainly misshapen.'

'Don't jump to rash conclusions, Fletcher. Your family has more twists and turns to it than a dog's tail. Talk to the monk when you next see him. Get his story, but don't complicate matters further by taking sides. I've a feeling this is very much between your uncle and your . . . monk.'

'So do I. My uncle has been unstable since I've been home. He pulled a pistol on me and nearly shot one of his guests. I'm afraid for Miranda and Lucy Jarvis. He has proposed marriage to Miranda . . . something she doesn't want. I've arranged to get them out of there tonight. I'll take them to my house.'

'Is that the Miranda the *Lady Miranda* was named after?'

The thought that he'd fallen in love so quickly still made Fletcher smile, despite his worry. 'We'd arranged to be wed this morning, but when we got to the church, there was nobody there to listen to our exchange of vows. We didn't know it, but the reverend was already dead. The monk appeared from the back of the church and said he was poisoned.'

'Are you sure *he* didn't kill the reverend?'

'I'm not sure of anything, but his words had the ring of truth.'

'Be careful, Fletcher. Monksfoot will be the first place Sir James will look for those young women. Most of your servants will do what Tom Pepper tells them, and he's in the pay of your uncle. You can't trust any of them.'

'There must be some who are honest.'

'I imagine so, but they're frightened of disobeying orders. The staff Silas gathered around him over the years mostly consists of scoundrels, and they took advantage of his illness. They'll scatter over the countryside like rats if they feel really threatened.'

'That will save me the trouble of getting rid of them. And my uncle's workforce?'

Oswald shook his head. 'You grew up there and would know better than I whom you can trust. Now, my friend, I'm going to give you a piece of advice,' and he tapped the missive on his desk. 'The dear departed has named names to ensure he has a place in heaven. Once I hand this over, all hell will be let loose. Your property might be seized, though your name wasn't mentioned. It will certainly be searched, and goods confiscated. I will delay handing this over as long as I can.'

Fletcher wanted to ask him to tear the document up and forget it, but he knew Oswald would never step that far over the line. Besides, there would be no point if there was a copy.

'You can take those young women to my home where they'll be safe. You should have a day or two before the authorities gather their forces together, and I shall quite enjoy a little female company.'

'Thank you, Oswald.'

'If there's any other way I can help, apart from placing my own life in danger, of course, do let me know. Oh, by the way, I have an account from the shipping agent handling the repairs of the *Lady Miranda*. It's sizeable, but they say the work is proceeding quickly under the direction of Joshua Harris. He's very thorough, I believe. They advise that the ship will be ready to move to Buckley's Hard for the refit within the week.'

'Thank you, Oswald. Tell them I'll visit them when she gets to the hard . . . unless I'm in prison. Now I must get back. If my home is going to be raided there are a couple of items I'd like to hide.'

'Do you intend to warn Sir James, Fletcher?'

'I don't know . . . He brought me up and was a father to me. In all conscience, I owe him *some* loyalty.'

'Yes, I suppose you would feel that, and I don't envy you the position you're in. And what about the monk – doesn't he deserve any? You haven't heard his story yet.'

'I don't know . . . I must think about it, and I must find him and speak to him about my past. Where would a monk be likely to hide himself?'

Oswald grinned. 'I can only say you have no imagination at all. Think about it, Fletcher. If you were a monk, where would you hide? It's obvious.'

'Monksfoot Abbey? You mean he's hiding under my nose. I'll be damned!'

'Could be worth a try. You could hide an army in that place. Silas would have known about your birth. He may have offered help to the monk over the past year or so. He would have enjoyed thumbing his nose at your uncle.'

'If the monk is there, I'll find him, because I'll tear the house apart stone by stone when I get back.'

When they stood to clasp hands, Oswald smiled. 'I'll whisper a few words in the right ears and stand to bail you out if need be. Don't carry a pistol; it will give anyone with a grudge an excuse to kill you. Good luck, my friend.'

It seemed like an inordinately long time before Caesar announced Sir James was home by joining her. Giving him time to settle himself, she went downstairs and knocked at his study door.

'Come in.'

He stood when she entered and waved her to a chair. 'Ah, Miranda, my dear. I can't imagine to what I owe this pleasure.'

'I can't find Lucy. She was gone when I woke this morning.'

'I see.' Walking round the desk, he seated himself on the edge and gazed down at her, his arms folded. 'I shouldn't worry too much. I'm sure she's safe.'

'Safe? Do you know where she is?'

'Where do you think she might be?'

'I thought she might have gone to look in the cellar and locked herself in. She was interested, because she's heard tales of giant pythons and was curious to see them for herself.'

'One shouldn't listen to gossip. For instance, just yesterday I heard a rumour that you were about to marry my nephew. Yet here you are without a ring on your finger and lacking the bloom of a new wife who is basking in the light of her husband's constant attention. In fact, you look quite pale and unloved at the moment.' He gazed at her for a short time, as if expecting an answer, and then prompted, 'I was about send for you, so you could explain yourself on this matter.'

The scales had dropped from Miranda's eyes with a vengeance since she'd read the journal. Sir James was no longer a heroic figure, but a middle-aged murdering coward. Knowing she would be leaving his home to be with Fletcher in a few short hours couldn't prevent the disdain she felt towards him showing in her eyes.

'Then I spared you the trouble, Sir James. And, as you advise, you shouldn't listen to gossip. Do you know where my sister is?'

He ignored her question and frowned. 'You disappoint me, Miranda . . . you really do. I offered you the respectability of marriage, a home and a title, and you bite the hand that feeds you.'

She felt a little desperate. 'I cannot marry you, Sir James. I don't love you.'

'Ah, love – a young man's ideal. It rarely lasts. I would be happy with love in the physical sense.' He reached out, taking her face between his finger and thumb. His eyes bored into hers, grey and cold. 'I want you in my bed, Miranda. I want your young, warm flesh yielding to my demands on it. There are many ways to make love and I'll teach you them all . . . the tender . . . the sweet . . . the painful . . . and the almost unbearable agony and corruptness of the dark side when the caress of the lash bites into your flesh.'

She began to struggle. 'You disgust me.'

Releasing her chin, he slashed a hand across her face. She cried out when the chair tipped over sideways, and he swore when she scrambled to her feet, her face hot and stinging. Caesar growled. It was deep, threatening and prolonged, coming from the depths of his throat. Despite the shock of being hit, she gentled the animal. 'Hush, Caesar.'

When Sir James went to place a hand over Caesar's snout, the dog snapped at it and drew blood. Jerking his hand away with a foul curse, Sir James wrapped his handkerchief around the wound.

'See what you've done to my dog, Miranda. You've spoiled him, made him feel important so he feels the need to challenge me – his master. I shall have to teach him a lesson . . . both of you, perhaps.'

He rang a little silver bell on his desk. When a manservant arrived, he said, 'Take the dog to the stables and tie him up, and send Mrs Pridie to me.'

'Please don't hurt Caesar,' Miranda said as the servant dragged the reluctant dog from her side.

'He must learn who's the master.'

She would leave – go to Fletcher at Monksfoot Abbey. She turned away from him. 'You're vile, and I'll never marry you. I'm leaving.'

'I really do think you should reconsider your decision,' he said when she reached the door. 'But if you do decide to leave me, understand this, Miranda: you'll never see your sister again.'

Hysterical fear rose up inside her and she fought to control it, so her throat dried up and strangled a scream. 'What have you done with her?'

'Nothing . . . *yet!*'

Mrs Pridie appeared. 'Bring Miss Jarvis to the stable yard in about ten minutes.'

'Yes, sir.' Mrs Pridie's hand slid firmly under her elbow. 'Come along with me, Miss Jarvis.'

She pulled away and gazed back at him. 'What are you going to do?'

'You'll see.'

And she did see. She saw a man devoid of any emotion whip an animal into submission. It went on for ten minutes. Caesar, tied to a metal ring set into the wall, had no means of defending himself. Around them, the horses fretted in their stalls.

Finally, the dog stopped trying to escape and began to endure, flinching every time the lash landed. His agonized yelps became squeals, then whimpers. He lay on his side, his body quivering and his tongue lolling out as he panted for breath. His rough coat was streaked in blood.'

Shocked and sickened by the cruelty of the beating, she pushed between them and screamed, 'Stop it!'

The spent tip of the whip caught her arm and laid a fiery welt across the pale flesh as Sir James snapped it back.

He gazed at her when she cried out. 'You're making a habit of saving those who are being deservedly punished. Now look what you've made me do. I must find a salve for it so it doesn't turn nasty.'

She wondered if there was a salve for *his* nastiness.

It seemed not. He took up a pistol and primed it before beckoning to her. 'Such devotion to each other is laudable, even if it is only a dog. I'll allow you to put him out of his misery, my dear. You just have to put the pistol against his forehead and pull the trigger.'

She could hear Roma and Nero's frenzied barking coming from the house as she crouched at the dog's side. Tears spilled from her eyes. She untied the rope securing him to the metal ring. 'I'm so sorry, Caesar.'

The dog's tail circled in a feeble wag, and he whined and gently licked her hand. He struggled to rise and stood there, all pride gone. His legs were splayed painfully apart, his usually proud tail curled under his rear.

Dragging her to her feet, Sir James placed the pistol in her hands. 'Oh . . . do spare me the drama of an emotional deathbed scene and get on with it, girl.'

She moved away from him, the weapon cold and heavy in her hands. 'I can't kill him . . . I can't.'

His eyes were merciless. 'You can and you will.'

The pistol wavered in her hands as she tried to take aim. Caesar lifted his head and gazed at her. His eyes were a beautiful, deep brown, and so trusting that she felt sick.

'Do it now, Miranda, else I'll beat him to death,' Sir James said.

She believed him. She must put the dog out of his misery. But why should he die when she had the power of life or death in her hands.

She found a spark of defiance and turned towards Sir James. The gun steadied in her hands. 'Come, Caesar.'

The dog limped to where she stood and pressed against her side, leaving smears of blood on her skirt. 'Go . . . Find Fletcher – he'll look after you,' she said.

The dog left and headed off towards the copse, and she hoped he'd make it.

Sir James gazed at her in amused surprise. 'I didn't expect you to turn on me. If you intend to kill me, do it now, for you'll never get another chance. You can't miss from that range.'

Miranda's finger tightened on the trigger, and they stared at each other. Her arms were beginning to ache from supporting the weight of the gun. The whip had landed across the muscle of her upper arm and it throbbed.

'The longer you put it off, the harder it will become.'

Her arms weakened a little more, and her hands wobbled. As the gun dipped, she jerked it up. It discharged. The noise startled her and the horses alike. The horses squealed and danced about. The bullet chipped one of the cobbles near Sir James's foot. It bounced up to bury itself in a wooden post.

He took a step forward and wrenched the gun from her hand. 'You'd never have found your sister if you'd killed me.'

'I never intended to shoot you. It went off by accident.'

Somebody had let the other two dogs out, for they came from the house, noses to the ground and baying as they cast around for the scent of the injured Caesar.

They came to heel at his whistle and he sent them back to the house.

He shrugged. 'Caesar will find a place where he can lie low and lick his wounds. The foxes will pick up his scent, run him down and tear him apart. If he escapes that, he'll come home again when he's hungry. Then I can beat him all over again.'

'You loathsome cur. You're cold-blooded, and I'll never become your wife,' she called out when he turned and walked away.

'We'll see.'

When she got back to the house, she went up to her room. Mrs Pridie brought her up some refreshment. She seated herself at the end of the bed. 'You've had a hard time of it.'

Tears spilled down Miranda's cheeks at her sympathetic voice. 'I don't know what to do for the best. I wish my mother and father were still alive.'

'Aye, you must miss them. That was a cruel thing the master did. I've sent someone after the dog, to make sure the creature ends up in safe hands.'

And what of Lucy? Was she safe? She sniffed at the tea in case something had been added to it.

'It's quite safe, I promise.'

'Do you know where Lucy is, Mrs Pridie?'

'I wish that I did.' The housekeeper lowered her voice to little more than a murmur. 'You should get yourself away from here.'

'I can't leave, not without my sister – and he knows it.'

A low grumble of thunder followed her words, cushioned within the bruised layers of the gathering cloud mass on the horizon.

They were in for a storm.

Eighteen

The storm had moved quickly over the district, offering a drenching downpour at just the right time for the corn crops to benefit from it. The gutters gushed noisily, the water expelled through the mouths of the grinning gargoyles situated at intervals around the roof.

The trees soaked up the rain and the leaves fattened into their full summer plumage, so green that it hurt the eyes. The clouds rolled away, taking the thunder with it. The sun came out and steam was sucked into the air. The land became dry underfoot, except for some dark patches in the undergrowth.

Fletcher called on Mrs Swift at the rectory to see if there was anything he could do to help.

There wasn't.

She was as uncompromising as ever, her lips pursed into a thin line. 'Sir James has arranged everything, and I'm to depart after the funeral. I must say this: I'll be pleased to leave this unholy place. If you want to see the reverend, he's lying in front of the altar. Perhaps you'd lock the door afterwards.'

He went across to the church. The reverend had his hands arranged one over the other on his chest. The gravediggers were already at work, preparing the dark bed that would swallow and start to consume his body, come morning.

The interior of the church was quiet and dim, and it smelled of dust. The weight of it lay across his shoulders and the quietness pushed against his ears. Goosebumps prickled along his spine. It felt as though he was being watched.

A beam cracked in the bell tower, making him jump. A bell rope swung. He checked the back door, bolting it from the inside, then went out the front and turned the key in the lock. The dog was lying in the porch. He stooped to the bloodied creature.

It wasn't the first time he'd seen a whipped dog, and it didn't take much imagination to know who had dealt the savage blows on this one.

'I have two choices. I could finish you off with a rock, or I could carry you home across my saddle and see if I can patch you up. Either option will hurt.'

Caesar lifted his head and whimpered.

'I hear you, Caesar. We'll see what we can do.' He took off his jacket to cushion the dog in and buttoned it around him. Lifting the creature across his horse's shoulders, Fletcher mounted behind him. They went slowly, the animal giving little cries of distress now and again.

Fletcher gentled him. 'I don't know what you did to deserve this, but my uncle has certainly turned you into a whipped cur.'

Dog and Dog waddled from the stables and gave duty growls when they saw him. At the same time, they wagged their tails and lifted their heads to have their ears fondled. They'd finally abandoned their daytime vigil outside Silas's room and offered Fletcher the dubious honour of their friendship during the day. At night, out of habit, they still slept in Silas's room, which had begun to smell like a kennel.

'What have you got there?' Tom said, sauntering out from the stable.

'One of my uncle's dogs – it's been whipped.'

'The poor beggar – it's Caesar. Leave him with me; I know someone who will doctor him.'

Fletcher took a stab in the dark. Tom and Silas had been lads together. He'd know just about everything there was to know, and wondered if he'd part with any of it. 'The mysterious monk, perhaps?'

Dark eyes challenged him. 'What do you know about the monk?'

'I've met and spoken briefly with the man. He's no apparition, and I need to talk to him.'

Tom shrugged. 'I haven't seen him lately, and I've never seen his face. Silas has entertained him over the past couple of years. Never could figure out what they were saying because they spoke in the Frenchie language. Silas told me he was a horse doctor, and he'd known him from the past. The monk used to come and go, usually when the moon was showing her dark side – as though he didn't want to be seen. Of course, rumours got around. We thought it would encourage strangers to keep their noses out of our business.'

'Then you don't know the monk's identity?'

Tom avoided his eyes. 'If Silas trusted someone, then so did I. He had more substance to him than any ghost, but I could only guess as to who he might be.'

'And your guess is?'

Tom shrugged and held out his arms for Caesar. 'Some French smuggler Silas had struck up a friendship with. Let's get the poor creature seen to.'

'Lead the way and I'll follow, since there's something I need to tell you. Did you know that Reverend Swift died last night?'

Tom nodded. 'Poor bugger. I heard he'd been poisoned, probably by his wife's tongue.'

Tom would not sound so flippant when he'd absorbed the next bit of information. 'The reverend made a deathbed statement, and I delivered that to my legal representative to deal with at his discretion. On the strength of that missive, I believe it's to be handed over to the proper authorities, and we'll shortly be investigated by the full force of the customs.'

Alarm filled Tom's eyes. 'When?'

'I don't know when.'

'Has your uncle been informed?'

'Not yet. I intend to do so later in the day, so you've both been served with fair warning and can act appropriately.'

'What does "act appropriately" mean?'

'That you can gather together your ill-gotten gains and leave town, or stand and fight. I'd prefer you didn't do the latter on my property.'

Tom swore. 'We have a large consignment coming in while the moon is on the wane.'

'I don't want to know.' Fletcher looked around him. He was in part of the house he'd never been in before. There were no windows, just a corridor with small alcoves and planks to serve as beds, he supposed. One had a mattress and a blanket. There were a couple of doors on the other side. A lone candle burned at the other end where the passage widened out into a common room. 'Fetch a blanket and spread it on that table, Tom.'

But Tom had gone, melting away into the darkness and leaving the lantern burning.

Fletcher did it himself. There was a table and two chairs. He rolled the dog gently on to the table and reclaimed his coat. When Caesar emitted a deep, painful sounding huff, it sounded like a man coughing, and the hair on the nape of Fletcher's neck stood on end.

Beyond that, steps led upwards towards a light. Another flight led down into darkness. The place smelled musty, of bat droppings and seaweed, but it was dry.

'Adrian Taunt, come out of your bloody hidey-hole before I dig you out. I'm sick of all this subterfuge.'

There was a chuckle, and a pair of sandal-clad feet came into view on the stairs. They belonged to a man in a salt-stained brown robe. He moved to where the injured dog lay, his hands moving gently over the animal as he whispered words of comfort to him. He sounded Caesar's lungs before he lifted his head. 'His heart is good and his lungs sound clear. He should survive if shock doesn't shut down his organs. Is this my brother's work?'

'If the baronet is your brother, yes.'

The man gazed down at the animal, then back to Fletcher. 'James is my half-brother; we had different mothers. I'll clean the dog up. His wounds will heal and he'll survive, and in a day or so he'll have got over his distress, won't you, boy?'

One wag of the dog's tail signalled agreement.

The man looked directly at him, his gaze travelling from head to toe and back again before he smiled. 'I didn't know I had a son until two years ago.'

'And I didn't know who my father was. Oh yes, I knew it was Adrian Taunt. I was told he was a soldier who fathered me, then went abroad and was never seen again. Your true identity was kept a secret. Even my mother would not discuss it. I never imagined you were a monk.'

'While I never imagined I was anything but, until two years ago.'

'Sometimes I thought it might have been my uncle who fathered me because we are so alike, and I was ashamed because of his kinship. Then Silas said I was related to him, and I thought he might have fathered me, and that Adrian Taunt was just an empty name to satisfy my curiosity. Now it's come full circle and I'm still ashamed. Perhaps they were right to keep me in ignorance.'

Adrian Taunt moved about, preparing a bowl with water and taking a jar of salve from a drawstring bag hanging on a hook.

Caesar hardly made a whimper as the man doctored him, though he yelped a couple of times when an occasional stitch was inserted.

The man thought to tell him, 'Every man has the right to know where he came from. You're related to Silas through your mother. She was Silas's second cousin.'

Fletcher stared at him. 'How could she be when Elizabeth is your half-sister – though you seem to have conveniently forgotten that fact on the occasion of my conception.'

The monk gazed at him with surprise in his eyes. 'Are you talking about Elizabeth Fenmore?'

'Who else?'

'Who else indeed! We seem to be talking at cross-purposes. Allow me to ask you something, and I'd like a truthful answer. Are you under the impression that Elizabeth gave birth to you, and we produced you between us?'

Puzzled, Fletcher gazed at him. 'She *was* my mother. Are you denying that you fathered a child on her?'

Adrian Taunt appeared horrified that someone thought he had. 'Most definitely I am denying it. Your mother was Rose Jones.'

'Rose Jones? I've never heard of her.'

'Rosie was Elizabeth Fenmore's maid. I fell in love with her, and when she told me she was with child, I offered her marriage.'

'So what happened to prevent the marriage?'

'Nothing. We wed in secret, in London. Both Elizabeth and James thought Rosie unsuitable, which she probably was, but she was eager to learn, and she was pretty and lively, and she made me laugh.'

That unravelled one puzzle for Fletcher. All this time he'd concentrated on finding out who'd fathered him, and he hadn't given any thought to the maternal connection.

The monk's smile faded. 'James was furious when he found out, but he seemed to accept it. He'd always lusted after Rosie himself and he followed us down to Marguerite House from London, and one day he caught me unawares. He'd always been stronger than I was, and he was consumed by jealousy because I'd inherited the title. He tried to burn the identity from my face and then he killed me.'

'Until you decided to resurrect yourself.'

'It wasn't by design. It just happened. I woke up one morning and I knew who I was, and what had happened to me.'

'I can't remember Rose Jones nor have I ever heard of her. Though I can recall Elizabeth.'

'Elizabeth didn't have any children of her own from her short marriage, and was widowed about that time. I expect she was forced to pass you off as her own child, to avoid a scandal. She was not a clever woman and would have done what James told her. He didn't like being crossed.'

'He still doesn't, and people are scared of him. What happened to Rose Jones — *my mother*? Do you know?'

'Something did. Silas wouldn't discuss it, but he opened his doors to me. It gave me time to see what had happened to the Marguerite Estate and decide what to do. James had kept it productive as a front for his illegal activities. As for the rest . . . I hope you're not involved.'

'One can't help being drawn in, though I've tried not to be. A man would have needed to walk around with his eyes closed not to see what's going on here. I've been legitimately involved with the shipping company for the past two years. I told my staff when I came here that the old ways are over for Monksfoot. Many of them are hand in glove with my uncle in ways I don't even know about. I came back here to try to reconcile with him, but now it's too late.'

Adrian's gaze went back to the dog. 'Perhaps it would have been easier to get on with the life I was living . . . but I must find out what happened to Rosie. He wouldn't have allowed her to live long after you'd been born.'

'Be careful of what you say, and to whom. My uncle has many irons in many fires.'

'Most of those will be extinguished once the reverend's missive gets into the right hands.'

'But you've returned home. Why?'

'To claim my birthright and to establish a kinship with my son — if he'll allow it.'

Fletcher cracked a wide smile and nodded. 'Are you sure you want to bring past events out into the open . . . Father?'

Adrian nodded. 'I must. James took everything from me, including everyone I loved. He'll do the same to you. The man has no conscience. He put a stop to your marriage by poisoning the reverend on the night of your lady's birthday.'

Fletcher felt a sudden stab of unease, and his brain unleashed the thought that, come midnight, Miranda would be safely under his own roof.

'There's a large consignment of goods coming over from France in a day or two in the dark of the moon. If the reverend's missive has reached the right desk, I think things will begin to happen then.'

'How do you know all this?'

'I've made it my business to know, by keeping my eyes and ears open. Trust me, Fletcher.'

After a moment or two of hesitation, Fletcher took his father's hand in a firm grip. 'I'll ask my housekeeper to prepare a guest room – if I still have a housekeeper. And sort out some clothing, so you don't frighten anyone.'

'I'll keep my robe until this business is settled. It's a good disguise, but it does need a wash. I'm afraid your clothes might be a little too big.'

'Silas's clothing should fit you, since he was about your height.'

A wry twist settled on the man's lips. 'I used to be taller.'

From that comment alone, Fletcher knew he would like him.

Simon Bailey rose from behind his desk when Oswald was shown in. A map of the Dorset coastline was spread out in front of him. 'To what do I owe this pleasure, Sir Oswald?'

Oswald placed the papers on the desk, the declaration uppermost. 'I've been entrusted with a deathbed confession, to be delivered at my discretion.'

'And you chose me – why?'

'After due deliberation, I came to the conclusion that you have the authority to act on the contents.'

Simon Bailey grinned. 'They must be important. Do you not have a clerk to act as delivery boy?'

'I do; however, this matter is more sensitive than most.'

'And your discretion veered to the side of legality on this occasion.'

'As it usually does.'

Simon waved Oswald to a seat and settled back in his chair. His glance fell on the signature and the seal and his eyes sharpened. 'That might be the Fenmore seal, but it's not Sir James's signature. How did you get this?'

'I reserve the right to withhold that information, and it's not something you need to know since it's a family matter. Also, if you deduce anything from that signature, I'd be obliged if you kept your thoughts to yourself. The confession itself is from the Reverend Swift, who died recently.'

Simon Bailey nodded. Drawing the paper closer to him, he used the shaft of his pen to lift the folds open, gingerly, as if he expected it to explode in his face. He finished reading it, then looked across at Oswald. 'Will you take some brandy with me, sir?'

When Oswald looked askance at the bottle sitting on the side table, Simon laughed and opened a cupboard. 'I imagine this one will suit your palette better. It's the best money can buy, though this particular bottle was a gift after I did a small favour for someone. I've been saving it for a special occasion.'

'Indeed, it will.' He accepted a glass and warmed it between his hands before taking a generous sip. It slid smoothly down his gullet, releasing its fruity aroma.

'Having learned since I've been here that one favour deserves another, is there any way I can reward you, Sir Oswald?'

Oswald smiled. 'Since you ask, there might be. Fletcher Taunt . . .'

'What of him?'

'He's a generally honest young man. He landed in the middle of this mess by returning from abroad to find he'd inherited Silas Asher's estate. Unwittingly, he found himself in an awkward position with his loyalties divided. I wouldn't like to see him hurt.'

'I understand, Sir Oswald.'

Oswald downed his brandy and stood. 'Good. Then I'll get on about my business.'

'How long before this missive becomes common knowledge?'

'At the moment, only four of us know that the package exists. It depends on how many of your people you can trust, I imagine. No doubt you'll have plenty to do, so I'll leave you to think things through and marshal your resources. There will probably be a commendation for you if all goes well. Will you be attending the reverend's funeral the day after tomorrow?'

'I wouldn't miss it. It's enlightening to observe a gathering of gentleman rogues in such surroundings. I must say, though, that the reverend has surprised me by turning out to be a villain, even a repentant one.'

'Crime always has a long reach. Villain or a victim — it's hard to tell in his case. I'll see you there, then. Good-day, Mr Bailey, and good luck.'

Nineteen

They were not waiting at the appointed spot, and his anticipation at the thought of seeing Miranda again plunged Fletcher into a pit of despair.

'Miranda,' he called softly into the velvety black night.

An owl hooted.

He waited for half an hour, and then moved up the carriageway towards the house. Lady Marguerite's House was a handsome and elegant building. Although he'd been born there, he'd never felt as though he'd really belonged. Now he knew why. It had been — still was — a house of lies.

Monksfoot Abbey, with its sturdy walls, suited him better. There was nothing fancy about it. No panelling or elaborate painted ceilings. It had been built as a hard-wearing house for hard-working men. Sturdy oak beams supported three rambling storeys. The windows were arched, as were the doors. He could have stood up straight in the fireplaces in the downstairs rooms, where uneven flagged floors had pathways worn through the most travelled areas. For all its roomy strength, there was a warmth and shabby homeliness to Monksfoot Abbey.

When he came in view of his uncle's abode, he was surprised to see light still burning in the study, since it was well past midnight. There were other lights — one in Miranda's room . . . another in the hall.

What if his uncle had harmed her? Fletcher picked up speed, his long legs carrying him towards the house at a fast pace. When he reached the front door, he pounded on it with both fists.

Jack Pridie opened it and tried to block his way. 'Your uncle is expecting visitors in a short while.'

At this time of night, they wouldn't be making a social call and would probably be armed. 'I won't take up much of his time.' He handed the man his hat, headed for the study and went in.

Sir James looked annoyed and said irritably to Jack, 'If any of my guests arrive, take them into the drawing room for now.'

He turned to Fletcher when the door closed behind Jack. 'This is very inconvenient, Fletcher. I expected you before this. Are you going to be tedious about something? If you are, get it over with.'

'You know very well why I'm here, uncle.'

'Ah yes . . . the delicious Miranda. You didn't really think I'd allow you to snatch her from under my nose, did you?'

'We love each other, and were to be wed this morning. As you probably know.'

'I make it my business to know everything.' He chuckled. 'How fickle of Miranda, when just this morning she consented to be my wife.'

Shock seared through Fletcher's innards. 'I'd hear it from her own lips before I'd believe it.'

'At this time she will be asleep, so come back in the morning.'

'I'm not leaving until I see her.'

'Very well.' He rang the bell on his desk and Jack came in. 'Ask Mrs Pridie to fetch Miss Jarvis down, please.'

A full five minutes ticked by on the mantle clock before Fletcher set eyes on Miranda. Her hair was a glossy fall about her shoulders, but her eyes lacked their usual sparkle. She looked as though she'd been crying for half the night.

Sir James came around his desk and pulled her against his side. 'My nephew here is under the impression that you intend to wed him.'

She turned her eyes his way and he saw pain in them. 'I'm sorry, I can't marry you, Fletcher. I'm going to wed . . . *him*.'

'You don't mean that, Miranda. You can't.'

His uncle's fingers dug into her waist under her ribs, and she winced. 'Yes . . . I do mean it. I . . . *love* him.'

The way she'd dragged it out made it sound more like 'loathe'.

'You love me; that's what you said.'

'No . . . no . . . please understand . . . I *cannot* love you.' She burst into tears, then tore herself from his uncle's grasp and ran from the room.

'She's overwrought. Go after her, Pridie; make sure she gets to her room safely. Give her a sleeping draught to settle her; I've prepared one in the scullery. Then come down and see my nephew out – through the servant's entrance, though.'

'I can see myself out.'

'No doubt you can, Fletcher. I hope you are now satisfied. A word to the wise: if you attend the reverend's funeral, I suggest you act more appropriately to your age. The girl doesn't want you, so from now on leave her alone. You might as well know that I'm going to have the wall between our properties rebuilt, and I will hold you personally responsible if it is damaged again. What's more, I intend to dissolve the company. My lawyer will contact yours in due course with regard to the sale of company assets. By the time all the debts are paid, there will be very little left. I believe Silas took out a loan on the Abbey not long before he died. I've already instructed the bank that I'm going to buy the mortgage.'

His uncle was whistling down the wind. Fletcher owned the Abbey free and clear. It had never been a company asset, since it had belonged to Silas. The deeds were in his possession and in his own name. The money he'd paid for it had been handed back in the form of a legacy. The *Lady Miranda* also belonged to him, since his own money had paid for it and his own money was paying for its repairs.

'And I'm going to sell the *Midnight Star* and *Lady Miranda*.' When his uncle smiled, Fletcher tried not to allow his dismay to show.

'You forgot to tell me about that little deal.'

'You won't get *Lady Miranda*. She's in my name and bought and paid for with my private funds. I started the shipping company from scratch, and can do so again if need be. I'm not going to allow you to destroy everything I've worked for over the past few years. You can have Silas's estate for the price I paid for it if you'll hand Miranda and her sister over to me.'

'Don't be pathetic, Fletcher; I've got you trapped there.'

'I can go the long way round and will still have access to the estate by sea.'

His uncle laughed. 'Do stop wasting time. Most of your workers are in my pocket; nobody will work for you. Get out, and don't come back. You and I are through, and if you step on my land, you'll be treated like any other trespasser.'

Fletcher gave him hard look. He was not about to hand over the two ships without a struggle. He'd worked too hard to get them.

The slap-down smarted, and although Fletcher was neither convinced nor satisfied by the little scenario that had been played out, he couldn't march up to Miranda's bedroom and drag from her what he knew to be the truth of her affections. He had no choice other than to leave.

He'd hardly got outside when Mrs Pridie came scurrying after him. 'Quick, take this. Miss Jarvis wants you to have it.' Pulling a bundle from under her apron, she thrust it at him. 'She said to tell you to read it.'

He detained her for a moment by catching hold of her sleeve. 'Look after Miranda as best you can, Pridie. And if you ever need a safe haven, you and Jack can come to Monksfoot.'

'I'll do my best, but your uncle has been difficult lately and thinks only of himself. Don't you worry about me. Jack has made a bit from what goes on, and we have something put by, so we're going to move on.'

'Sooner might be a better time than later. Good luck then, Pridie.'

'And to you, sir.' She kissed his cheek, then turned and slipped inside, locking the kitchen door securely behind him. Fletcher was tempted to creep around the house and wait, to see who his uncle's guests were, but he didn't. He could quite easily guess. It was sufficient to know that Miranda still loved him. If she didn't, she wouldn't have bothered sending him a message.

Miranda stood at the window gazing out. She was done with crying.

Dawn had brought cloud and an early drizzle, but when the rain cleared and the sun came out, the mist rose and every leaf was washed clean. Spiders' webs had transformed into lacy chandeliers quivering with refracted light. It was the type of morning for optimists, and Miranda would have loved to share it with Lucy.

She felt sluggish and bad-tempered after getting hardly any rest, and was tempted to crawl back under the covers to seek the oblivion of sleep. She began to wish she hadn't poured the sleeping draught away. A glance in the mirror displayed a face that was as haggard as she felt. Fletcher stood behind her and she wished he were anything but an image on the portrait. Something dark moved in the depths of the glass. At the same time, there was a gentle touch against her shoulder.

Heart beating fast, she spun round and grimaced. Her imagination was playing tricks again. But, then, *was* it her imagination? It might be the ghost of Lucy. Perhaps she'd been killed and was coming back to let her know. Fear nearly swamped her and she bit back her rising hysteria.

She washed and dressed, and then braided her hair, dragging it back from her forehead. She had no interest in adopting the role of lady of the manor with Sir James by her side, and saw no reason to try to look attractive for him.

Gazing up at the portrait, she shivered, hoping Mrs Pridie had lived up to her promise of being trustworthy, and that Fletcher was in possession of the journal. 'I love you and I believe in you, Fletcher,' she whispered, and blew him a kiss. 'Please believe me when I say that the monk is on your side.'

Her glance fell on her sister's lacy pink shawl, which was hanging over a chair. Picking it up, she held it to her face, before pulling it round her shoulders for comfort. 'Where are you, Lucy?'

The house was as quiet as the grave as she went down the stairs. There was usually a maid about, but not today.

As she descended, she noticed the cellar door was ajar. She hesitated and looked around. There was a sense of waiting about the house. The steady tick of the clock was a reassuring noise.

The dogs came from the kitchen and nosed about her ankles, looking for a scent of poor Caesar, perhaps. A faint waft of breeze came through the cellar door, a mixture of dry mould and salt.

She was tempted to brave the darkness, despite the creatures that reportedly lived down there. It was a cellar, nothing more. Sir James used it as a dispensary, and if the creatures didn't hurt him, they wouldn't hurt her.

Nero pushed at her hand for a caress, but Roma was nosing at the shawl.

'I know it's not what I usually wear; it belongs to Lucy.'

She remembered the dogs could track. Pulling off the shawl, she held it to their noses and whispered, 'Good dogs . . . find Lucy.'

'Stay,' Sir James said from the top of the stairs, and the dogs instantly sat. He smiled at her, as though the night before had never happened. 'You're a resourceful young woman, Miss Jarvis. I think I may have underestimated you.'

'The door was open and I was going to close it,' she lied.

His glance settled on her head. 'I don't like your hair like that.'

'I don't care whether you like it or not.'

His voice became as tetchy as hers. 'You're being petulant, Miranda; it's a lovely morning – don't spoil it. Come and walk the dogs with me. You can help me compose my eulogy for the reverend.'

'I'd rather be anywhere than in your company.'

'Then allow me to please you in that regard.' Taking her under the elbow, he thrust her towards the cellar door and pushed her down several steps. Taking a silver vesta case from his waistcoat, he struck a flame and applied it to a candle in a lantern. 'There you are, my dear. You and your sister have always been too curious, and I wouldn't want you to miss anything. As long as the candle lasts, you should be safe.'

'You have my sister hidden in your cellars.' Fear flew at her. 'Is she still alive?'

'It's possible. You might even find her if you look hard enough. I'll be back in the morning to let you out, unless you find another way. Enjoy yourself.'

He went back up and stood there a moment, framed in light, and then the door closed behind him. The key turned in the lock with a solid clunk.

'Let me out,' she said against the door panel, but all she heard was the sound of footsteps walking away.

She sat on the steps and found herself gazing at racks of bottles – more spirits than a man could drink in one lifetime, though it wouldn't take long to sell it on to a middleman and absorb it into the market. He was allowing her access to his secrets, allowing her to come to her own conclusions. She already knew more than was comfortable, and the time would come when she knew too much. Then he would dispense with her. The man must be insane to do what he was doing to her and Lucy.

She saw no sign of a dispensary – but, then, she hadn't expected to. Why would he even have one here where there was no natural light? Besides, Mrs Pridie had said it adjoined the kicthen.

There was a door. It was open. Beyond it stretched archways of bricks. They supported the floor of the house above. She would be able to stand up straight, but anyone taller would be forced to stoop. The weight of the house above exerted an imperceptible downwards pressure. There was tension, too, a constant minutiae of adjustment as the house pulled this way and that. The archways were overburdened in some places and cracks had zigzagged down them, following the mortar and allowing bricks to shift sideways.

What if it collapsed on top of her?

'Then you'll be squashed,' she said out loud. Releasing the obvious didn't reassure her one little bit, since her voice was high and breathless with fright.

When she heard a noise in the darkness that sounded like a footfall, prickles crept up Miranda's back and she began to perspire.

The candle flickered and she remembered the draught . . . and Sir James saying there was another way out. She intended to find it!

Gingerly, she stepped forward, knowing that while there was brickwork, then she was still under the house. She was brought to a sudden halt by a wall of stones.

There was a furtive movement at her feet and her imagination exploded. *Snakes . . . spiders . . . giant rats!*

Too frightened to look down, she was frozen to the spot with fear.

There was a tiny squeak and a mouse found courage to streak up the wall in front of her. It disappeared into a hole.

She gave a hysterical giggle and her breath came out in a relieved rush. She felt her way along the wall. Her head brushed against a sticky mass of web and she jerked it away, shuddering and pulling at it as it clung to her face and hair. 'Ugh.'

Not stopping to check the contents of the nest, she moved in the other direction and came across a door. A flight of steps led down into the earth.

She sat on the top one and gazed into the bottomless pit, trying to pierce the darkness to get her bearings. The cellar door was on the left side of the house and the adjoining rooms were the kitchen and pantry complex. Beyond that was the stables . . . further still was the church with its small cemetery where the reverend would be buried tomorrow. Ugh, she hoped no graves blocked her way.

There was a faint sound of water running. It was the chalk stream that ran through the meadow, she thought, but the thought also held some caution. It went underground for a while before turning into a spring just before the old cemetery. But it had been raining. What if the stream swelled to fill the tunnel? Best if she turned back, since Sir James had said he'd let her out, come morning.

She turned and was about to retrace her steps when she heard a faint sob.

'Lucy!' she yelled and her voice echoed from several directions.

'Miranda . . . I'm scared.'

'Where are you?'

'I don't know. I went to bed and I woke up here. I thought I was having a nightmare . . . but it's going on too long. It's dark and I'm hungry and thirsty.'

'Try not to be scared, Lucy. I think we're in the cellars under the house.'

'How did I get here?'

'I don't know,' she lied, for she knew very well who had done this to her sister. Sir James had drugged them both on the night of her party and had then taken Lucy from her bed as she slept. And the crime was being used as a lever for a forced marriage. As soon as she got Lucy out of here, they were going to Fletcher's house where they could hide.

Half an hour later, she'd explored several tunnels, and the candle was burning low.

'My lantern won't last much longer,' she called out. 'I'm at the top of some steps going down. Call out now and then, so I've got a direction, and tell me if you see the light.'

Miranda advanced carefully down the stairs. The stream stopped her progress. 'I must have come the wrong way. I'll have to go back.'

'Don't leave me by myself,' Lucy begged. 'Even your voice is better than nothing. I can see a light through a crack, but it's very faint, like a candle guttering in melted wax. I think it's you.'

Disregarding her own safety, Miranda waded into the water and along the tunnel. It gradually deepened until it reached her waist, then her breasts, so she had to lift her arms to keep the lantern out of the water. The flow was quite strong, as though it had started to go downhill, and the bed of the stream was slippery. Beginning to feel panicky, she called out to her sister, taking comfort from hearing her voice. 'Are you still there, Lucy? Talk to me now and again.'

Her sister began to recite a poem, and her voice came from above. Miranda placed one hand against the tunnel wall to steady herself while she tilted her head to look up. She saw the light of day and gave a cry of relief, for another couple of steps and she'd be submerged if she wasn't careful. Her hand closed around something wooden and she swung the lamp round. A ladder!

Her feet suddenly slipped from under her. She let go of the lantern, which was swallowed by the rush of water. Plunged into darkness, she gave a terrified cry and made a grab for the ladder with her free hand. Her fingers hooked over a rung on the ladder. The flow of water lifted her legs so she floated; her skirt was saturated with the water and trying to pull her under.

Gradually, she managed to pull herself upright, and after a short rest to recover some energy, she took a step upwards. She rested and looked up. She could still see daylight, but there was hardly any strength left in her body, especially her arms. As she couldn't go back along the tunnel against the flow of the water, she had no choice but to go up.

It seemed to take all day. One step and rest, another step and rest. Her muscles ached from the effort, and her teeth chattered from the cold – or was it nerves? A metal grid was over the top of the hole, obviously there to stop anyone from falling down the hole. When she pushed it, it swung open on creaking hinges and clanged against the flagged floor. There was a frame with a bucket and handle. It was a well.

She closed the grid and stood there for a moment, her skirt leaking a river of water on to the floor. It weighed her down and she allowed it to, sinking face down on to the dirty flagstones to rest. After a while, she found the energy to look around her. She seemed to be under the church in a crypt, for there were lines of stone tombs with effigies on them.

A faint light came through small dirt-encrusted windows near the floor. Shrubs had been planted on the other side, which served to keep anyone from looking out – or looking in! Several brandy kegs and some packages told her this place was used for the storage of smuggled goods. Had the reverend been involved in it, too?

Lucy must be in one of the tombs. She shivered, and tears ran through the dirt on her face. How macabre a hiding place it was; her poor sister must be terrified. She knocked on the nearest one. 'Lucy?'

No answer.

She tried the next one . . . then the next. A ludicrous picture came into her mind, of a corpse opening the lid to poke his skull out and say, 'Ah, I have visitors at long last – do come in.' She stifled a hysterical giggle.

'It's not funny,' she told herself loudly, but it must have been, because she giggled again as she banged the heel of her shoe against the container.

Unexpectedly, it provided her with an answer. There was the effigy of a woman on the lid. Her nose was missing. Miranda jumped when there was a muffled knock in return and Lucy yelled, 'Miranda . . . I'm in here! See if you can find a door.'

She didn't want to tell Lucy she was in a tomb, and might be sharing it with a pile of mouldy bones. 'There is no door.'

'There must be – otherwise how did I get here?'

She had a point. 'It's got . . . well, it's got a *lid.*'

'So it's a chest of some sort.'

'Something similar.' Lucy didn't need to know exactly what sort of chest until she was free of it. The place was creepy enough without adding that sort of terror to the brew. She couldn't imagine what being locked in the darkness of a tomb for two days would be like.

Miranda desperately pushed at the lid, but it wouldn't shift. She needed something to insert under the edge to lever the lid off. Her glance went round the chamber and fell on a grapnel attached to the end of a rope. 'I'm going to try something, Lucy.' Cover your eyes tightly with your hands, else the dirt might fall in them.'

Placing one of the points of the grapnel under the lid, she took hold of the rope and pulled as hard as her strength allowed.

It didn't move even a fraction.

'You're pulling it in the wrong direction, my dear; allow me to help.'

Sir James! The voice scrambled her brain. 'To get this far, and all for nothing,' she whispered. She fell to the floor and, holding her head in her hands, began to howl with the misery she felt.

Twenty

Miranda was gathered into strong arms, and although she had no strength left in her own to fight him with, she balled her hand into fists and struck him several weak blows wherever she could land one.

He set her on her feet and, catching her fists, he kissed one and then the other. 'It's me – Fletcher.'

Now she flung herself against him and hugged him as tight as she could. 'How did you know I was here?'

Pridie saw my uncle push you into the cellars and heard him say that Lucy might be hidden down there. She sent a message over as soon as she safely could.'

'My father knew we could get into the tunnels this way. Not through the well, though. It's too dangerous. There are steps at the back of the crypt that take you directly down to the main chamber, though the door is kept locked. It branches off to the right and emerges through the Fenmore family tomb in the old cemetery. Now, tell me, why are you trying to get the lid off that stone coffin?'

'To let Lucy out. She's hidden in there!'

'A strange place to hide.'

'Your uncle put her there,' she said with some exasperation. He drugged her and hid her, but she can't remember him doing it, or how she got there, or, indeed, how long she's been there. He's been using her as a hostage to force me into marriage with him.'

'Let's start by getting her out, then. You've met my father before, I believe.'

A smiled touched her lips. 'Briefly – and unless I'm mistaken, I should say welcome home, sir.'

There came a furious thumping on the lid of the coffin, followed by Lucy's muffled voice. 'I can hear voices. Let me out!'

Fletcher ran a finger down Miranda's cheek, then set her aside and beckoned to his father, who'd been watching them with a smile on his scarred face. 'Can you help, sir?'

'Easily. Take the edges and slide the lid longways along the grooves. Make sure your fingers are safely out of the way, though. I'll push and you pull.'

Fletcher banged on the side. 'We're going to get you out now, Lucy.' The lid rumbled as it moved, and Lucy sneezed as dust rained down on her.

Shivering in her wet clothes – or was it simply nerves making her tremble? – Miranda watched on. She couldn't stop crying. She felt like screaming. Her body was racked with shivers, and she couldn't believe she'd crawled through tunnels and had been up to her ears in water. And was that little moaning sound coming from her own mouth?

Lucy sat up and gazed around her. 'Where are we? I've still got my nightgown and robe on. Did I walk in my sleep? And how did I get into this coffin?' Amazement came into Lucy's eyes when she set eyes on her sister. 'Miranda, you look an awful fright. Where am I? Have we died?'

Miranda began to laugh and cry at the same time. 'We're in the church crypt, and Sir James brought you here. Do I look dead?'

'You don't look very alive.' Lucy gave an uncertain laugh. 'Sir James wouldn't do such a horrid thing. He's always been kind and he likes me . . . us. He said he wished I was his daughter . . . and when he married Miranda—'

An impatient snort came from the intended bride and her tears were forgotten in the heat of her reply. 'I'd rather eat a raw lizard than marry Sir James.'

Fletcher outdid her. 'I'd rather eat a dozen lizards than allow you to, when you've promised yourself to me. We would have been wed by now if the reverend hadn't departed.'

Lucy gazed from one to another with a smile, then turned to stare at Adrian Taunt in a rather critical matter. 'Who are you, sir? You look like Sir James, except for the scar.'

'This is Adrian Taunton Fenmore – my father.'

Lucy's eyes couldn't have grown any wider. 'Good gracious, you must be the elusive Adrian Taunt, referred to as letter A in R.J.'s journal. That's the writer of the journal I found. I call her Ruby Johnson in my novel.'

'Her name was Rosie Jones, and she was my wife. What do you know of her?'

'Very little, except what's in the journal. I was writing it into a novel. I've just got to the last chapter, but it has a sad ending. She gave birth to a son . . .' Her glance went to Fletcher. 'That must be you. When they took her son from her, she was afraid. She heard someone coming for her when she was in the middle of a sentence and she stuffed the journal down behind the window seat.'

'Who came for her, do you know?' Fletcher said gently.

'How could I? The journal ended there. But I can remember the last entries. It was so sad . . .'

'Tell me,' Adrian Taunt said.

Lucy thought for a moment and her face softened. 'As well as being sad, it was so romantic . . .

E was crying. She said she would look after my son as though he were her own. I long to hold him in my arms, just once, before I join my beloved A, and I pray that my son will grow into manhood knowing he was loved.

S has not visited, though he promised to plead my case with J. He has too much to lose, is in too deep, and has chosen to turn his back on my plight. I curse them and their offspring both.

It is night. He will come for me soon, for the full moon brings with it the curse of his madness. I have opened the window to heaven. The air is soft and humid and the garden is bathed in silver light. Beneath the window the terrace is a hard bed.

I hear his footfall on the stair—

Lucy stopped speaking and gazed at them with tears in her eyes. 'I think she then pushed the journal into its hiding place and threw herself from the window. I think that's what she meant when she said the terrace was a hard bed.'

She looked at Adrian for confirmation and he nodded. 'There was a small terrace there, with a seat.'

'It's a rose garden now. Do you know who S is?'

Fletcher drew in a deep breath. 'Silas, I imagine.'

Adrian nodded. 'The curse Rosie put on them came true, for both men lost their wives and children. Silas was Rosie's second cousin. He could have put a stop to it, the devil take his soul. We can use the journal as evidence to help prove your claim, Fletcher.'

Lucy gave a small, frustrated wail. 'The journal is in our room at Marguerite House. I'll never see it again once Sir James finds it.'

'It's not lost, Lucy. When I realized what the journal was about, I asked Mrs Pridie to give it to Fletcher. Do you have it?'

Fletcher shrugged. 'It's at the Abbey, in my desk drawer. I haven't had time to read it yet. I've been more concerned about getting the pair of you away from my uncle.'

Lucy gazed from one to the other. 'Sir James put me in here, didn't he? He betrayed my friendship.'

'James doesn't have friends, and I'm afraid he has betrayed all of us.' Fletcher held out his arms to her. 'Come on out of there, Lucy. I'll take you both back to the Abbey.'

'But I'm in my nightgown. And Miranda looks as though she's been through a storm.'

'You can stay there if you'd prefer.'

Lucy shuddered and rose from her container in a hurry. 'And share a bed with a corpse? No, thank you.' She looked back over the lip of her former bed when he lifted her down. 'Oh . . . there isn't one – how disappointing.'

'No, it's not. The thought of anyone sharing a bed with the dead is just awful, Lucy, and macabre. I shudder to think of what would have happened if I hadn't got to you. The water was up to my neck and I slipped and dropped the lamp, and only by luck managed to grab the ladder on the inside of the well.'

'Goodness, Miranda, you must tell me all about it. Think how dramatic a scene it will make for my next novel.'

'I don't feel like being dramatic. I just feel like going to sleep for a week and forgetting all about it. It's been awful with the poor reverend losing his life and you in danger of your life. Sir James whipped the dog, and the poor creature cried, but he couldn't get away because he was tied up. And I was forced to watch it.' She held out her arm, where the welt stood up proud from her skin. 'Sir James inflicted that when I tried to stop him. He laughed when I freed poor Caesar and sent him to find Fletcher. He said the foxes would find him and tear him apart, and that's when he locked me in the cellar.'

She felt like stamping her foot until she saw that Lucy's lip was trembling and knew the girl had been putting on a brave front.

Fletcher put an arm round both of them. 'Caesar found me,' he said, 'and although he's in a bad way, he'll survive. I'm going to try to get the pair of you out of the district, where you can take shelter with a friend of mine while we sort this out. The problem is, my uncle will have his men stop anything on the roads and make a search.'

There was a shuffle and Mrs Swift stepped out of the shadows. 'I know a way of getting them out.'

'Mrs Swift! May I ask how long you've been eavesdropping on our conversation?'

'Long enough to realize you have the welfare of those young women at heart, which is more than your uncle does. He deliberately led my husband into deserting his calling and exploited his weakness. I have reason to believe he caused the death of Ambrose, and before he had time to repent his sins.'

Adrian Taunt put a comforting arm round the woman. 'Rest assured, Mrs Swift; your husband did repent. He confessed to me and I wrote it down, and even though your husband has passed from this life to the next, the reverend will be the architect of reform in the district.'

She gave a faint smile. 'I believe you because I saw a friar in the church once. He was praying, and devoutly.'

The part of Adrian's face that could smile smiled. 'Ah yes . . . I'd heard there's a ghost hereabouts, and I knew that the monk was not the ghost people referred to.'

'There was nothing insubstantial about this particular friar. He was no spirit from another world, but a living, breathing man brought ashore by a French fishing boat. He had your face, which is distinctive whichever way you look at it, and he went towards the home of that rogue, Silas Asher.'

'Why didn't you report me?'

'Whom could I trust? Most men I was acquainted with were as corrupt as the next, and to keep silent is to survive. Even my husband was part of it. I feared for him if I spoke out.'

'Yet you find the courage to say this to me now.'

'You are a devout and sincere man, Adrian Taunt.'

'I've spent the last twenty years as part of a religious order and God is part of my life, as is prayer.'

'I watched you come and go on occasion. Every month you would visit and stay for two days. You went into the church tower and used it as a vantage place as you kept a watch on Marguerite House. It was clear you were waiting for a glimpse of someone.'

Adrian gazed at his son and smiled. 'You were right, Mrs Swift. Why did you not tell him the truth about me?'

'I didn't know what was truth and what was falsehood. When I saw you praying in the church early one morning, candlelight illuminated the damage on your face and beyond. It was as if the wound had peeled away. Underneath the scar, I clearly saw your face and I remembered a troubled young man who had recently returned to confront a man he believed he had wronged. I thought he had enough problems to face.'

Mrs Swift had absorbed what was going on and had learned too much in the process, Fletcher thought. Thank goodness she had said nothing. But that hadn't been enough to save the life of her husband.

'How did you know that the friar was my father, Mrs Swift?'

'I knew because your birth and death – and the supposed manner of events surrounding that death – were recorded in the church registers. The previous cleric was very conscientious about such matters.'

'You make me ashamed, Mrs Swift. I came here with nothing but revenge in my heart for what I had lost.'

'No doubt the Lord will guide your hand in that, Sir Adrian.' Mrs Swift's glance moved to Fletcher. 'There is a confession by Elizabeth Fenmore, sworn before the last cleric. It discloses the details of your birth, young man. Elizabeth Fenmore had never married, and she died shortly after she made her confession. The cleric recorded that her conscience was sorely troubled. I asked my husband to give it to you, but he wouldn't. By then he had lost his spirit and given in to his demons. He said it was best to let sleeping dogs lie.'

Fletcher kissed her on the cheek. 'My thanks, Mrs Swift. I've been looking for something to prove my identity for a long time.'

'Then you will have it, Mr Taunt, for it's obvious the Lord intended that the pair of you should be together as father and son. I'll take these girls to the rectory, give them a bath and find them something to wear – it won't be fancy, mind. To be honest, I could do with the company.'

Lucy's stomach rattled inelegantly. 'Will there be anything to eat and drink? I'm absolutely famished.'

'Lucy hasn't eaten for three days,' Miranda told her, apologetic for her sister's lack of manners in the face of Mrs Swift's unexpected kindness.

'I understand, my dear. I have some pea and ham broth on the stove.'

Fletcher placed a hand on her arm. 'I'm not going to just hand them over. I need to know your plan.'

'It's simple. After my husband's funeral, Sir James is providing me with the use of his closed coach to take me to my sister's house. It will have the Fenmore crest on the door. We will be accompanied by the bishop's vehicle. Nobody will dare search us. The young ladies will hide themselves inside my coach.'

'And if they're caught?'

'In that case, you must be prepared to offer a diversion, but I have great faith in the Lord to get us through without harm.'

Adrian chuckled. 'I like the irony of your plan. I'm sure we can manage a diversion if we need one; in fact, I can almost guarantee one. You seem to have uncovered a talent for being devious, Mrs Swift.'

She smiled. 'You don't know how devious I can be. Kindly present yourself in the church at ten, gentlemen. Now come along, young ladies. Let's go and get settled in before someone thinks to search the church. Close the lid to that coffin before you leave. They will be using it for contraband before too long and it will look out of place if it's gaping open.'

'We'll return later and take up residence in your hall. I won't feel easy leaving you to fend for yourself. Someone might take it into their heads to search the rectory.'

'As you wish, Mr Taunt, but my windows have stout shutters and my doors bolt from the inside.'

'I'm scared,' Lucy said quietly. 'I'll feel better if you're with us, Fletcher. Sir James will set his dogs to find us when he knows we are missing.'

'We both will,' Adrian Taunt said, 'and we'll use Caesar as a blind. They'll sense his distress and will follow his scent first. But they will probably follow your scent through the tunnels as far as the water and go no further.'

They gained the rectory unseen, and there was enough food in the larder to sustain them for a day or so.

Mrs Swift smiled. 'I preserve fruit and vegetables to give to the poor of the district, and the reverend used to help me deliver it. And there are eggs, and enough flour to make bread. And I used to collect clothing for them to wear.'

There was a box full and they found skirts, petticoats and bodices, carefully patched, but meticulously clean.

The men returned to the rectory, carrying Caesar. The dog limped when they set him down. He wagged his tail when he saw Miranda and thrust his nose into her hand.

Adrian said, 'I hope you don't mind, Mrs Swift. He needs looking after.'

'That's Sir James's handiwork, if ever I saw it,' she said sourly. 'That man will have a lot to answer for when he finally stands before his maker. She made a soft nest of blankets for the dog and dug the ham bone out of the broth. Caesar licked it clean and then went to sleep; his front paws anchoring the bone in position in case it decided to stray.

They spent an uneasy night together, the storm raging around the house.

The day dawned warm and soft. The funeral was well attended, mostly by acquaintances who liked to be seen offering their respects at such events. Simon Bailey was present, with two other customs officers.

Afterwards they chatted about an expected delivery of brandy at Christchurch and Bournemouth Bay, and a raid they were taking part in that night, not bothering who overheard or troubled by the fact that the information would be all over the district by nightfall.

The cemetery attached to the church was covered by a myriad of jewel-coloured flowers – the blush of foxgloves and irises so golden that they outshone the sunshine. Hedges were embroidered with dog roses, and the smell of honeysuckle drifted in the air, busy with the sound of bees and the flight of butterflies.

Carriages lined the outside of the weathered stones of the wall surrounding the cemetery. The cart containing Mrs Swift's worldly goods had already departed, rumbling off towards Poole. Sir James was efficient.

Miranda and Lucy were concealed behind a family mausoleum near a break in the wall. An angel stood on a plinth above them, giving her blessing with two raised and crooked fingers while Mrs Swift issued her directions.

'Wait until the church doors are closed and the carriage drivers are inside the church, and then use the wall to hide your movements as you sneak into the carriage. You know which one it is.'

Miranda had begun to admire Mrs Swift. She was strong and brave, though opinionated. 'Thank you for being so good to us.'

Tears glistened in the woman's eyes, as if she wasn't used to being paid a compliment. 'Oh, I knew the pair of you would be trouble as soon as I set eyes on you. It was plain that your mother was a decent, God-fearing woman who'd taught you some manners. That sort of innocence always attracts men of a certain type. And it was plain Sir James had some plan of his own – and just as he was about to offer for Sarah Tibbets, or so she would have us believe. She should count her lucky stars the scoundrel didn't get a ring on her finger.'

Instead, Miranda had got one on her finger – the one that had belonged to her mother and put there by her own favourite scoundrel.

It seemed forever until the door to the church closed on the mourners. The horse turned a dark-fringed gaze their way, and the dark interior of the closed carriage pressed suffocatingly in on them when they scrambled inside.

Miranda hoped the horse wouldn't take it into his head to move off. But, like all Sir James's animals, it was well trained and behaved itself. They shrank into their respective corners when Mrs Swift got in, her wide black skirt and the black curtains drawn across the carriage windows, effective in hiding them from sight.

'Thank you, Sir James, you've been so kind,' she simpered when the coachman handed her in. 'The bishop will be part of our entourage. And has kindly offered to precede us . . . such an honour.'

'I'm pleased to be of help, dear lady,' he said, his voice sounding totally sincere.

★   ★   ★

Watching them go, Fletcher heaved a sigh of relief and headed for his horse. He intended to follow, off road and from a safe distance, and make sure they got there safely.

He'd barely reached the outskirts of Poole when he heard horses coming up behind him.

He spun round to be confronted by Simon Bailey who was flanked by two of his men. 'Mr Taunt, you're under arrest. Best you come without making a fuss.'

'And if I don't?'

Simon smiled widely. 'Someone might shoot you.'

'I'm unarmed.'

'Accidents happen, Mr Taunt.'

'Obviously.'

He gazed from one to the other, wondering if he should make a run for it – but to what end? He hadn't done anything illegal recently – at least, not anything he could remember.

'I hope this isn't going to be some nuisance trespass charge my uncle has concocted against me.'

Bailey and his men exchanged a glance and laughed. 'I'm given to understand you became a married man barely two hours ago. You wouldn't want to disappoint your bride by dying before she has a proper wedding night, would you?'

A smile flitted across Fletcher's face when he thought of Miranda in her shabby patched skirt and her mismatched bodice, her eyes dewy soft with love and gazing into his while they took their vows before the bishop. Mrs Swift had gazed on smugly, pleased by the outcome of her own meddling. Lucy had wept.

'How the devil could you know about my marriage?'

'Let's say I attended the wedding. I was quite touched.'

Fletcher felt a little desperate. 'Look, Bailey, my wife and her sister are in the carriage up ahead. I need to convey them to a place of safety before I can allow myself to be arrested.'

'One of my men is looking out for them.'

'What man? I can only see my uncle's second . . . *coachman.*' He recalled former suspicions because the man was too friendly with Bertha, the Monksfoot Abbey cook. His suspicions had never progressed past that. Not that she was much of a cook. He shrugged. 'Barnstable is one of your men? I'd never have believed it. He's humping my cook. Bertha will brain him with the skillet when she finds out.'

Simon Bailey's eyes lit up, and he looked as though he found it hard to control his laughter. 'Come, come, Mr Taunt, you're being a bit hard on them, especially since it's obvious that you believe in true love. Now . . . come along with me and I'll lock you in a nice safe cell until it's all over . . . because my men will be going in hard.'

'I can think of better places to be, so would prefer not to. I have unfinished business with my uncle.'

'So does the crown, so join the queue. I'd be grateful if you had anything useful to tell me.'

Fletcher began to laugh; the man certainly had a sense of humour. 'I can sense Oswald's hand in this. If you think I'm going to allow myself to be incarcerated without reason, you can think twice. There's nothing you can charge me with.'

Simon's grin had a touch of the piratical about it. 'It wouldn't take long to think of something.'

'Shoot me if you must, Mr Bailey, but I'm unarmed, and it will have to be in the back. I'm not a bad judge of character, and I doubt if that would sit well on your shoulders. I'm returning to defend my house and home, and to sort out a family problem, something I'm not looking forward to. Smuggling is your sport, not mine.'

He turned and headed back towards his home, his spine prickling and knotting even at the thought of a bullet tearing into his flesh.

'Try to keep out of my way, that's all, Mr Taunt,' the man called after him.

Bastard! Fletcher thought, but he allowed himself a grin. Damn it all, there was something he liked about the man!

Twenty-One

Sir James had put it about that there would be a gentlemen's wake for the reverend that evening. Very little mourning would go on, but plenty of drinking and gambling.

Fletcher hadn't expected to be invited, so when his uncle told him he was welcome to attend, he was suspicious. Was it just another of the man's eccentricities or, as he suspected, an attempt to undermine him again? 'I'm entertaining a guest.'

'A woman?'

Fletcher scrambled to give his father the first name he came up with. 'A man. His name is Fryer . . . um . . . Hadrian Fryer.'

'Hadrian Fryer? I had no idea there was a stranger in our midst. Bring him by all means, Fletcher. I might have some special entertainment for a select few of us.'

He couldn't help saying, 'Will Miss Lucy be playing the piano for us, then? Or Miss Jarvis?'

'I was thinking more along the lines of sport: use them as hostesses for the evening, then auction them off as slaves. It will entertain the men.'

'I thought you liked them, uncle.'

'They turned out to be rather tedious. The younger one is empty-headed and prattles. As for Miranda, she disapproves of everything I do for her and needs to learn how to be grateful. But she has had her chances. I found the pearls I recently bought her thrown into a corner. I imagine I shall find a place of employment for them somewhere.'

And Fletcher could imagine where that place would be.

Blood beginning to boil, Fletcher had made a show of looking around him while he took a steadying breath. 'I expected them to be at the funeral.'

'The creatures are probably still abed. They will turn up for the evening entertainment, I promise.'

And that had alerted Fletcher to the fact that his uncle hadn't. checked on them yet, but was confident he knew of Lucy's whereabouts. As for Miranda, it was only by luck that she'd found a way out of the tunnels. Thinking she was still down there, his uncle would send the dogs down to flush her out.

Now Fletcher stood at the window and gazed down over Axe Cove. It looked totally peaceful. The tide was out, the beach had been cleared of seaweed, and the sand stretched in little ripples to the water's edge. There, seagulls fished amongst the froth. On the horizon, a smoky purple smudge heralded the approach of evening.

He loved it here – in its summer peacefulness and its winter fury, and all the stages in between.

The channel in and out of the cove was a dark blue slash of

water. He'd always known that the stream servicing the well in the crypt ended up in the Axe. When he'd been a boy, and his uncle's shadow, for he'd hero-worshipped the man, he'd been with his uncle and Silas in the crypt. They were directing the workers to stack bolts of fabric and other goods that had been unloaded from the *Wild Rose*. At the time, Fletcher had no idea that the activity was an illegal one.

He'd climbed down the ladder to drop a piece of wood into the well, one he'd fashioned into a boat. His little craft had been sucked under. He'd found it a couple of weeks later, floating in the cove.

His uncle had thrashed him when he'd come back up the ladder. 'If you go down there, you'll be swept away, and one day Silas will discover your remains lying on the beach, with the seagulls pecking your eyes from your head.'

Hands held over his sore buttocks, he'd said defiantly, 'How will Silas know it's me?'

Silas had laughed. 'The bones will have your name on them, my lad. Fletcher Taunt from Marguerite House.'

The power of the current had fascinated him. When it rained hard, the water came up the well, and once it had spilled over on to the crypt. Sometimes it formed a whirlpool as it retreated. If the summer was dry, it became a trickle. The water was clean and cool and tasted fresh. But the thought of Miranda being sucked into that stream made him shudder.

His uncle had loved him then, after a fashion, but when he'd grown into manhood and developed a mind of his own, he'd suddenly become a rival.

The *Wild Rose* was resting on the sand, kept upright by the ropes tying her to the shore. Fletcher had warned Tom off as best he could, but would that stop the man from taking the lugger out? Tom had always been a law unto himself.

It would be a simple matter to stop him. All he needed to do was loosen a plank and the incoming tide would do the rest. As soon as it ebbed again, he could repair it. Fletcher was tempted.

He turned to his father. 'I was thinking I could sink the *Wild Rose* to stop Tom taking her out.'

'Why bother? Tom knows the risks, and you've warned him. If people believe the rumour that the raid will be in Christchurch, then they deserve to get caught. Even if they don't, it won't stop them coming across. If the reverend was right, this is a big push. It's the dark of the moon, and the smugglers will try to take advantage of it. The authorities will be stretched to the limit.'

'There will be bloodshed.'

'Blood is shed every day along this coast. It always has been. Too many good men are killed just going about their lawful business. Men like my brother think they're above the law, and the more they get away with it, the worse it becomes. I understand that smugglers will never be stamped out entirely. The customs service and revenue men do their best to keep it under control when it gets too organized.' He placed a hand on his son's arm. 'I know your conscience troubles you, Fletcher. When it does, just think of Miranda and Lucy – two innocents who accidentally wandered into the spider's web. It doesn't take much imagination to know what my brother had planned for them.'

'I've got them to safety. My uncle has not noticed they're missing yet and intends to entertain his less savoury friends with their presence. I hope to be there when he realizes they're missing. What are your plans, sir?'

'I will find the opportunity to bring things to a head before midnight. That's when people expect the ghosts of the dead to walk abroad with their heads tucked under their arms. If we time it right, it will be a double blow.'

'May I ask you something . . . can you actually detach that head?'

Adrian chuckled. 'I admit that sometimes it feels as if it belongs to somebody else. I used to have a silk mask to wear, so I didn't frighten the ladies. It invited more curiosity, since people wanted to know what was under it.'

Fletcher said, 'What will you do if your brother doesn't hand over the title and estate? He won't, you know. Not without putting up a struggle.'

'If I can shame him in front of his friends and get him to admit to what he's done, then that will give me satisfaction. After that, I'll do things the long way, and have a legal representative prepare a petition to set before the House of Lords.'

'He might shoot you, and will probably shoot me. His guns are pin-fired and he's a good shot.'

'And you don't want to visit your maker before you've enjoyed your wedding night, aye?'

Fletcher chuckled, for he'd already tasted a little of what was to come. 'There's that.'

Adrian smiled. 'Not all of my brother's staff are loyal to him, or even dishonest; they are just too scared to defy him. I've arranged for the cartridges to be removed, and if all goes to plan, we'll have time to get out of there and run as if the devil's after us.' He picked up his robe. Mrs Targett had taken charge of it, and it was now clean. He draped it over the dog.

'Are you wearing that over your evening suit? It will be covered in dog hairs.'

'Only on the inside; if it has Caesar's scent on it, the other dogs will be intrigued, and it might stop them attacking me if ordered.'

'Not so my uncle.'

'People usually think twice before shooting a monk, and you did tell James that my name was Hadrian Fryer. The cowl and mask will stop him recognizing me at first. Remember, he's not seen the result of his handiwork; I want to catch him off guard.'

It was with some trepidation that Fletcher entered his uncle's house at the stroke of eleven. There was an air of expectation about the men present, and some of them were inebriated. His uncle's dark eyes had something in their depths, a sort of feverishness.

'I thought you were never coming. Where's this mysterious guest of yours?'

'He had some business to attend to and will be along in a little while.'

'Rather an odd time to do business . . . unless it's a little monkey business, of course. I have no intention of waiting any longer.' He held up his arms. 'Let's get on with the entertainment, shall we, gentlemen? Just remember, the young women are of exceptional quality, so be prepared to make a good bid on them.'

A cheer went up and they followed their host out into the hall, all of them knowing the prey was the two Jarvis girls. Disgust filled Fletcher.

His uncle whistled and his two remaining dogs appeared. A shawl was waved under their noses, and the dogs wagged their tails when he opened the cellar door. His uncle turned and smiled at him. 'Fetch her,' he said, and the dogs put their noses to the ground and went down into the darkness. 'In the meantime, the rest of you can go and hunt out the second wench. I have her tucked away in the church crypt, the one by the well.'

They went off, baying as loudly as a pack of dogs, leaving behind a man who was the worse for wear from drink, collapsed in the corner of the couch. He was one of Simon Bailey's men.

Sir James flung himself on to a couch and gazed up at his nephew. 'Are you not joining them in the hunt, Fletcher? I thought you would like the prize.'

For the first time in his life, he felt like killing someone with his bare hands. 'I think not, uncle. I've only just got here and I haven't had a drink yet. I'd better wait for my guest. I'll put a bid on when the time comes.'

'I must say, you don't seem at all perturbed. I thought you might have some idea of playing the hero and rescuing the prey. I was looking forward to it.'

His uncle wouldn't be disappointed in that, if everything went to plan. 'I don't see any point in being upset. I thought you intended to wed her.'

'I toyed with the idea. I even thought I might be in love with her a little, but she wasn't biddable, and she disappointed me once too often.'

'What will you do with them afterwards?' he said, as the man began to move away.

Cocking his head to one side, his uncle could barely keep the disdain from his eyes. 'I imagine I'll think of something. There are many places where enterprising young women can be placed to earning a living, and they owe me a debt that needs paying off.'

It wasn't too long before the dogs came back. 'I ordered you to fetch her, you dumb fools. Where is she?'

The men came back, jostling each other and grumbling. 'What sort of idiots do you think we are, Fenmore? The tomb is empty, and so are the others, apart from a few bones.'

There was a high-pitched giggle. 'Ingram thought he saw the phantom monk down there and it disappeared.'

A nerve twitching in his jaw, Fletcher's uncle turned to stare at him. 'Where are the sisters? What have you done with them? You can't just take them, since they're my wards.'

'That's not true. Miranda is my wife. We were married this morning by the bishop. Her sister prefers to live under her care.

What sort of man would treat two young ladies under his protection in such a scurrilous manner?' Fletcher saw a faint movement beyond the door in the darkness of the cellar and felt a yawning relief. Having been ruled by his uncle for most of his life, he felt inadequate to properly deal with him.

'How did you get them out?'

'During the reverend's funeral they were concealed in your own carriage, hidden there by Mrs Swift and accompanied by the bishop's conveyance. Did you really think I was going to allow you to debauch two innocent young women? You should be ashamed of yourself . . . You all should be ashamed of yourselves.'

Some of the men shuffled their feet, and another gave a shamefaced laugh. 'Hoist by your own petard, aye, James. Well done, young man – a fine evening's entertainment. I think I might head for home.'

'Allow me to introduce my guest first. Adrian Taunton Fenmore. My father.'

Someone choked on his wine, the significance of the name obviously not lost on him. Andrew Patterson – his uncle's lawyer!

His father stepped out of the darkness, the cowl concealing his face.

Most of the men pulled back and there was some nervous laughter. A couple headed for the door, to be prevented from leaving, for the drunk in the corner of the couch had miraculously sobered up and stood, his hand on the pistol under his tunic. Simon Bailey had sent an armed man to look after him!

'What foolery is this? Adrian Fenmore is dead,' James shouted, and gave the bell-pull a vigorous jerk to summon a manservant. 'I'll have him thrown out.'

'Your threw me over the cliff over twenty years ago . . . That was after you'd rubbed my face in the hot ashes of a fire.'

'What sort of trick is this, Fletcher? Let the imposter show me the scar.'

When the cowl was thrown aside, everyone fell silent.

'*Adrian!*' James whispered. 'It cannot be. We took your broken body out to sea and drowned you.'

'We?'

'Silas Asher owed me a favour, and although he took your

death hard, I gave him no choice. Why didn't you come back sooner?'

'Because I had no memory. Like a baby, I couldn't feed or look after myself. I was taken in by a religious order and gradually gained bodily strength. Two years ago I regained most of my faculties and remembered that my wife had been with child. All that time I had a son I'd never met. When Silas learned I was still alive, he allowed me a roof over my head whenever I needed one. Between us, we devised a plan that would allow me to regain my title and estate.'

Fletcher cut in. 'Sir James kept my mother a prisoner until I was born. They passed me off as the child of Elizabeth Fenmore.'

'Who was your mother?' someone called out.

'A lady called Rose Jones. She was Silas Asher's cousin, and maid to Elizabeth Fenmore.'

'Lies . . . all lies. You can't prove anything. This man is an imposter,' James shouted, and he lunged for the gun he kept in the drawer in the table. When it didn't fire, he threw it against the wall and headed for another from his study. That one didn't fire, either.

'The pins have been removed,' Adrian told him.

'I'll see you in hell before I give you as much as the time of day, Adrian. As for the rest of you, I know too much about you for your own good. If one word of this gets out, I'll visit you when you sleep and cut your throat, and the throats of your wives. I'll also feed your children to my dogs.' He rang the bell again. 'Where are the damned servants?'

Nobody had an answer for him. An awkward silence descended, and the men shifted from one foot to another. 'You're insane, James,' Adrian said. 'You've always been insane.'

'Get out . . . all of you, get out. You're a pack of leeches trying to suck the blood out of me.'

His gaze fell on the dogs, which were sniffing around Adrian's robe, and he kicked out at them. 'If you stay long enough, you can witness what my dogs can do.'

But Adrian had made sure the dogs would obey him. 'Heel,' he said, and when the dogs sat and gazed up at him, their tails thumping on the floor, he opened his palm and allowed them to nose for a small meaty reward he had hidden there. 'Good dogs.'

A few of the men had left; the rest were lingering out of curiosity.

Adrian warned his brother, 'I'll be back, James, and with the force of the law behind me.'

'Do your worst, Adrian. Marguerite House will never be yours. As for Rosie Jones, she might have gone willingly to your bed, but she was just as exciting when she was forced. You know . . . I do believe she enjoyed being forced. Once a whore, always a—'

Adrian's fist shot out and Sir James sprawled on his back, blood spurting from his nose.

A cheer rang out and a passage was cleared for Fletcher and his father to make their escape.

Adrian clicked his fingers and the dogs followed after them, looking back at their master only once.

'I'll shoot you when you come back, you mangy curs,' he muttered.

Outside it was the darkest of nights – a night that allowed no shadow to escape. In the small cemetery overlooking the sea, a blue flame burned steadily.

Roadblocks had been set up. Anyone found abroad was detained and questioned by soldiers. Men were searched, goods confiscated and the carriers were handed over to revenue men, then carted off in wagons to the barracks compound, where they would be placed under armed guard.

Out beyond the bay, the French fishing boats unloaded their cargoes, tying the rafts containing the brandy kegs in a long string to float them ashore. A number of small boats came from along the coast, and rafts containing brandy and taxable goods began to be towed towards the shore, where a small number of men began to take the various goods to their destinations. It piled up on the beach.

Fires of driftwood were lit along the cliff top.

The Royal Navy cutters watched the contraband boats come and go, and in the streaky yellow light of dawn they formed a barrier behind the boats, to trap them within Lady Marguerite's Cove. Along the cliff tops, soldiers stood shoulder to shoulder with customs and revenue men. Those who tried to escape were rammed and sunk. Shots were exchanged with the French.

It was a bloody fight – one the authorities would win.

Come dawn, armed soldiers followed Simon Bailey into Lady

Marguerite's House, now deserted by the servants. They conducted a search for Sir James, the soldiers descending into the wine cellars and twitching at every noise, having heard the rumours of venomous wild life.

They found neither man nor beast and went no further.

Going back into the hall, and wondering where else to look, they gathered in the hall, unfamiliar with the layout of the house. As Simon gazed up the dark staircase to the landing, there was a draught, and a flirt of a woman's skirt. She came down the staircase and headed towards the solid study door.

He could see the staircase through her and chills ran down his spine.

Sir James was seated behind his desk, enjoying a brandy. He looked up and smiled. 'Ah . . . Rosie Jones, I can't see you but I can sense you, and I know you're there. Have you come for me? I wouldn't have hurt Fletcher, you know. He looks like me, and I always thought he might have been my son.'

Taking a gun from his desk, he held it to his temple, and then swore when he remembered it had no firing pin. He turned to get one from the drawer.

When the soldiers began to batter down the study door, he stood and pushed a coal from the grate. It landed on a trail of black powder that crackled across the room and disappeared behind the panelling. Smoke rose.

The door gave, and he pointed the gun at his brother and smiled. 'I never could get the better of you, Adrian. I must warn you, though. I have several barrels of gunpowder scattered under the foundations, and the fuses are alight. In a few minutes, the house will be blown off the foundations and will bury us both.'

The soldiers scattered and headed for the door.

Adrian smiled and shook his head. 'You've forgotten I grew up in this house, and so did Fletcher. We both know our way about the tunnels, and the explosives have been removed.'

'Are you sure about that, brother? Believe me, you wouldn't have found them all.' James's fingers closed around a firing pin and inserted it into the weapon. It was typical of his brother to carry no weapon and he smiled as he took aim. He wasn't going into hell alone and intended to enjoy this moment of cold blood as the instrument of his brother's death. This time he'd make sure of it.

Stepping out from the shadows, Simon Bailey lifted his gun in one fluid motion.

James didn't hear the shot that killed him.

The three men gazed at each other, then Simon said, 'Do we intend to stand here to discover if we become dead heroes, or shall we do the cowardly thing and run like hell?'

Fletcher shrugged. 'On this occasion, I'd be inclined to trust my uncle.'

They were running like hell across the garden when the first explosion blew them off their feet.

Nothing much had been left of Lady Marguerite's House except for the stables, and they served as a place of storage. They'd removed as much of the reusable building material as they could, and already, the trees and ivy had begun to grow over the ruin and were reclaiming it, healing the gash in the landscape.

The body of James Fenmore had been laid to rest in the family tomb overlooking the sea. He'd left his fortune to Fletcher, who'd engaged an architect to rebuild Lady Marguerite's House, but on a smaller scale and in a different position, so as not to interfere with traffic. It would eventually house his new estate manager.

There was no stain on the family name. Indeed, to those who knew Sir James – as he was still referred to – he became a legend in the district, the gentleman smuggler who helped the poor and had died fighting the authorities that sought to oppress private enterprise. The tales of the dangerous animals he kept became more fanciful each time they were mentioned.

Lucy had written a novel about it. As had her first book, her second, *The Gentleman Smuggler*, was published under her pen name, Lucian Jarvis.

Arms about each other's waists, Fletcher and Miranda gazed out over the sea. They smiled at each other when the *Lady Miranda* came into view. They'd been on board when she'd sailed on her maiden voyage to Boston almost a year since. It had been a highly sensuous and delightful introduction to married life.

Much to Lucy's disgust, she had been left behind on that

occasion, well chaperoned by Mrs Swift, whose offer of her services had been taken up by Sir Adrian with a sigh of gratitude.

Freed from the tyranny of her husband's weakness, the widow became more relaxed and pleasant, and a delightful sense of humour had emerged. Her honesty and her lack of guile seemed to intrigue Sir Adrian.

Though her task had come to an end, Mrs Swift hadn't bothered to move out of Monksfoot Abbey and nobody had thought to tell her to . . . including Lucy.

'Your father and Mrs Swift seem to enjoy each other's company. Do you think they might wed?' Miranda asked her husband.

'They might. Mrs Swift doesn't seem to mind his scars, and she's well read and can supply him with intellectual debate, which he seems to thrive on. To be honest, he's not half the farmer his brother was.' He gazed down at her. 'Did you know Simon Bailey has designs on your sister? He wants to call on her.'

Miranda smiled. 'He already calls on her.'

'With our blessing, I mean.'

'Lucy is nearly eighteen and can decide for herself. After all, I did, and look what a bargain I got.'

'Did you? I thought it was me who got the bargain.'

'Let's agree to disagree on that. Tell me about Simon; is that why you offered him the management of the shipping company?'

'Could be . . . and could be I'll offer him a partnership if he proves to be as capable of running it as I think he is.'

'What if a marriage between them doesn't come about?'

'It won't make any difference. If a man's good at his job, he gets the reward he deserves – and the issue of Lucy will have no bearing on the matter.'

'Simon's a determined man, and Lucy has always liked him, you know. But what of Sarah, his sister? Lucy doesn't get on with her.'

'I understand that Sarah is being courted by a widowed professor with a couple of children who need mothering. You're not giving your sister enough credit; she has a sensible head on her shoulders when it's needed. Now, enough of others, I'm more interested in us, Miranda.'

'What about us?' she teased.

'I wondered if . . . I've noticed . . . damn it all, Miranda, we've been married for a whole year and there's something different about you. You haven't stopped loving me, have you?'

'How could you think that when I've adored you for every second we've spent together?' She chuckled, then reached up to caress his cheek. 'Spring,' she said.

He looked puzzled. 'What about spring?'

'That's when the daffodils bloom and the ducklings hatch and the lambs gambol in the meadow. That's when the mist absorbs the scent of bluebells, the cuckoo spits, and the showers shiver with pleasure of being born on the wind. That's the season we'll welcome a new love and life into our hearts.'

He stared at her, and then his eyes filled with tears. 'You mean . . .?'

'I mean our infant will be born halfway through April; is that plain enough, Fletcher, my love? Now tell me you love me.'

The grin that had appeared on his face grew wider and he gently pulled her into a hug. 'I love you,' he said, and the kiss they exchanged seemed to last for ever.

Around them in the stirring of summer air, pollens drifted in the perfume of roses. The earth was turning, going about its business of renewal. The poppies were blood-red splashes, dancing with the harebells and mayweed to celebrate the new life to come.